SUBTERFUGE

THIN BLUE LINE

I0544795

Also by Melanie P. Smith

Warrior Series

Dusk

After Dark

Serendipity (Novella)

Dawn

Shadows

Intrepid (Novella)

Chaos

Exposed

Progeny

Thin Blue Line Series

Mount Haven

Moondance Ridge

Novels

Hidden Lakes

Paige Carter (Police Procedural)

Season 1

Season 2

SUBTERFUGE

Thin Blue Line
Book 3

By:
Melanie P. Smith

MPSmith Publishing

Copyright © 2018 Melanie P. Smith

Edited by LaPriel Dye
First Edition, First Printing

*No part of this document or the related files may be reproduced or
transmitted in any form, by any means (electronic, photocopying,
recording, or otherwise) without the prior written permission of
the Author.*
*This book is a work of fiction. Names, characters, places and
incidents either are products of the author's imagination or are
used fictitiously. Any resemblance to actual events, locales or
persons, living or dead, is entirely coincidental. All trademarks
are the property of their owners and are acknowledged by the
proper use of capitalization throughout.*

0 9 8 7 6 5 4 3 2 1

www.melaniepsmith.com

Dedication:

To all the unsung heroes in blue. Thank you for your service.

Chapter One

Agent Skeeter Perkins pulled the rented sedan off the main highway and slowly made his way up the rural back road. He focused on his destination, a secluded oil field, as he maneuvered around locals desperately trying to sneak a peek. This was normally a sleepy little town about thirty miles outside of Houston where nothing of consequence ever happened. A body was big news in these parts. An event the locals didn't want to miss. Mixed in with the curious but harmless natives, were various news outlets; reporters and cameramen a little more creative in their zest for that one great shot. Skeet knew the competition was fierce and each station sent their best men and women in hopes of scooping their rivals as they reported the breaking news. Confirmation the murders were connected had reached the national syndicates. Anchors with the biggest networks debated everything from the mental stability of a serial killer to safety tips for the average American.

Skeet hit the button to roll down the driver's side window and casually flipped open his credentials as he approached the stoic lawman positioned to block the public from entering the scene.

Subterfuge

Within seconds, he was waived forward, around the barricade, and onto a make-shift parking area among the tall weeds.

He stepped from the vehicle and paused to take in his surroundings. The medical examiner already had a transport wagon parked among the marked units; various paramedic vehicles; and unmarked sedans that, most likely, belonged to the Violent Crime Detectives already working the scene. His forensics team hadn't arrived yet; but, he knew they couldn't be far behind. Unfortunately, that meant his boss, Supervisory Special Agent Frank Dumas, would also be arriving any minute. Skeet wasn't in the mood to deal with the pompous fool. He had a scene to process and a sadistic killer to track. With any luck, the media whore – also known as SSA Dumas - would spend his time hobnobbing with reporters in hopes of getting the proverbial fifteen minutes on screen.

Skeet turned his back on the vehicles and surveyed the area. Texas truly was filled with wide open spaces, another world completely when compared to his hometown of Chicago. And, still, violent and senseless death tainted the air as it destroyed the lives of another unsuspecting family. The sun had nearly set over the horizon replacing the clear blue, serene space overhead with a vibrant orange display that looked mystical and surreal somehow. Skeet was taken by surprise, amazed he could pause at such a horrible time to enjoy the beautiful and magnificent splendor Mother Nature offered... in comfort? Balance? Now, that was a question for another time and place. He sighed, took a deep breath and tried to focus on the task ahead as he surveyed the area. Birds chirped in the distance and a gust of wind kicked up, flapping the bottom edge of his leather trench coat before moving on to create a small dust devil that finally settled in a crop of aspen a few yards away. It would have been a peaceful, pleasant evening if not for the body. Another innocent girl traumatized and discarded by a madman. Skeet knew the scene all too well. He didn't have to see it to know what he would find just over the ridgeline. At least, the girl was out of sight; protected from the gawkers, cameras, and the madness. He closed his eyes and once again tried to focus; to relax his mind and utilize all of his senses. He felt a slight breeze in the air as it gently flitted across his warm skin, smelled the dust and smoke from the oil rigs, and listened to the cheerful tune of a nearby bird as he tried to prepare himself for the offensive scene that waited just a few yards away. He'd never been to Texas before; but he thought, under different circumstances, he might actually find it pleasant and relaxing.

He sighed deeply, only allowing himself a few seconds before he straightened and moved forward. His long strides took him to the yellow tape, and the uniformed officer stationed to protect the inner perimeter, in a matter of seconds. "Agent Skeeter Perkins," he offered before the man could turn him away. He flipped open his credentials and waited.

The sober lawman nodded once and held out a clipboard. "Anyone that goes beyond this line has to sign the log," he advised.

Skeet took the clipboard, perused the names scribbled on the official record, and added his own signature before handing it back. "Any idea where I can find Sgt. Rodriguez?" Skeet asked, referring to the local homicide sergeant.

"I believe he's still with the body, sir."

"Thanks." Skeet took a step forward, bent slightly and swung below the yellow police tape that was currently keeping all but essential personnel away from the dump site. He slowed, careful not to slip on the slight dip in terrain before moving in beside Rodriguez.

"As you can see, he's finished with our first victim," Rodriguez said in frustration. "You were right, we couldn't save her. Our Forensics Unit has already documented the scene. I was waiting for you; but, we're ready to roll her on your cue."

Subterfuge

"Give me a minute," Skeet said softly. He crouched down and leaned forward, shining his flashlight over the girl's lifeless body as he searched for clues. He knew they wouldn't find any. The man who considered himself a scientist was too careful, extremely meticulous, and probably a little paranoid. He cleaned every inch of the body carefully before he discarded his victims... usually out in a field in the middle of nowhere. So far, he hadn't left a single clue. Once the man was confident all evidence was removed, he loaded up his subject, transported her to a carefully selected drop point, and disposed of her lifeless form. Then, he moved on to the next young, naïve girl. An attractive, vulnerable woman he had carefully selected and abducted before his previous 'experiment' finally succumbed to her injuries. After only a few seconds, Skeet straightened and took a step back. "Go ahead."

Two men from the Medical Examiner's Transport Team moved forward.

She'd been beautiful, Skeet thought as they carefully rolled the body onto its stomach. Even the dull, cloudy film that now covered her eyes in death couldn't hide her good looks... or her innocence. So much potential snuffed out by a monster. He watched the two young ME techs take a few steps back, anger and pity evident in their eyes as they stood and waited a few feet away. "Document the number," Skeet said soberly as he skimmed over the shallow cuts and burn marks to focus on the permanent ink. It was an offensive symbol; one the killer used to debase and devalue each human life he touched.

A man with a large camera stepped forward and snapped a shot of the red number twenty-two tattooed on the girl's left hip, just above her buttocks. 'The Scientists' twenty-second victim. The media had penned the name and fighting it was futile. Skeet had learned long ago that once a serial killer was given a moniker, it stuck permanently. Anyway, he had more important things to worry about. Skeet hadn't located all the bodies yet and that fact still haunted him. There were six families out there who had no idea their loved ones had been murdered. Six sets of parents still holding out hope their little girl would find her way home someday. Skeet wouldn't stop until he gave them closure. He just hoped the knowledge would bring them peace instead of more pain and heartache. He had to believe knowing was better than uncertainty.

Skeet frowned as his gaze returned to the offensive numeral. "It looks fresh." He crouched again, reached out and touched the girl's palm. "This girl was killed no more than an hour ago — if I had to guess."

"I agree," Dr. Avery Moss said as he moved in closer to the body. "I'll run the tests and see how close we can pinpoint time of death, but rigor mortis hasn't begun to set in. See here, her shoulders have turned pale and the skin is still clammy and cool. Post Mortem lividity has begun; but, it hasn't reached the point of fixed lividity yet. That will take another seven to ten hours, at a guess. We all know the body has been moved; but, I'll document my findings and nail down TOD for trial once we get her to the lab."

"Thanks," Skeet said, placing a supportive hand on the ME's shoulder. "I can see the blood has begun to settle creating those red spots on the back of her shoulders, her buttocks, and the heels of her feet. Once we get the photos we need, they can roll her again. I know you'll want to transport the body on her back to preserve the evidence as much as possible."

The group watched as the cameraman took one last shot, sighed deeply, and stepped back. "She's all yours, Doc."

Skeet stood and glanced toward the designated parking area. His forensics team had just arrived. He turned his attention to Sgt. Rodriguez and realized his colleague had also spotted the van. "I'll talk to Krueger and have him coordinate with your guys. The chance of finding anything is slim; but, we have to run through it."

Subterfuge

"Yeah," Sgt. Rodriguez sighed. "We do. I'll go tell Harvo to play nice with the feds. When I'm done, we need to speak to the complainant and see what he knows."

Skeet followed the sergeant's gaze and spotted a middle-aged man sitting on the tailgate of an old pickup truck. Two officers in uniform flanked him. Even from this distance, Skeet could see the guy was white as a ghost and teetering on the verge of shock. In that condition, they'd be lucky if the guy remembered his own name; but, they needed the details before he had a beer with his buddies and muddied the facts with exaggerated tales conjured in his mind to impress his friends. Skeet had only taken two steps towards the traumatized man when a heated discussion caught his attention. What looked like a motorcycle cop was arguing with one of the brass. Skeet took a detour, determined to move the conversation to a more secluded area.

"I need to speak to the fed," the motor cop insisted.

"I said it can wait," the lieutenant countered.

"Is there a problem?" Skeet asked, stepping in closer to the duo. Both men abruptly stopped and turned to study the newcomer.

"Are you the federal agent in charge of this case?" the motor cop asked.

"I am," Skeet held out a hand. "Agent Skeeter Perkins."

"Deputy James Beck," the cop said as he gripped Skeet's hand in a firm shake.

"I'm not sure what this is about," Skeet turned to glance at a single cameraman that had left the designated media area and was slowly creeping closer to the small group. "But, I'd appreciate it if you could move this discussion to a more... private area."

The lieutenant looked up, scowled and headed for the lone cameraman. "Derek," Lieutenant Hancock growled. "This is your last warning. Either get behind that line, with the rest of the vultures, or I'm going to have my deputy cuff you and transport you for interfering."

"You can't..." Derek began.

"Oh," Lt. Hancock interrupted, "I can, and I will. I'm afraid I'll have to confiscate your camera as well. Evidence. I suspect that cutthroat producer of yours won't be too happy if his footage is locked up, safe and secure in a tamperproof evidence bin — all weekend. Your call," Hancock shrugged. "You have ten seconds to decide."

The cameraman turned and stomped back to the designated media area grumbling about the public's right to know.

Skeet grinned in approval — a man after his own heart.

"Sorry about that," Lt. Hancock said when he returned. "Derek has aspirations. He tends to push and manipulate his way over, under, and through a story until he gets a fresh lead. When that doesn't work— he sneaks."

"I'm used to it," Skeet assured him. "Now, if you'll excuse me. I have to go talk to a man about a murder."

"Before you go," Deputy Beck said quickly. "I was wondering if I could have just a few minutes of your time."

Skeet glanced at the man still sitting on the edge of the pickup and decided the guy could probably use a couple more minutes, anyway. "Sure, but a few is all I have."

"This can wait," Lt. Hancock said impatiently.

"No need," Skeet motioned for the deputy to proceed. "I'm here and I can spare the time."

Subterfuge

"Well," Deputy Beck began. "I work traffic, Motors. This month, it's my responsibility to put out the trailer. The speed trailer," he added at Skeet's look of confusion. The deputy pointed up the road to a small digital display mounted to a trailer parked on the side of the main highway.

"Okay," Skeet nodded. "I'm not sure how traffic control pertains to my homicide; but, go ahead."

"That trailer has been out here since Wednesday," Deputy Beck explained. "In that same spot."

"Again," Skeet began. "I'm not sure how..."

"It has a camera," Beck explained. "The Sheriff was able to pull together the funds for a state-of-the-art camera system for the trailer. We have a problem with speed racing — mostly on this road and sometimes a few streets over on Mapleview Drive."

"A camera?" Skeet considered. "Day use only, or night capabilities? What kind of light gathering sensor does the thing have?"

"That's the thing," Beck continued. "In addition to teenagers thinking they're the next Vin Diesel— Fast and Furious," he added when his lieutenant frowned. "We also have parents who think little Johnny is a saint. Even when we catch the kid in the act, mom and dad insist we have the wrong boy. We must have misunderstood their son's intentions. Johnny would never race on a public roadway. You know the drill. The parents spin their sob story; the case worker falls for it and demands leniency; and the juvie judge goes easy on the kid; which only reinforces the bad behavior. Anyway, Sheriff Conway was able to scrape up enough funds to buy a system that works at night. It was a necessity since that's when the little darlings start their innocent fun. We needed a way to capture the driver's face and a clear shot of the plate.

Now, when the misunderstood delinquent flies by the trailer, we have clear video to show mom and dad."

"How long?" Skeet asked. "How much video is retained on the system?"

"Like I said, I parked the thing out here Wednesday morning," Beck said soberly. "The hard drive will hold twenty-four hours of constant video; maybe, a little more. I normally swing by at the end of the day and download the footage, then wipe the drive and start fresh for another twenty-four."

"You're telling me you have a record of every car that drove this roadway over the past twenty-four hours?" Skeet clarified.

"More," Beck shrugged. "Like I said, I download the files daily. I have every vehicle that has driven this road since O-nine-hundred Wednesday morning. I'm not sure if anyone told you; but, that turnoff up there," Beck pointed to a T-intersection a few hundred yards away. "Well, that's the only way into this place. This side road continues for nearly a mile but then it dead-ends. I thought you should know, your killer had to drive right past my camera."

"And, we have video," Skeet smiled.

"And, we have video," Beck affirmed.

"I'm going to need everything," Skeet decided. "Everything you have since you posted that thing Wednesday morning. Can you help me with that, Deputy Beck?"

"Absolutely," Beck assured him. He glanced at the lieutenant. "Guess it was important after all. I'll head in, get started right away. Just send someone over to the main office. Maybe, give me an hour or so, and I'll have the discs ready."

Lt. Hancock narrowed his eyes at the deputy but decided to let the remark go. The kid was right, this might be important.

Subterfuge

And, if the video helped identify the killer, everyone involved in this cluster would be happy.

"I'm going to send Fulmer over to assist you," Skeet decided. "He's our resident e-Man. Best electronic guru on the planet if you ask me. He'll work with you on this, copy the footage, and coordinate any paperwork you need to make it official."

"I'll be waiting," Beck said before he turned and strolled away.

Skeet mumbled a thank you to the lieutenant then made his way across the field to join Sgt. Rodriguez. They had a witness to interview.

"What was that little tiff about?" Rodriguez asked when Skeet finally arrived. "You should probably know Hancock and Beck have history. The L.T. is constantly riding him over something or other. I kind of feel sorry for the guy, can't catch a break no matter how hard he works. And, Beck, he's solid, a hard worker, sharp too. He's wasting away in traffic, if you ask me."

"I agree," Skeet shrugged. "It appears we have video. If we get lucky, we might finally learn what our Mad Scientist looks like."

"Seriously?" Rodriguez glanced up the road. "I'd forgotten about that. Sheriff Conway finally had enough funds in the coffer to spring for the good stuff. He wanted a clear shot of the little turds using his highway as a raceway. Most parents around here like to believe their kid is pure and innocent. I can't count the number of misunderstood youth this county has. It's a travesty, I tell you. Us cops? We're out to get them... don't know why; but, apparently, there must be a reason."

Skeet grinned. "Let's talk to the witness. I think he's settled as much as he's going to."

* * * *

It was several hours later when Skeet finally arrived back at his hotel. The witness hadn't seen much; but, he had spotted a white van in the area. It was the reason he left the oil field and headed out to investigate. Skeet had grilled him as much as he dared under the circumstances. But, Dustin Rutledge had known the victim and he was more than a little traumatized by the entire incident. Who could blame him? Dustin was a longtime friend of Amanda's father, Nate Perdue. He described Amanda as a sweet, caring teen that walked her neighbor's dog when the eighty-year-old woman had her knee replaced; and she mowed the single mother up the road's lawn once a week during the summer. In other words, the girl had fit their suspect's preferences like a custom-made glove.

For the most part, the witness was a bust. He confirmed what Skeet already knew; Amanda fell smoothly into type; and, the unsub had access to a van. But, Skeet was still hopeful. This time, they had finally caught a break. He was positive they now had video of the killer. All they had to do was narrow it down. If he could get a clear shot of this Scientist, he was sure he'd be able to identify him — eventually. He was realistic enough to know they wouldn't save the next girl. The one the Scientist had probably started on tonight. But, maybe, just maybe, his killer wouldn't get a third girl. It was the best he could hope for. The pattern was well established. 'The Scientist' hadn't deviated, not once, and there was no reason to believe he would start now. He'd move into a city, set up his lab and abduct three young woman. Each was tortured, using various means, to see how long they could last under duress; then, given a number and discarded. When their bodies started to give out, after some trigger that only the killer knew, he'd

pick up his next subject.   He never started on the second victim
until the first one succumbed; but, he always had one waiting.
Once he finished with his third victim, he'd pick up stakes and move
on.

Skeet was determined to stop him this time.   If luck turned
his way, they might just catch this mad scientist before he devastated
the lives of another family, before he gathered up his tools and
disappeared for another month.   Skeet figured the killer used that
downtime to locate and outfit his new digs, maybe transport his
equipment and select his first victim in the new location.   He
hoped, with everything he had, Houston would be the last area the
man terrorized.

* * * *

Skeet climbed from the uncomfortable bed and headed for
the kitchenette.   He hadn't slept well, and he desperately needed
coffee…good, strong coffee and, about a gallon of it.   He settled in
and flipped on the television, it was always beneficial to see what
the media was reporting about your current case.   He instantly
regretted his decision.   All the morning shows were asking the
same questions.   *Why hadn't the FBI captured the man terrorizing
young women across the nation?   Was Agent Perkins in over his
head?   Had the world-renowned profiler risen up the ranks due to
luck, rather than talent?*   He shut it down, settled against the back
of the chair and tried to clear his mind completely.   Had he ever
called himself a hero?   No.   Had he ever said he could catch
anyone with the slightest lead?   No.   Had he claimed to be the best
profiler the world had ever known?   No, he had not.   It was the
same networks, the same commentators, now criticizing his
progress that had made him into some modern-day hero.   He wasn't

a hero, he was a cop. Skeet sighed and once again tried to force the disgust and the resentment from his mind. He had a long day ahead of him and he wanted to start fresh, not angry at the world. He would find his mad scientist in spite of the restrictions his current supervisor had placed on him, in spite of the image the media was portraying, in spite of the odds. He had to, it was the only acceptable outcome.

It was nearly an hour later when Skeet stepped into the temporary office and glanced around. Where were all the men? He made a beeline for Dumas' office and found that too, was empty. He turned and spotted Agent Kirkwood just outside the door.

"Hey, Skeet," he paused and frowned. "Dumas said you wouldn't be attending this briefing. Something about overtime, budget constraints, blah, blah, freakin' blah."

"He did, did he?" Skeet seethed. "I guess he'll just have to deal with disappointment, then. Any idea what enlightening words of wisdom he intends to impart?"

"No idea," Kirkwood frowned. "Did he try to shut you out again?"

"Try is the operative word," Skeet shrugged. "Don't worry about it. I can take it."

"What do you say I send you a personal invite, in the future I mean? I'll tag you anytime he calls us in," Kirkwood offered. "I don't like his games. None of us likes the way that man treats you. He doesn't even try to hide it."

"Thanks, I appreciate it; and, yes," Skeet decided. "I'll take you up on that offer. But, keep it to yourself. I don't want Dumas to get wind and shift his wrath to you. No good deed..."

"Right," Kirkwood grinned and stepped into the conference room.

Subterfuge

Skeet stepped in behind him. It took exactly two seconds for Dumas to spot his least favorite agent and scowl.

* * * *

"I was told there was a budgetary issue surrounding this operation," Skeet said casually once Dumas had finally ended his hour-long dissertation on responsibility to the public and emotional distance. "Don't you think the last hour would have been better utilized tracking our killer?"

"As I recall," Dumas said through gritted teeth. "You were not actually invited to this meeting. I wonder, Agent Perkins, what have you done to generate leads and locate the next victim this morning?"

"I'm glad you asked," Skeet said, standing and moving to the front of the room. "May I?" he snatched up the laser pointer his boss cherished more than breathing before he slipped a disc into the laptop and brought up a file. "I have cataloged the video Deputy Beck provided and split it into sections. Each of you will be assigned one section." He picked up a stack of papers and handed it to the agent sitting on the end of the first row. "Use these forms, document the license plate, color, registered owner, and make and model of each vehicle. Our killer is in there — somewhere. I've taken the last three hours of video; most likely, our guy is somewhere in that block. But, we've always believed our target scopes out his dump site prior to disposal...at least a day or two before the kill. Pay particular attention to any white vans. The Wit said that's what brought him into the area in the first place; it's the reason he stumbled onto the body so quickly."

"Agent Perkins," Dumas was furious. "I wasn't aware you received a promotion; one that comes with the authority to hand out assignments."

"That's because I didn't," Skeet said, unconcerned. "You asked, I complied. I planned to go over all of this with you earlier today; but, well... you scheduled this impromptu meeting and somehow, I guess I didn't get the memo. It was just a lucky break for all of us that I came in early. Makes it easier to divvy out assignments." He turned to the room and smiled. "Does anyone have concerns about my request?"

A variety of responses filled the room. "Nope... Not me... Sounds like a good strategy... Count me in..."

Skeet turned back to Dumas. "I'm also going to need at least two additional data techs to join the team."

"Not possible," Dumas said immediately. "Budget cuts, Perkins. I told you already, this time we are running thin. There's no room for extravagance."

"I need those techs," Skeet insisted. "We have hundreds of missing-person reports to comb through. If we can't determine the identity of his current victim, we have no hope of saving her."

"Focusing on the victim will not provide any insight into our killer," Dumas said as if he were speaking to a misbehaving child. "We've covered this already. Knowing Amanda Perdue was his first target here in Texas did nothing to find the location of his operation."

"Actually," Skeet said, narrowing his eyes at his boss. "Documenting when and where the man abducted his victims in Louisiana helped us locate the structure he used to work on them; and, it provided valuable insight into the man, his motives and his lifestyle."

Subterfuge

"And yet," Dumas said smugly. "He still got away and has already killed again. You won't be getting additional manpower, Perkins. Make better use of the people you already have." With that, he turned and left the room.

"I'm sure I can get Amy to help," Agent Troy Vance offered. "Her boss isn't as... uptight as our SSA. I have no doubt he'll approve the OT."

"Let me talk to him first," Skeet decided. "I need the help; but, I don't want Amy paying the price for her dedication and cooperation. We both know Dumas will pitch a fit the instant he sees her. Plus, we would need to coordinate travel, accommodations, and other expenses. Someone would have to pay for all of that."

"Well," Vance considered. "What if we just sent the details to her? She'd be more comfortable in her own space anyway; and, if Carter approves it, Dumas doesn't actually have to know."

"I'll talk to him," Skeet repeated. He liked the idea; but, he also felt the supervisor needed to know exactly what he was getting into before he agreed. He pulled out his phone and punched in the number. In less than five minutes, Skeet was grinning.

"Success?" Vance asked.

"Carter came through for us, big time," Skeet told his friend. "Thanks for the suggestion. We got Amy; but, he also threw in Miles and Josie. Apparently, all of them jumped at the chance to make a little extra. They're going through the missing-person database as we speak."

"Carter's the bomb," Vance sobered. "And, Dumas?"

"Carter said he has the funds in his own budget," Skeet relayed. "Claims there's no need to run it by anyone — especially

Dumas. As head of the department, he has the authority to authorize OT if he feels it's a priority. He's decided this case deserves the attention. He told me it was covered, I guess it's covered. I agreed to let him handle things his way. It's a win for us and Carter is thrilled. Apparently, I just presented him with the perfect opportunity to exact a little payback, whatever that means."

"Jabrowski case," Vance said absently.

"Are the rumors true, then?" Skeet asked.

"If by rumors, you mean did Dumas go behind Carter's back, basically steal the report off his desk, and take credit for all the work Carter put in tracking the hidden money? Then, yes, the rumors are true."

Skeet just shook his head in disgust.

"I can see words have failed you," Vance smiled. "I think I'll just take a moment to sit here and fill in the blanks myself, in the vast recesses of my own mind. There are so many that seem appropriate."

Skeet laughed and made his way to his desk.

* * * *

It was past eight o'clock in the evening when Miles phoned the conference room, confident he'd located their current victim. "I'm sending an email to you right now with all the pertinent data. I've contacted the Records Department at Houston PD already. Once the report comes through, I'll forward it on. I think we might get it tonight. I stressed how important it was to get the data immediately and the woman assisting me was extremely helpful."

Subterfuge

"Good work," Skeet told him. "All of you. I really appreciate you staying late to track this down. I won't forget how much you've helped us on this case."

"No prob," Miles said cheerfully. "We're happy to help. Don't hesitate to ring if we can jump in with anything else."

Skeet moved to his computer and opened the email already waiting in his inbox. Their current victim was Darla Thompson, a senior at Clear Lake High School in Houston, Texas. She'd gone missing two days ago. He clicked out of the email, not satisfied with the basics provided in NCIC, prepared to wait patiently for the actual report. The National Crime Information Center database, or NCIC, was a good resource if you were looking for the big picture; or, trying to match a person with a report; but, Skeet needed the details. And, for that, he would need to contact the detective assigned to Darla Thompson's case. His computer beeped again and Skeet clicked on a second email from Miles, surprised to see the Houston report had already arrived. He skimmed through it quickly, jotted down the details he wanted to include in the team's daily report, then fired the update off to all those involved with the task force. He printed off the entire document, set it aside for later, and went back to the video Beck had provided. He wanted to find that damn van. Needed to. The prospect of actually seeing an image of the man they'd been chasing, for far too long, had kept him motivated throughout the day. It was still driving him to work - just a little longer - before he called it a night.

Nearly an hour later, Skeet was starving, exhausted and jubilant. Exactly forty-two minutes before the body was reported by Rutledge, a white van approached the speed-trailer, slowed, and cautiously made a right turn onto the back road where Amanda's body was found. The man once again slowed, backed onto the open field and vanished in the thick shrubbery. Thirteen minutes later, it pulled back onto the roadway, made a left onto the highway and disappeared. "Gotcha," Skeet said in triumph. The video was crystal clear. The guy even rolled down his window and leaned outside to glance around before he backed off the roadway; oblivious to the fact his every move was being recorded.

He was younger than Skeet had expected. He'd created an extensive profile of the sadistic killer nearly a year ago, early on, during the FBI's original case. His official assessment put his target between the ages of twenty-five and forty. Unofficially, he thought the man was probably in his late thirties somewhere. He'd been wrong. This guy couldn't be more than thirty... thirty-two tops. He looked more like twenty-seven or twenty-eight. Some people looked young for their age; but, Skeet didn't think that was the case with this guy. He had dirty blonde hair and vibrant blue eyes — cold, dead eyes if you looked close enough.

But, Skeet figured the women he abducted probably didn't look. They were young, trusting and this mad scientist was attractive. A girl that age wouldn't see past the surface to the monster lurking inside. He had most likely coaxed them into the van somehow, maybe with a little innocent charm, maybe a request for help like Bundy had used. Once he got them where he wanted them, their life was altered forever.

Skeet worked another two hours before he called it a night and headed home. He'd been able to splice the video and grab a fairly good screenshot while he was at it. Feeling proud of his accomplishment, he attached both the video and the photo to another email and sent it out to the team. With any luck, one of the others would spot the same vehicle a day or two earlier when the suspect selected his dump site. It would be nice if he exited the van, maybe wandered around a little. They could get an idea of height and weight that way. If not, Skeet would settle for the face. Tomorrow, first thing, he was going to start contacting the locals. He'd need to reach out to each department where previous bodies had been found and see if they had the ability to run an image through their local systems. Scrolling through millions of driver's

Subterfuge

license photos manually would take months considering how many victims there were, how many agencies, how many different states were currently on the list. But, he had to start somewhere.

They could always release the photo to the media. He'd have to think about that. Once the guy saw his picture plastered nationwide, he'd probably work to change his looks; darken his hair, add a mustache, or buy brown contact lenses. There were too many ways to alter a person's appearance these days. No, he wasn't ready to release that photo just yet.

* * * *

Skeet's eyes felt like sandpaper as he moved slowly to his temporary desk and settled in. He was about to snag a cup of coffee when his phone began to ring. "Perkins."

"Hello," Dr. Moss said in greeting. "I'm glad I caught you. I wasn't sure what time you got in."

"Right about now," Skeet admitted.

"Well," Moss continued. "I found something. Can you make a trip to the morgue this morning?"

"Sure," Skeet stood. "Anything you can tell me over the phone?"

"There was a strange particle embedded inside the wound on our victim's head," Moss advised. "The skull was fractured and cleaned post mortem, but a particle of some sort remained. It appears to have snagged on the skull and didn't come loose during the cleaning."

"What kind of particle?" Skeet asked as he started his vehicle.

20

"That, I don't know," Moss sighed. "I have it here, wanted to send it to the lab; but, they're telling me to get in line. It could be at least a week before we have anything concrete on the item."

"Keep it," Skeet told him. "I'm on my way. I'll take it to our lab. Krueger can identify anything. I'll be there in ten." He disconnected the call and tried to resist the feeling of elation that wanted to break free. If the particle was unique, they'd just caught their second break. After twenty-one flawless murders, he finally had a solid lead — maybe two. But, he wouldn't get ahead of himself. The particle might not be unique, it might be something she picked up in that field.

* * * *

Skeet stood next to Amanda Perdue's body, magnified goggles secure, head bent, brow furrowed. Dr. Avery Moss was thorough. He'd spotted an anomaly in Amanda's body that hadn't been present in the others. Well, it hadn't been detected by his predecessors. Skeet straightened to consider. "I've always believed he was impotent - it explained the lack of sexual assault."

"Amanda is no exception," Moss assured him. "She wasn't raped or abused in that way. I tend to agree with you. I think this man is incapable of that kind of invasion."

"So, how did her uterus sustain that injury?"

"Now there's a question," Moss said, perplexed. "I'm still working on that. But, if you look closer — it's barely visible — she has the same burn mark on her left ovary."

"A burn," Skeet said slowly. "An internal burn that didn't injure her outer skin, blood vessels, anything. Do you think he's developed a new tool? Something like a laser or an x-ray machine?"

"I think this man is sick and twisted," Moss studied Perkins. "I think anything is possible. Medically, something like that would never be allowed; but, he's not restricted by rules and regulations. He's using it for his own pleasure, his own morbid experiments, nothing is off the table from what I see here. Whatever he used, it damaged the flesh and the muscle around the organ. The damage is so extensive it would never have healed properly, not without severe scarring. This girl was tortured to the point her body simply gave out, then she was cleaned up, drugged, and tortured again. If I'm right, and I am, the process that left that mark was intense and very painful. I would very much like to see him stopped... before another girl ends up on my slab."

"Just another area where you and I agree," Skeet focused on Amanda. It was an awful way to die, worse when it was someone so young and vulnerable. He knew he would see her in his nightmares; remember every burn, every cut, every bruise. She would join the other fifteen victims he had located over the past year; her image would haunt him forever; not just until the case was closed. He glanced over and saw the doctor was watching him.

"I just realized something," Moss said. "I've been wallowing all morning; well, since last night really. I even stopped the autopsy and tried to escape the image of this girl's death. I rarely do that... take a break before I've finished. It's a matter of professional standards I guess you could say. I went home, got a little drunk and tried — unsuccessfully I might add, to sleep. When that didn't work, I rose before the sun and returned; determined to finish the unpleasant task of documenting the cruelty a madman inflicted on an innocent girl. And, I remembered something I'd let myself forget. Life is precious. Still, I worked and felt sorry for myself. I even cursed fate a little before calling you in."

"I'm sorry you have to deal with this," Skeet said sincerely.

"And, that's what I realized just now," Moss put a hand on Skeet's shoulder. "I'm dealing with one girl. One tragic, brutalized, heartbreaking body. You have dealt with so many... twenty-two, I guess." He glanced at the tattoo. "Do you want me to analyze that as well? I assume your team already has pretty much everything on the ink, the method, the... well, everything."

"I'd appreciate it," Skeet said softly. "We do — have it. But, it's important to document it all; every time. It's important... she's important." He ran his hand through his hair and wondered how this kind, intelligent doctor had broken down all his defenses. He never showed his emotions, never admitted how much each of these girls broke his heart just a little more, never let a case get personal.

"I know it's none of my business," Moss added. "But, I think you are walking a fine line here. I think you have internalized far too much of the madness. I think you have done that; because, I know I have. My heart aches for this girl and her family. My blood boils with hatred for the man that did this. You are a controlled man, Agent Perkins; but, even a strong man needs someone." He glanced at Skeet's ring finger and studied the simple band. "I hope when you leave here, you can go to her, and let her in... lose yourself in the love and forget the evil for just a little while."

"I hope so, too," Skeet sighed. "Now, if you'll grab that particle sample, I'll get out of your hair."

"As you wish," Moss reached into a secured case and pulled out a small baggie. "I'll call you if I find anything else, including answers."

"Thanks," Skeet said, anxious to get outside. He needed air, he needed a minute to understand what had happened in there, a

Subterfuge

minute to lock away the pity and compassion he'd just received from a stranger.

* * * *

"It's come to my attention that you disobeyed my order and utilized additional personnel, from another department, after I very clearly denied your request," Dumas barked the instant Skeet stepped into the room.

Skeet sighed and focused on his boss. "Carter made that decision, you'll have to take it up with him."

"Do you seriously expect me to believe you had nothing to do with it?"

Skeet shrugged, dropped into his chair and pulled up the file on Darla Thompson.

"I could easily have you removed from this case, Agent Perkins," SSA Dumas said softly, leaning forward to invade his subordinate's space. "One more incident, one slight disagreement, and you're gone. You'll be lucky to work anything more complicated than a domestic on an army base."

"Clearly, you have never actually worked a domestic," Skeet said casually. "If you had, you would understand just how 'complicated' they can be. Sir," Skeet added, undeterred. Dumas could try to remove him; but, it would never happen and they both knew it.

Dumas straightened to his full height. "In the future, I expect all updates to go through me, to get approval before they are distributed to the other members of this team."

"I assume that directive has been given to the entire task force," Skeet pushed. He couldn't help himself. The irritating man had grated on his last nerve. "I mean, we all know how a discrimination complaint can impact a career," he shrugged, knowing Dumas desperately wanted to be promoted. "But, I'm more than happy to comply... once I get your official memo."

Dumas' face turned a bright shade of red before he pivoted and practically stomped to his office.

"Guess he changed his mind," Skeet said softly.

Several hours later, Skeet was running his suspect's face through the FBI's facial recognition program when Ryan Fulmer stepped up to his desk. "Heard you had some trouble this morning," the computer expert said soberly. "He won't succeed, you know? He barks, has that little dog syndrome I suspect; but, he won't be able to boot you from the team. He knows it, we all know it. I doubt he'll actually try."

"Doesn't matter," Skeet sat back and rubbed his aching eyes. "What brings you to my neck of the woods, Ryan?"

"I already ran your guy through the system," he nodded at the computer screen. "He's not in there. We pretty much knew that; but, it had to be done."

Skeet used his mouse to click a few buttons and the search was terminated. "Any ideas?"

"A few," he shrugged. "Working on it; but, everything I've come up with takes time. We don't have a lot of that to spare."

"Right," Skeet frowned.

"Vance did hit on your guy," Fulmer advised. He slid a sheet of paper onto the desk. "Full body shot. You called that one. Wouldn't want to dispose of a body just anywhere, I suppose. The cocky SOB spent ten minutes scoping out the area, based on the height of that van and the measurements I took when I went back out this morning..."

"You went back out to the scene?"

"Had to," Fulmer explained. "You want my results or not?"

"I want them," Skeet studied the man standing a few feet away from the van. He'd guess the guy was around six foot, one ninety maybe.

"Your Mad Scientist is five feet nine, one eighty — eighty-five, tops."

Skeet nodded. "The plate?"

"Stolen," Fulmer said. "Just like before... well, I guess after. This picture was taken the day before our guy returned with Amanda Perdue's remains. Both come back to vans registered in the area. But, here's the thing. I mapped everything out and I'm sure he's working within this area," Fulmer dropped a map of Houston and the surrounding area on Skeet's desk. "I pulled the report on the plate theft. The prick stole it on his way out to scout the site. Based on the time frame, he has to be somewhere within that circle."

Information was running through Skeet's head. They were getting close, they were closing in. He could feel it. "I agree. Can you send me that map? E-mail it..." he paused to glance at his ringing phone.

"Perkins."

"Before I make your day," Krueger began. "I just want to let you know, I like me a good bottle of whiskey now and again."

"What do you have?" Skeet demanded.

"That item you dropped off this morning?" he began. "I've identified it. It's a small piece of shale."

"Shell?" Skeet frowned. "As in sea shell?"

"Not shell," Krueger laughed. "Shale. Sedimentary rock, you moron."

"Okay," Skeet didn't know how that was going to help.

"It's what was on the shale that you might find interesting," Krueger continued. "Black soil mixed with minute traces of buffalo grass and alfalfa meal,"

"In layman terms?" Skeet pressed.

"It means I can narrow the location down to two places," Krueger said. "One is an old factory, shut down just over six years ago. The black clay was constantly shrinking and swelling until the foundation finally became unstable. Houston zoning officials condemned it, deemed it unsafe."

"And, the second?" Skeet didn't think the killer would camp out in a drafty and condemned, ancient factory.

"The other is an old farmhouse," Krueger advised. "It's only been vacant for a year. Belongs to the Stubbins."

"Where are the Stubbins?" Skeet asked.

"Thought you might ask. Agnes died about eighteen months ago," Krueger provided. "Her husband, Joe Stubbin, is currently residing at Garden Terrace. It's a senior center for those with Alzheimer's and early onset Dementia. Joe went downhill fast after his wife passed. The property is currently vacant. There's a civil case pending, seems the kids are battling with each other over what to do with the place. I've sent you my findings," Krueger advised. "Call me if you need anything else."

Subterfuge

Ryan Fulmer gave Skeet a pained look once he disconnected the call. "Uh, there's something you should know."

"What?" Skeet asked absently.

"Dumas is monitoring your data."

Skeet's head shot up. "Define monitoring."

"He put in an order for full access to your system," Ryan told him. "It had all the proper approval, so my tech complied with the order. If Krueger sent you the results, Dumas has them as well."

"I can deal with Dumas," Skeet decided. He was pissed... beyond livid. More furious than he'd been in a very long time; but, he'd set it aside for the case. Then, once this was over, he'd deal with SSA Dumas. The man had gone too far this time and he was going to have consequences. "Can you do me a favor? Forward the paperwork to Burns."

"Skeet," Fulmer objected. "My guy didn't have a choice. The order came through, he had to comply."

"I agree," Skeet assured him. "And, so will Stan; but, I need him to know Dumas gave the order. It would be better if it came from you, rather than me."

Fulmer grinned. "Already done, twenty minutes ago."

Skeet was about to respond when his phone chimed again. He glanced at the display. "I have to take this. Perkins."

"Skeet," Stanley Burns said coolly.

"Yes, sir," that should alert his long-time friend he wasn't alone.

"I need to talk to you, privately," Burns added. "Whatever you're doing, excuse yourself so we can talk."

"Give me a minute to find an empty room and I'll call you back," Skeet clicked off.

"Burns?" Fulmer asked.

"Yeah," Skeet stood.

"Conference room is empty," Fulmer also stood. "I'm going to work with Vance for a bit. Watch your step, Dumas is on a mission. He's determined to bring you down for some reason." He shook his head. "The entire Bureau knows Burns is a close friend. Well, everyone it seems but SSA Dumas. How is that even possible?"

"I'm stumped," Skeet smiled. "I mean, he's a trained observer after all. It simply defies logic."

* * * *

It took nearly thirty minutes to calm Burns down. His friend and mentor, who also happened to be the Executive Assistant Director in charge of Criminal Investigations, was even more livid about the intrusion than Skeet had been. Skeet promised to watch his back and notify Stan immediately if Dumas crossed another line. He hadn't wanted to make that promise; but, Burns insisted. It made Skeet feel like a tattle-tale child; but, he'd keep his word if necessary, and decide what to do about the bigger problem once the case was complete. Unfortunately, it was time to find a new home.

He stepped into the large office Dumas had procured and waited for his boss to acknowledge him. It took two full minutes before Skeet's supervisor glanced up and motioned for him to proceed.

Subterfuge

"Krueger identified the tiny substance found in the victim's skull," Skeet told him. "Based on his findings, Fulmer's analysis, and my profile... the only possible target is an old farmhouse on the outskirts of town."

"I disagree," Dumas settled back in his chair. "I'm just putting the final touches on a tactical operation at the abandoned factory. I didn't plan to include you; but, if you insist on participating, I suppose I can find something for you to do."

"You're making a mistake," Skeet began.

Dumas held up a hand. "Save it. I'm still in charge here and I say we're hitting the factory. Briefing is in fifteen minutes - in the conference room."

Skeet stood in the doorway, frustrated, furious and out of options. His boss was wasting time — time Darla didn't have; but, there was nothing he could do to stop him.

* * * *

The large group was gathered in the conference room, listening as Dumas presented his plans for the Op. Skeet thought it had a lot of holes; but, he kept his mouth shut. It didn't matter, the suspect wasn't there; so, safety wasn't really an issue.

"Are there any questions," Dumas asked, not expecting any.

Lt. Travis Carrigan, the SWAT Commander with Houston PD, motioned with a subtle wave of his hand. "That place is unstable," he began. "We need to scout the property prior to hitting the building to make sure the electrical is still safe and the structure can handle the extra weight."

"That's not necessary," Dumas dismissed him. "Anything else?"

"Yeah," Carrigan snarled. "Where are you putting the marksmen?"

"Lieutenant," Skeet was surprised that with one word, Dumas had conveyed impatience, condescension, and arrogance. "The target will not have a weapon," Dumas provided. "It's not necessary to position marksmen on this particular mission."

"With all due respect," Carrigan said blandly. "It's always necessary."

"I have a question," Skeet jumped in. "When you find the factory empty, will we be regrouping here to formulate another plan before we hit the farmhouse; or, will we do that on-scene? I'd like to be prepared," he added and resisted grinning at the anger evident in his supervisor's face.

"Agent Perkins," Dumas warned.

"What farmhouse?" Carrigan demanded.

"Our particle guy, Krueger, he identified two possible targets," Skeet explained. "The factory, and an old farmhouse that is currently vacant and tied up in some civil case. It belongs to the Stubbins, I believe."

"I know that place," Carrigan said carefully. "Why do you think that's a possible target?"

Before Dumas could shut the topic down, Krueger jumped in and explained his reasoning to the local SWAT expert. Ryan Fulmer added his findings to the mix as well, explaining how those two properties were the only ones within his target area that fit Krueger's findings. Carrigan turned to Skeet. "I'm told you're the best profiler the Bureau has on tap."

Subterfuge

"Those reports are highly overstated," Dumas snapped.

Carrigan ignored him. "Do you agree with this?" He motioned to the board that contained the op plan. "Do you think the factory is the most likely target?"

"No," Skeet told him. "I do not. I believe our killer likes his creature comforts. He would not lower himself to hide out in an old, drafty factory. He'd want a home, seclusion and... everything that goes with that. He would need access to water, electricity, heat as well as privacy. In my opinion, the farmhouse is the most likely target. But, I was overruled by my supervisor."

"I see," Carrigan was silent as he considered the situation. "I'm afraid our agency cannot assist you in the current operation," he told Dumas. "I'm not comfortable with the lack of preparation, the lack of intelligence, and your lack of concern for my men's safety. I wish you luck at that factory and hope you get your man. But, as you just stated, there is no reason to believe the man is armed. The threat level is low, it doesn't meet our threshold; and therefore, there is no need to utilize SWAT on this warrant." He stood and left the room.

"Perkins," Dumas said softly. "Effective immediately, you are off this team. You are now banned from all investigative activities; including the warrant service tonight. You are also barred from speaking to anyone on the task force. Do not test me on this. If you come within one mile of that factory, I'll have your job."

Skeet stood and left the room. He didn't care about the factory. He was happy to steer clear, he did care about the case. He cared about a young girl that was currently being tortured beyond what any human could endure. He cared about Darla Thompson; and, he cared about the third victim. Because, his gut told him the Scientist had already abducted another one.

"Perkins," Carrigan pushed away from the wall and stepped up next to him. "We need to talk."

"I'm afraid I'm not on the task force any longer."

"Idiot," Carrigan shook his head. "If our guys can get us a warrant for the farmhouse, you want in?"

Skeet froze. "I do."

"You'll catch hell for it," Carrigan warned. "That man in there is afraid of you, he clearly feels threatened by you, and I think he'll go to any length to ruin you. I could use you, though. I want your knowledge and your experience; but, I also know that might cost you. I'm just going to say you're welcome to join us; and, unlike that man in there, we'd be honored to have you."

Skeet was surprised and a little confused by the praise. "You don't know me."

"Doc Moss does," Carrigan shrugged. "And, I'm a good judge of character. Some people have it..." he glanced back at the door to the conference room, "some don't."

"You get that warrant and I'm in," Skeet decided. "How are you going to get around the low-threat level?"

"In your opinion, do we need SWAT on this?"

"I recommend it," Skeet considered. "There's no evidence to suggest our suspect owns a gun; but, he does have a large collection of knives as well as other lethal instruments he routinely uses to torture his victims. We both know there are a lot of options, dangerous weapons he may have readily available other than a firearm. I don't believe he would hesitate to use any number of them if cornered."

"Well," Carrigan grinned. "Lookie there, the threat level just jumped significantly. I'm going to call Rodriguez. This is his case and it's up to him; but, I'm fairly confident he'll agree and move forward immediately. I'll tag you as soon as I can with an answer."

Skeet watched the lieutenant disappear down the hallway. He was grateful to be included; but, Carrigan was right, this was going to be dicey. He'd have to call Stan, a call he wasn't looking forward to; but, a promise was a promise and Skeet always kept his word.

* * * *

It was several hours later when the local team pulled up to the farmhouse. The judge had a few questions once he learned the feds were hitting a warehouse with the same goal in mind. He also wanted to know why the local homicide sergeant hadn't tapped the same magistrate, suspicious they were judge shopping to get what they wanted. Rodriguez had smoothed it over, scored the warrant, turned the information over to Carrigan; who sent a couple of his men out to scout the property, and then scheduled a briefing. In just a few hours, they had hashed out possible problems, discussed entry options and generated not one -- but two entry plans in case anything went wrong. Skeet had to admit, he was impressed. These guys were professionals and they knew tactics better than anyone he had dealt with in the past.

He was standing on the edge of the property, camouflaged by the trees, when the entry team detonated a liquid explosive they had attached to the front door and rushed inside as a cohesive unit. The men telegraphed their progress over the police radio as they worked. They moved swiftly through the main level of the home, checked each room carefully, cleared closets, the attic, anywhere a person could hide out or ambush an intruder. Once they completed a thorough search of the main level, the team moved to the stairwell.

"Visibility is limited," Skeet heard over the radio. "We're going to try to get eyes on and see what's below us."

Skeet held his breath. His gut told him Darla was below them; but, was the suspect waiting for them as well? Several agonizing minutes passed, and the radio remained silent... eerily so. He focused on the house, would he know if someone was hurt? Had the killer set traps to preserve his space and his work?

"Target is clear," came a voice over the air. "We need medical and the bolt cutters. Also, send in a detective to secure the scene."

"Agent Perkins, Tac 10," came Carrigan's voice over the air. "I need you to respond to the residence. One of my guys will escort you into the basement."

Skeet frowned but complied. They agreed before the group arrived that he'd wait on the outskirts for the tactical team to finish up inside and the detectives to approve it, before he entered the residence — something was wrong.

* * * *

Darla Thompson was unconscious – or dead. Skeet realized that the instant he saw the horrific room. She was naked and chained to some kind of platform. The Scientist must have built it himself. The base contained nearly an inch of clear liquid. Around the edge was a flat, narrow lip just wide enough to fit a person — if they didn't move or shift their body too much. The SWAT guys had moved a large piece of plywood onto the platform and placed the girl's body on top of it. Skeet took several steps forward before Lt. Carrigan blocked his path.

"The liquid is some kind of acid concoction. Looks like she moved as far to the side as she could on that flat section, clearly trying to avoid the liquid; but, once she passed out, her legs shifted and slid into the acid, which then started to eat through," he swallowed hard. "It looks like the skin and most of the flesh on the bottom of her feet is gone, completely. Our tactical medic did find a pulse; but, it's weak. They're working to get those chains off; but, he's rigged some kind of electrical current to them. It's low voltage, and appears to be powered by that box over there. Now that we have the bolt cutters, my guys are trying to work through the shock to cut those chains off. Rodriguez also went upstairs to look for the breaker box. We thought if he could find it, we would just shut down power to the entire home."

Skeet took a deep breath and focused on the job at hand. He could be horrified later. Right now, he needed to shut down the source of the electrical current. "I might be able to help with that." He moved in behind the group of officers working to free their victim, and studied what he recognized as a controller for an electrified fence used by ranchers to keep their livestock contained. He guessed that made sense, it would be an easy way to funnel limited power without electrocuting his prisoner. Within seconds, he had the wires disconnected and the hindrance that was slowing down the men neutralized. "That should make things easier, test it to be sure; but, there shouldn't be any power going to that..." he paused not knowing what to call it. "Hideous prison now."

One of the men tested the nearest metal chain, realized the power had been shut down, and quickly cut the last binding from the wall. They couldn't get the leather manacles off; but, at least, the girl was free. Several men lifted Darla from the platform and gently set her onto a nearby stretcher. The medics rushed her up the stairs and out to the ambulance waiting near the door.

The initial shock had passed, and Skeet was now studying his surroundings. He moved in next to Carrigan and casually bumped the man's ribs.

Carrigan jumped, then turned. "What?"

"We're being watched," Skeet casually glanced around the room hoping the Commander would spot the camera.

"The SOB has to be close," Carrigan decided. "Let me see if we have anyone that can work on that."

"Fulmer is in my car," Skeet admitted. "He insisted on coming, and since he wasn't needed at the other location, I agreed. Send him in. If anyone can track that, he can."

It took less than five minutes for Carrigan to move back in next to Skeet. "He said he's working on it. Doesn't want to come in. Said he doesn't need to. Rodriguez decided to stay outside and help him."

* * * *

The man the world now knew as the Scientist stood on the other side of river, fuming. How did they find his workshop? How did they locate him? They'd never even come close before and he hadn't packed up his tools, his journal, his life's work. He studied the tiny monitor, focusing on the man in the dark, leather coat. Agent Skeeter Perkins. Maybe, he'd underestimated his rival. Didn't matter. They may have found his laboratory; but, they didn't find him. They didn't know who he was. They didn't even know what he looked like. He watched as the men in combat gear freed his latest specimen and lowered her to a stretcher. The

Subterfuge

woman had been a disappointment; but, she was still his. His property, his test subject, his lab rat. He needed to finish documenting her failure. Wanted to witness the moment she took her last breath. They had no right to be here. He kicked at the dirt in frustration, glanced toward the waiting van, and sighed.

Agent Perkins may have foiled his latest research trial; but, he didn't thwart his mission, hadn't foiled his objective, hadn't stopped his purpose. The agent had certainly interfered. Had obstructed his work and delayed his progress significantly; and, for that, he would have to pay a price. A high, personal price. One he, a professional scientist, would enjoy exacting — immensely. He set the hand-held device with the attached monitor on the driver's seat, paused to glance at the bundle lying motionless in the cargo section of the van with regret, then walked away. It took less than three minutes to reach the waiting car — his get-away vehicle. *One should always have a plan.* He was still furious forty minutes later when he stepped onto his private plane and gave the pilot their next destination. Not even thoughts of revenge soothed his mood tonight. He still had most of the data he'd collected, it was stored in his private cloud account; but, the last test - the subject he'd spent so much time nurturing - was lost completely. He hadn't had time to transfer his personal notes to his electronic ledger. Fury engulfed him, grew inside and threatened to explode... to the point he wanted to scream, to lash out and destroy everything in his wake. It was all gone, his tools, his private notes, his life's work. Yes, Skeeter Perkins was going to pay dearly for his actions tonight... and he'd never see it coming. The Scientist settled in to develop a plan.

Chapter Two

Skeet sat at his desk, skimming the internet for the first flight back to Chicago. He wanted out of this place. He wanted a cold beer, his favorite recliner, and his wife. Angela was home waiting for him now. She'd been on the road for nearly three weeks this time. A grueling tour with four exhibitions to display her amazing work. He was proud of her for abandoning her safe career as an internet consultant and following her passion; but, he missed her terribly. The only thing that had gotten him through so many weeks apart was this case. But, his work here was done — yet, incomplete. Angela had called him the previous evening, excited to announce every one of her paintings had sold. He wasn't surprised, his wife had talent – amazing talent. He had told her as much the first day they met. He remembered that day like it was yesterday; the attraction had been instant. He smiled, remembering how she stood out in a crowd, even though she was doing her best to blend in. The sun was bright that day, highlighting the champagne, golden honey and sun-kissed blond hair that she had pulled into a messy ponytail. She was wearing an old t-shirt and cutoff jeans, both were covered in fresh paint. He was sure, if he

Subterfuge

could get close enough, the woman would smell as sweet as honeysuckle in the summer breeze. He had sat on that uncomfortable bench watching her from a distance, long enough that he felt like a voyeur, before he gathered enough courage to approach her. That was the day she shared her masterpiece with him. At the time, she'd been self-conscious and insecure. Now, especially after the success of the past month, she was confident and determined to make her mark. He was more than happy to support her dream, no matter the personal cost. Over the past few weeks, the cost had been intense loneliness.

Exhausted and still a little frustrated, he leaned back and ran his hands over his face. He wished he could see things differently; but, no matter how he came at it... the mission had failed. Oh, they'd rescued the girls. Fulmer had traced the signal from the camera to the rolling hills behind the Stubbin's farm, across the river, and a few feet into a stand of trees. There, they located the van — and Jessica Messina. The girl was unconscious, handcuffed to a bar that had been welded to the stolen van, and abandoned. He was grateful she'd been located so quickly, and grateful Darla was still breathing. He supposed that was something, although her chance of survival was slim in the long run. Darla had extensive damage. Too much damage. One of her kidneys had failed, her feet were a distorted mess from the acid; and, like the first victim, she had mysterious burns on the inside of her body. At least, if she died, she'd be surrounded by family... not chained to a wall, cold and alone. He glanced up and sighed when Dumas stepped into the room.

"Perkins," he barked as he walked by. "In my office."

Skeet stood and followed the bane of his existence into the elaborate space.

"Why are you here?"

"I was just leaving," Skeet said soberly. "I'm out of here as soon as I find a flight home."

Dumas reached into the inside pocket of his suitcoat and pulled out an envelope. "You're already booked on a flight, leaves tomorrow night at twenty-one hundred."

"I was thinking of leaving much sooner," Skeet argued. "We're done here. There's no reason to drag this out. I need to get home. We need to figure out where the Scientist is headed. Plus, I still haven't identified him. We don't know his name, where he's from, where he now resides. That video is key."

"You leave tomorrow," Dumas corrected. "And, since you insist on working a case that is no longer your responsibility, I suggest you spend your time going through his latest hideout. You let him escape, if he kills another girl — it's on you."

Skeet gritted his teeth but somehow managed to remain silent.

"You disagree?" Dumas settled against the back of his chair. "I've already sent a report up the chain outlining your insubordination and informing the administration of your mistakes. I also let them know our killer was able to escape because you disobeyed a direct order and hit that farmhouse without approval."

"First," Skeet forced air through his nose and told himself to keep his cool. "I didn't hit that farmhouse. I merely accompanied the local police department on a warrant they were serving on a potential target. A warrant that pertained to our case... and theirs."

"Tell it to the review board," Dumas shrugged. "I'm finished with you. I want you off this case, I made that clear in my report. You are arrogant, insubordinate and cocky. You refuse to work with the team and can't handle direction — or, correction. I just hope another family doesn't suffer because you let a madman slip through the net."

Subterfuge

"How do you figure?" Skeet was truly curious how the man justified blaming him for the cluster tonight.

Dumas studied Skeet for several seconds. "If I have to explain it to you... well, I guess you're not as smart as everyone seems to think you are. Agent Perkins, you created this mess. You undermined my operation, went off half-cocked to play cowboy, and lost the killer in the process. I on the other hand, coordinated a successful search of an abandoned factory. I personally obtained the warrant, I led the team, and I eliminated one of two possible targets."

"The wrong target," Skeet mumbled. He had eliminated that target before anyone even stepped foot in the place.

"Once I determined the building was clear, I began the process of obtaining a second warrant - on our other target," Dumas continued undeterred. "That's when I learned the local police had already petitioned the court and was granted a search warrant on said location. Before I could step in, before I could call you off, regroup, and plan for another mission tomorrow night... you and the rest of your band of hotheads stormed the farmhouse, tipped off our suspect, and left the place empty handed."

"Somehow," Skeet said softly. "I think Darla Thompson and her family would disagree. I'd add in Jessica Messina and her family as well. My band of hotheads, as you put it, rescued two women tonight. What do you have to show for your efforts?"

"That's quite enough," Dumas warned. "We both know, had we waited as I intended to do, the killer would be vulnerable right now. He'd be completely oblivious to the fact that we were closing in. And, less than twenty-four hours from now, he would be locked up tight awaiting trial for his heinous crimes."

"I don't know that and neither do you," Skeet disagreed. "What I do know, is that if we had waited — as you planned to do — Darla Thompson would be dead. And, at this very moment, Jessica Messina would be suffering. She would be stripped naked, chained to a platform, and forced to endure excruciating pain and torture. The likes of which you can't even imagine."

"Darla Thompson will most likely die anyway," Dumas waved a hand in dismissal. "And, the girl could survive one night of pain if it meant capturing the individual who killed so many others."

Skeet stared at the man sitting before him, dumbfounded and in utter disbelief. That's when it hit him - he simply could not take any more. Not tonight, not ever. He couldn't work for a man like Dumas. If the review board didn't transfer him off this team, he'd submit an official request of his own. He was good at tracking killers, excelled at profiling, could easily slide into the mind of the worst monsters society had ever seen... and he was done. He'd rather guard a cornfield in Iowa than work one more minute for a man that would willingly subject an innocent girl to torture just to have his way. Skeet slowly turned and headed for the exit. He stopped at his desk, gathered up his case files, and took a minute to shut down the computer. He didn't even pause to glance back as he walked away. He was done here, and he needed air.

Skeet had just stepped outside the building and was approaching his rental car when his phone rang. He glanced at the display, saw it was Stanley Burns, and let it go to voicemail. He didn't have the energy to deal with him right now. As he pulled from the lot, he briefly wondered if his mentor was calling to give him support, or censure. Didn't matter, he couldn't handle either one at the moment. The instant he stepped into the run-down motel and shut the door, he settled onto the bed and called home. He needed his wife, needed to hear her sweet voice and desperately wished he'd booked the redeye before Dumas had cornered him. Too late now. He'd waste his time in Houston, then he'd fly back

Subterfuge

to Chicago and demand a vacation. They could debate his actions, and his future, all they wanted. Skeet knew he had done the right thing.

"Hi, baby. I miss you," Angela said in greeting.

* * * *

Officer Rowdy Cooper pulled on the last door and relaxed. The local elementary school was secure; another false alarm. He glanced down at his K9 companion and gave the command to go play. Knight could use a break. And, to be honest, so could Rowdy. He'd been busy tonight. For some reason, they were always busy during a full moon. Something about the bright orb brought out the crazies, and tonight was no exception. He glanced at his watch and decided to give his favorite German shepherd a few more minutes of freedom before clearing his detail. The mutt needed a short break to run free and mark a few trees, Rowdy was willing to oblige. He leaned against the front of his truck, relaxed and content as he waited.

Several minutes later, he straightened and sighed when his radio beeped three times, followed by the familiar voice of his favorite dispatcher. "Break time over," he said softly when he recognized the address. He was only two, maybe three, blocks away. "Knight," he called. "Truck." Within seconds, they were locked up tight and ready to roll.

"Dispatch, Kilo 3," Rowdy said into the mic.

"Kilo 3," came the quick response.

"Assign that open door to me and show me enroute."

"Copy."

"ETA, one minute. And, clear me from the alarm at the elementary school. Everything is Code 4 and secure."

"Copy, cleared at twenty-two fifteen," dispatch acknowledged.

Rowdy slid to a stop in front of the residence and frowned. There were several lights visible through the windows and a door was standing wide open at the side of the house. "Kilo-3, show me arrived," he said into the mic.

"Do you want a back?"

"I'll advise," Rowdy answered before moving to the back of his unit and releasing his dog. He gave the command to heel and proceeded to the side of the house.

Rowdy could hear music coming from inside the home. He moved cautiously to the side of the open door and called into the darkness. "Police, are you okay in there?" No answer. He tried again, still no answer. He glanced at his dog then stepped into a large kitchen. So far, there was no sign of anyone. As he peered around the corner, he again called down the hallway. "Police, is anyone home?" No answer. He moved into what looked like a living room and called out again. A lamp was glowing in the far corner, but there was still no sign of the owners. He was about to head down the long hallway when an envelope caught his attention. "Agent Perkins" was scribbled across the front; in bright red, bold letters. Was the owner a cop? Agent meant federal — FBI, DEA, ATF— the options were limitless. His gut clenched, and instinct told him something was seriously wrong. "Skeeter or Angela Perkins? This is the police, is anyone home?"

Rowdy and Knight made their way down the long hallway and moved into the first room to the right. It was designed as a bedroom, but someone had made it into a workspace. An artist

45

Subterfuge

lived here, a painter. "Well," Rowdy told his dog. "We found the radio. Stay." He moved cautiously across the room and hit the off button, thankful for the instant silence. Knight was standing just inside the doorway waiting impatiently for his next instruction. "Find him," Rowdy said, giving his partner the command to do a thorough search of the residence. One glance at the room told Rowdy there was trouble. There were obvious signs of struggle everywhere. A paint can was tipped on the side, liquid oozed out and spread several inches across the floor. The easel was tipped over and the enormous canvas was upside-down on the floor. The most obvious sign was the blood. Not a lot, just a smear here and there — on the back of the chair, on the door jamb and a few smears and small drops on the floor. He was pretty sure they wouldn't find anyone inside the residence. The perp and his victim were long gone; but, he had to check.

Once the upstairs was cleared, Rowdy and Knight moved to the basement. Within minutes, he found the point of entry. A window was broken in what looked like an office. Glass was scattered over the carpet, the desk, and an expensive leather chair. "Shit." He reached for his phone and dialed his brother. Coop was on call tonight and he needed a detective. He shifted his attention to his dog, Knight had caught a scent and was trying to jump onto the sill and climb out the window. "Heel, boy," he said absently just as Detective Andy Cooper answered the call.

"Not likely," Coop laughed.

"I need you on my detail," Rowdy said soberly. "I think we have an abduction."

"On my way," Coop pulled into the nearest parking lot. "Give me the address so I don't have to look it up."

Rowdy rattled it off then paused. "Uh... Coop?"

"What's wrong?"

Rowdy had exited the house through the side door, pulling it shut behind him. He glanced around to make sure he hadn't attracted attention from the neighbors. So far — so good. It was a quiet neighborhood and he hadn't seen a soul since he arrived. Confident he could do the search without anyone compromising the scene, he made his way to the back of the house. When he reached the corner of the residence, he gave his dog a pat and once again ordered, "find him."

"Are you still searching?" Coop asked, confused when he overheard the command.

"Yeah," Rowdy watched as his dog approached the broken window, sniffed the ground and took off across the backyard. "Get here fast, bro. I think the guy's a cop."

"You think?" Coop asked, making a sharp left. "Why don't you know? Hold on. Dispatch, Car 201, show me unavailable and responding to Kilo 3's detail."

"Copy, twenty-two nineteen."

"There was an envelope on the mantel addressed to an Agent Perkins," Rowdy said as he left the manicured lawn and made his way through a tiny gate. On the other side, the property was lined with large trees before it emptied out onto a small service road. Knight was pacing back and forth along the roadway. Every once in a while, he'd turn, focus on Rowdy and whine before heading in the opposite direction.

"Okay," Coop considered. "As in, out of place and left by the perp?"

"Yes," Rowdy pulled out his flashlight and studied the ground near the roadway. He wasn't going to find a clue he could use in that mess. There were tire tracks everywhere... tons of them.

Subterfuge

He moved to restrain Knight and froze, his dog was sniffing at a rag, pushing it around with his nose like a toy. Rowdy snapped on the leash and pulled Knight a few feet back. "Stay," he ordered before crouching to study the small piece of cloth more closely. "Where are you, Coop?"

"Just pulling up to the residence," Coop said as he parked behind Rowdy's truck and shut down the engine. "Where are you?"

"Around back," he stood and waved his light, making a circle toward the residence. "Can you see me? If so, bring an evidence bag."

"On my way," Coop ended the call and made his way to his brother. "What are you doing out here?"

"Did you bring the bag?" he waited while Coop reached into his pocket and passed Rowdy a plastic baggie.

"What is it?" Coop moved forward to study the cloth more closely.

"The woman was a painter," Rowdy provided. "Looks like she was listening to some tunes while she worked on her current piece. Bad guy breaks a window in the basement, sneaks upstairs and a fight ensues."

"Signs of a struggle?"

"Tons of them," Rowdy confirmed. "And, there's blood, not a lot, mostly smears and a few small drops. I think one, or both of them are injured. If I had to guess, that blood belongs to one of them. Maybe dropped by the victim before she was shoved into a waiting vehicle."

48

"Okay," Coop took the evidence and shoved it back into his pocket. "Let's take a look inside."

"The home is owned by Angela and Skeeter Perkins," Rowdy provided. "I ran it before I approached the open door. Wanted to know who to call out to if I had to go inside."

"We need to confirm his status with the Bureau," Coop moved forward and spotted the envelope. He reached into his back pocket and pulled out a pair of rubber gloves. The envelope wasn't sealed and most likely didn't have any prints; but, Coop was careful not to touch it more than necessary. The letter inside was short and to the point. "Agent Perkins, you took my girls — I took yours."

"FBI?" Rowdy asked, looking over Coop's shoulder to read the note.

"Yeah," Coop sighed. "You don't recognize the name?"

"Should I?"

Coop shook his head in resignation, his brother never was big on current events. "He's some bigshot profiler with the Bureau. Young guy on a fast-track to the top and supposedly brilliant. They say he can find a killer faster than a speeding bullet; if you buy into all that national media hype."

"I'm going to put Knight back in the truck," Rowdy decided. "The work space is the first door down the hall, to the right. Go ahead and check it out. While I'm out there, I'll call dispatch and have them track down this Agent Superman, or his boss."

"Can you also have forensics respond?" Coop asked. "We'll need them to photograph everything, the broken window downstairs, the blood, and the chaos in the workroom. We need photos and samples of all of it."

"On it," Rowdy said before disappearing out the door.

Subterfuge

* * * *

"You're going to pay for that you stupid whore," the Scientist practically screamed as he pushed the woman into the passenger's seat and snapped on the restraints. She couldn't answer because he had tied a large strip of cloth around her mouth before pulling her from the residence. After the fight they'd just had, he wouldn't take any chances. The streets were empty; but, if the woman started shouting, the neighbors were sure to come running. He was out of time and needed to get far away from the area before someone called the police. Especially since he wasn't able to close the back door when they left. He knew if he let go of the hostile woman – even for a mere second to secure the residence, she might escape; and, he couldn't risk that. He climbed behind the wheel, reached into the back seat and snatched up a small towel.

His nose was still bleeding, and his face felt like it was on fire. He knew it would be more of a challenge, abducting the wife of an agent; but, he hadn't been prepared for this. The woman had struck him on the side of the head with the two-by-four that held her canvas in place. She'd made contact before he even saw it coming. He'd seen stars, actually saw bright flashes of light from the impact. He had almost regained his composure when she struck out again, catching his nose with the make-shift weapon. Blood gushed instantly down his face; but, he reacted immediately. As he knocked the piece of wood from her hand, she stumbled forward and collided with a shelving unit. He watched, amused, as her hand caught the jagged corner of the metal shelf and sliced a large gash across her palm. He saw the pain in her eyes just before she landed face first on the floor. In the subsequent fight, her blood had ended up on various surfaces throughout the room. Another little gift he'd left for the interfering agent.

He turned to the woman sitting next to him, still furious she had resisted, and backhanded her across the face. He couldn't start his experiment yet anyway and he needed the release. It helped, a little. Calmer now, he put the car in gear and drove away.

* * * *

"Burns," Executive Assistant Director Stanley Burns answered his cellphone. His tone telegraphed his impatience with the interruption so late at night. "This better be important."

"Um," a male voice came over the line. "This is Agent Norris. Sir, we have a situation. I'm working the emergency line this evening and Chicago PD is looking for Agent Perkins. Their dispatch center called earlier, and I informed them he was unavailable. Now, uh… it's a detective, and well he's rather insistent. Says it's an emergency and he needs to make contact right away."

"Do you have a number?"

"He's still on the line," Norris advised. "Said he's not hanging up until I connect him with Perkins or his supervisor. I tried to call SSA Frank Dumas; but, I couldn't reach him."

"Transfer him to this number," Burns decided. "I'll take care of it."

"Thank you, sir," Norris said in relief. "Here he comes."

"Burns," Stan said when he heard the familiar click that indicated the transfer had been successful.

"I'm trying to reach an Agent Skeeter Perkins," Coop told him impatiently. Seriously, how many people did he have to go through to talk to one damn agent?

Subterfuge

"I'm afraid Perkins is out of town at the moment and unavailable," Burns gave the company line. "Can I help you with something?"

"I have a family emergency and need to reach him right away," Coop said reluctantly. "Are you his supervisor?"

"In a manner of speaking," Stan said. "What kind of emergency? Has something happened to Angela?"

"You know his wife?" Coop asked to clarify. "Personally?"

"What is this about?" Burns demanded. "Who did you say I was speaking to?"

"My name is Detective Andy Cooper," he provided. "I'm with the Chicago Police Department. And, as I said, it's imperative that I reach Agent Perkins right away."

"What happened to Angie?" Burns settled onto the couch, worried and afraid of the man's answer.

"Before I answer that, I really do need to know who I'm speaking to," Coop evaded. "It would also be helpful to know your relationship to the family."

"You are speaking to Executive Assistant Director Stanley Burns of the FBI," Stan barked. "And, my relationship is both professional and personal. Agent Perkins works for my division and we are close friends; practically family. What happened to Angela?"

"I'm afraid she is missing," Coop told him. "Is there any way you could send Perkins or a representative to his home right away?"

"I'm on my way," Stan said before disconnecting. He jumped to his feet, stopped momentarily to inform his wife he was leaving, then rushed out the door.

* * * *

The instant Stan stepped inside Skeet's home, he knew it was bad. The house was full of people, cops mostly mixed in with a few forensic guys with cameras, evidence bags and swabs. They were taking samples and scouring through everything Skeet owned. He paused to ask for Detective Cooper and was directed into the living room.

Coop glanced up and spotted the middle-aged man, stress and fatigue written all over his face. "Special Agent Burns? Director Burns?" he reached out a hand in greeting. "I'm sorry, I'm not sure how I should address you."

"Burns is fine," he glanced around the room and saw the note lying on the wooden coffee table. All the color instantly drained from his face and he stumbled back two steps before he reached out and gripped the arm of the couch.

"I assume you understand what that means?" Coop motioned to the letter.

"Angie. Sweet Angela has been abducted by a madman," Burns whispered as he lowered himself onto the couch. "How am I going to tell Skeet his wife's fate is in the hands of a killer?"

"Why don't you let me do that," Coop suggested. "How do I find Skeeter Perkins? I'd also like to know everything you can tell me about this killer."

"He's not available," Burns said, glancing at his watch. "He's on a flight at the moment, returning from Houston. It was scheduled to land at twenty-three-twenty this evening. There was a slight delay; but, the last I checked it was back on schedule."

Coop glanced at his watch. Didn't give him a lot of time, but if he left now, he might barely make it to the airport in time. "Alright, why don't you stay here? My team will be processing the evidence for a while. I'll head to the airport, find Agent Perkins and break the news to him. I can bring him back here, or I can take him somewhere else if you prefer."

"No," Burns stood. "We'll do this together. It's going to kill him. You have no idea what this is going to do to Skeet. And, poor Angela... what she must be going through." He closed his eyes in agony. How had they not seen this coming?

"Okay then," Coop turned. "I'll drive."

* * * *

Skeet made his way down the long tunnel that led to the airport boarding area. He was so glad to be home and couldn't wait to hold his wife again. He had only taken a few steps when he spotted Stan and a stranger. *What was this about?*

"Agent Perkins?" Coop held out a hand. "Detective Cooper, Chicago PD."

Skeet glanced at Stan and froze. His friend was pale, too pale, and the look in his eyes was guarded and... full of agony. "What happened?"

"There's a private room just over here," Coop suggested. "Let's take this inside."

"I want to know what happened," Skeet demanded.   "I'm not going anywhere until I know what happened."

"Let's go inside," Burns directed.   "Right here," he slid open a door and practically pushed Skeet inside.

Skeet turned on the cop, fear and anger in his eyes. Something was wrong.   Angie. Something terrible had happened to his wife, he knew it... felt it all the way down to the marrow of his bones.

"I'm afraid your wife is missing," Coop said softly.   "An individual broke into your home and abducted her earlier this evening," Coop paused.

"No," Skeet shook his head.   "She's trained, she knows how to handle herself."

"It gets worse," Coop told him.   "He left you a note."

Terror flowed through him and he knew.   "What note?" he choked out.   He had to see it, had to be sure.

Coop pulled out his phone, found the photo of the note he had snapped before leaving the Perkins' residence, and set it on the table in front of the agent.

Skeet couldn't breathe, the man he'd been tracking for over a year now, a madman that tortured and killed the innocent, had abducted Angela.   Skeet had brought danger into his home, for what?   He jumped to his feet and moved to stand next to the window that looked out over the tarmac.   Angela wasn't the killer's type, it was revenge pure and simple.   Revenge against him. Would he wait, settle into a new home, gather new tools; or, start immediately with the torture?   There was no way to know.   A single tear trickled down his face as reality set in.   His beautiful Angela was going to suffer unspeakable pain — because of him.

Subterfuge

"Skeet," Stan moved forward and placed a hand on his shoulder.

Skeet stiffened. He had to get out of here. He had to think. He had to find his wife. He was going to kill the monster responsible for this. He'd rip him to pieces with his bare hands without a second thought, or one shred of guilt over his actions. If that meant losing his job, he didn't care. "Take me home." He turned and locked eyes with his mentor. "I need to go home. I'm going to find my wife."

"I have a few questions," Coop began.

Skeet turned on him, glared at the detective that had delivered the news, hated the messenger as much as the monster at that moment. Somewhere in the back of his mind he knew that wasn't fair; but, it didn't change the way he felt. And, it didn't matter. All that mattered was getting home and walking through the scene. He swallowed hard, his home; their sanctuary, the place they'd shared so much happiness. Now, it was the place his wife had been abducted. He had to gather evidence and track the murdering lunatic before he killed the only woman Skeet had ever loved.

* * * *

Rowdy straightened when he saw his brother's vehicle pull up. He spotted the two men inside the car and instantly knew they were the feds. He snatched up the coffee he'd saved for his brother and made his way across the front lawn. "I thought you might need this by now," he said as he passed the large container to Coop.

"Thanks," Coop said absently as he continued to watch Perkins. The man was clearly on edge. He had a look of trouble in his eyes and Coop worried they'd be arresting him before this was over.

"You must be the boss," Rowdy said, offering a hand to Stan.

"Executive Assistant Director for Criminal Investigations, Stanley Burns," he said in greeting.

The corner of Rowdy's mouth twitched; but, he forced his face to remain neutral. Seriously, how many freakin' adjectives did one guy need in a title? "Executive pion for the animal utilization, behavioral modification, and pinhead adjustment unit...but you can call me Officer Cooper. Or Rowdy, I mostly answer to Rowdy."

Stan grinned. He liked the kid. "You can just call me Burns. And, for the record, I think I prefer the way you guys do it. Sergeant, Lieutenant, Captain, Chief... much easier all around, but what do you do?"

"Well, Burns," Rowdy said casually. "Things slowed down a bit... out there in the city. But, the media and the curious neighbors haven't. The unit Coop left to guard the scene was getting a little frazzled. I decided he might need some help. On my way back, I snagged up a few coffees to go. Figured the old man and the rest of the team could use a hit about now. Tell me how you like it, and I'll snag you one while they're still hot."

Stan glanced around, spotted the police line keeping the media and the growing number of on-lookers at bay, and decided it was best to take this inside. "I appreciate that, cream and one sugar."

"I assume you are Agent Perkins," Rowdy turned to the man who hadn't said a word. The agent was close to his brother's age... mid-thirties if Rowdy had to guess. And, he was a mess, the guy looked exhausted and completely wiped out. Rowdy didn't blame him, he was sure Coop would have that same broken expression if

57

Subterfuge

anything ever happened to Maggie. He absently wondered if cops should get married at all. Rowdy didn't have to worry about such things, he was carefree and completely unattached. Probably always would be. At least, for the foreseeable future. He liked women... pretty much all women and didn't see a reason to settle for just one.

Skeet was frozen in place, he couldn't take his eyes off his house... or the side door. The place Angie had been forced from their home; frightened and alone. It took a minute to realize the cop was talking to him. Had he asked him a question? Right, his identity. "You can call me Skeet."

"Okay, Skeet," Rowdy moved to block the view of the house. "How do you like your coffee?"

"What?" Skeet said in confusion. Coffee? Why was he asking about something so trivial? Skeet ran his hands over his face and realized it was an offer. One that felt like a lifeline right now. He could use a cup, desperately. "Black."

"Easy enough," Rowdy turned back to Burns. "There's a crowd forming, and those cameras will reach us up here. You should get inside, and I'll hook back up with you in a minute."

"Let's go," Coop put a hand on Perkins back and propelled him forward. They went in through the front door, straight past the foyer and into the living room.

Skeet let Stan direct him to the couch, then lowered himself onto the cushion. He somehow answered all of the detective's questions, somehow kept it together as he described the man who had abducted his sweet wife, somehow managed to grip the insulated cup the second cop handed him. All the while, he wondered how he was going to escape. He needed to get out of here, now. He wanted to head into the office and gather his files.

Dumas would block him, he was sure of it and he needed that video, the screenshot of the killer's face, the profile, the reports, he needed everything. And, he knew, without a doubt, Assistant Director Stanley Burns would try to stop him. If his mentor knew what Skeet planned, he would do everything in his power to stand in his way. So, he couldn't know... no one could.

* * * *

Rowdy wasn't sure how he knew the agent was going to try something, he just knew. He stepped outside the house and took a look around. The crowd had thinned substantially; but, the media was still holding out, hoping to get a few crumbs before the morning news report began. Not his problem, the Watch Commander could deal with those vultures. His thoughts returned to the fed. The look that man had under the surface was raw desperation. Oh, he tried to mask it. Had gone along with his boss all calm and controlled like, but it was a ruse. A good one. Rowdy was a trained observer and he almost missed it. You couldn't blame the guy. At some point, if he hadn't already realized it, reality was going to hit; and, the agent would see the writing on the wall. The guy was about to get benched. No good cop would allow that, not when the life of the woman he loved was on the line. And, something told Rowdy, Skeeter Perkins was a good cop.

Rowdy took another few seconds to survey the area, then walked casually to his truck and pulled away. He'd set up on the service road, the same narrow escape route the suspect had used to flee unnoticed by anyone; then, he'd wait.

* * * *

Subterfuge

"If that's all," Skeet stood. "I need some air."

Coop studied the man closely; the guy was holding it together better than he would have. He couldn't imagine the fear, the sheer terror this man had to feel knowing a monster had his wife.

"Skeet," Burns began.

"No, Stan." Perkins took a long breath, then turned to face a man he considered family, prepared to lie. "I can't take one more minute on that couch. I need a break. I need a few minutes alone. I'll stay out back, away from the cameras; but, I need this."

"Okay," Stan agreed. "But Skeet," he waited. Several seconds passed before Skeet could face his friend. "I expect you to remember who you are. I know how difficult this is. I know the only thing you want to do right now is tear that man to pieces a little at a time. Don't forget why you became an agent in the first place. Don't forget all the hard work, all the victims you've stood for, all the cases you've closed, or the men you've put behind bars. And, most of all, don't forget your wife is depending on you. I've held Dumas off so far; but, if you cross the line… it's out of my hands. And, Angela can't afford that kind of lapse in judgment… not by you."

Skeet swallowed hard, nodded and escaped.

Stan watched him go. It was the hardest thing he'd ever done. He wasn't stupid, he knew Skeeter Perkins was about to disappear. He just hoped the man could regroup and start thinking with his head instead of being consumed by emotions of the heart. What he said was the absolute truth… Angela needed Skeet right now more than she'd ever needed her husband before. Perkins was her only hope, regardless of what policy and procedure dictated. In spite of the men, including Dumas, who envied Perkins' talent and would do everything in their power to shut him out. Stanley Burns knew, without hesitation, that his friend and colleague was the only man that could bring this monster down. "I'll head out, see what I can do about the media."

"I'll contact Lt. Sinclair and have him meet you up front," Coop pulled out his phone. "If you give them a coordinated statement, maybe they'll finally clear out for a while. If your man actually comes back, he could use a little space to breath."

Stan couldn't deny what he knew in his gut, so he didn't try. "Officer Cooper? Any relation?"

"Kid brother," Coop said flatly.

"I like him," Stan said honestly. "We have a task force, a talented group of agents that have been tracking this guy for over a year now. I intend to push your administration until they assign you to my team. I'm also going to ask for that brother of yours. Any objections?"

"None from me," Coop grinned. "But, Rowdy, well he's more of a chase 'em down and book 'em kind of guy. I can't promise he'll be interested."

"I think we could use a man of action at this point," Stan provided. "Now, let's get rid of those cameras." He turned and stepped outside in search of Sinclair.

* * * *

Skeet walked out the side door and slid behind his house. He was sure he could make it to the exterior gate, slide silently into the trees and take the back-access road to the next street up. From there, he'd walk a few blocks and call a cab. The more he thought about it, the more urgent it became in his mind to head into the office and copy his entire case file. If Dumas hadn't heard about this

Subterfuge

incident already, he would in a matter of hours. Once he did, Skeet would be riding a desk. As soon as Skeet reached the solid line of trees, he glanced back over his shoulder, confirmed the coast was clear, and stepped into the open.

"Going somewhere?" Rowdy inquired.

Skeet jumped in surprise but recovered quickly. "What are you doing here?"

"I think the better question," Rowdy pushed forward, off the hood of the truck he'd been leaning against and stopped directly in front of the agent. "Is what are you doing here?"

"I live here," Skeet said immediately.

"Yeah?" Rowdy asked moving his head from one side to the other. "Where's the bed?"

"Funny," Skeet said, not in the mood for the exchange. "If you'll excuse me, I'm in a hurry."

"Alright," Rowdy shrugged. "Get in, I'll give you a ride."

Skeet frowned. "Why? Never mind, I don't need your help."

"Are you sure about that?"

"Positive," Skeet tried to move around the cocky cop; but, the man blocked his path again. "What do you want from me?"

"Nothing," Rowdy told him, never taking his eyes off the man's face. "It's more about what I can give you."

"I'm listening," Skeet said reluctantly.

"Get in," Rowdy pointed to the side of the truck. The two men stood face to face, neither one willing to give an inch for several seconds. Finally, Skeet turned and climbed into the truck.

"Where to first?"

"You say that like you believe I have an agenda," Skeet scowled. "What exactly do you think I'm doing here?"

"You tell me," Rowdy started the truck. "I'm just the driver."

Skeet studied the man for several seconds then took a calculated risk. "I need to go into the office," Skeet said as he stared out the windshield. "I need my files."

"I wondered how long that would take you," Rowdy replied before pulling away.

"How long what would take?"

"Are we going to do this all night?" Rowdy asked, a little annoyed

"Okay," Skeet relented. The guy was perceptive, he should respect that. "I realized it on the way back from the airport. Burns will try to keep me involved; but, my immediate supervisor is already looking for a reason to give me the boot. Once he hears about Ange, he'll assign me to desk duty. I'll be lucky to have fifteen minutes in the men's room without an escort."

"So," Rowdy said as he pulled into the federal lot and shut down the truck. "What's the plan?"

"You still on duty?" Skeet began to relax and wondered why he was trusting this stranger.

"Yeah, until O-four-hundred."

Subterfuge

"Look, this is going to take a while," Skeet told him. "Go ahead and take off. If you're free in an hour, you can come back. If you're tied up, I'll catch another ride."

"I could do that," Rowdy shoved open the door. "But, I think I'll hang out here instead. The mutt needs a break to run a bit, and things have cooled down. If I get something hot, I'll tag you. Otherwise, it's a nice night to do a little star gazing. You know, in the spirit of professional cooperation and all."

"I'm serious," Skeet pushed out of the truck. "If you need to bolt, I'll be fine."

"Copy that," Rowdy also exited the truck and moved to the rear gate to release his dog.

Twenty minutes later, Skeet had all the digital files copied, including the video and the photos. He pulled the Scientist's journal from his pocket and debated. Technically, the thing was still signed out to him. He had logged it out in Houston, so he could study it on the flight home. But eventually, probably sooner than later, Dumas would track him down and insist he turn it back over. Skeet needed the information in that journal. With a sigh, he moved to the window and glanced down at the lot. Rowdy Cooper was still entertaining himself by playing with his dog. He couldn't ask the guy to wait, it wouldn't be right. He shoved the journal, the discs and the hardcopy of his personal file into his briefcase and headed for the door.

"Got everything?" Rowdy asked when Skeet approached.

"Sort of."

"Problem?" Rowdy frowned.

"I have something," Skeet admitted. "A piece of valuable evidence I carried with me on the plane. Once Dumas gets wind

I'm personally involved, he's going to block me, he'll shut me out of the case completely, and demand the journal gets returned immediately. I need a copy, but it's fairly large. Plus…"

"Yes," Rowdy pressed.

"I can't use the office copier, it requires a code. There will be a record of use and I can't risk that. I need to find somewhere I can make a complete copy of the book and do it before my team arrives to start the day."

"Other than that, do you have everything you need?" Rowdy asked.

"Yes."

"Then get in," Rowdy moved to the back of the truck and secured Knight. "We'll head to my office and take care of it. What's the plan once we're done? I'm not sure you should stay at your place. Too many memories… it's going to interfere in a big way."

"I hadn't thought that far ahead," Skeet considered. "But no, I can't go home. Because of the memories; but, also, because I can't risk it. If the Bureau realizes I took my case files, it's over. They'll seize them and shut me out for good. I need to find another place to crash for now."

"Okay," Rowdy entered the highway and maneuvered toward his office. "You'll stay with me."

Skeet stared at the cop in shock. "You don't even know me."

Rowdy shrugged. "You're a cop. One that caught the attention of a sadistic prick with a grudge. That's all I need to know."

"It's really that simple?"

Subterfuge

"It is to me," Rowdy slowed, turned into the parking lot of a discreet looking building and flipped off the engine. "I have a small but comfortable guest room and an empty loft that would be perfect to set up as a war room. We can bring in a folding table and I think there are a few unused whiteboards here at the office. I'll grab them while you copy that book of yours. We'll have the place set up before I check off duty. Then, we get a couple hours down before you go over the details and we come up with a plan to get your lady back."

"If only it were that simple," Skeet stopped just outside the door and waited.

"Oh," Rowdy grinned. "It's not going to be simple, because I have to break the news to my brother."

"The detective," Skeet realized.

"Yeah," Rowdy pointed to the copier and turned to leave. "But, I think I'll wait until he has breakfast. He'll be more reasonable on a full stomach... after he's had a couple cups of coffee.

Chapter Three

Skeet woke and made his way to the kitchen. He hadn't expected to doze off at all; he was so worried about Angie. Well, more like terrified of what she might be going through at this very minute. He didn't have time to sleep. He had wanted to work straight through the night; but, Rowdy insisted they take a break. He finally relented, thinking he'd just relocate to the guest room and continue to push through on his own. Exhaustion had won that battle and he spent nearly all of his down time comatose. He needed to get back to work... after he found some coffee. As he approached the doorway, he heard arguing. So, the good detective wasn't on board with the plan. Maybe, he could help. "Detective," he said as he stepped into the room.

"Agent," Coop narrowed his eyes and watched the man's every move.

Skeet selected a mug, poured a cup of coffee and settled in at the table. "Progress?" he asked Rowdy.

Subterfuge

Rowdy shrugged. "Does it matter? We hashed it out already. I'm creating my own task force — a team of two. Three, if the obstinate investigator pulls his head out long enough to see the light."

"For argument's sake," Coop said patiently. "Let's say I agree to participate. How does that help? I mean all three of us are already a part of the bigger unit."

"All three?" Skeet glanced at Rowdy and then back to Coop. "They've added both of you to the task force? Officially?"

"My division commander notified me this morning," Coop told them. "Said Rowdy had been approved by his division as well. Burns told me he wanted both of us last night, I just wasn't sure he could pull it off."

"And, I haven't agreed to participate," Rowdy countered. "I think we'll be more effective here."

Skeet laughed, something he hadn't been sure he could do any more.

"What's funny?" Coop demanded.

"Oh, this is going to be good." Skeet focused on Coop. "Dumas is going to blow a gasket when he meets your brother. Rowdy will irritate the hell out of the man. I'd lay odds he doesn't last a day. He might end up hating the local K9 officer even more than he hates me."

Rowdy frowned. "I'm likable."

"Dumas is a pompous, back-stabbing, dishonest..."

"We get the picture," Coop frowned. He hated working with the type of man Skeet was describing. It always gave him a headache.

68

"He'll hate everything about you, Rowdy," Skeet continued. "Your sense of humor, your perception, your decision to become a lowly street cop instead of striving to work for the F...B...I." Skeet lowered his voice in a sort of mocking reverence as he relayed the initials. "And, because you will irritate him beyond his limits, he won't tolerate you on his team. He'll fire you before the day is over."

Coop considered. "And, that takes care of two, gives you the opening you wanted to work on this without interference from a man that is only looking for recognition. You can work the case without this Dumas guy constantly watching over your shoulder; scrutinizing every move."

"Why two?" Rowdy asked.

"Because Skeet is already out," Coop said absently. "He just doesn't know it, yet."

"I know it," Skeet disagreed. "It's just not official, yet."

"Which will leave the level-headed, adult to monitor the official team's progress and report anything new."

"You're bringing Jonesy in?" Rowdy asked.

Coop didn't bother with a response. "And, I'll stick. I've dealt with more than my share of men like Dumas. I'll remain on the team, bring back information and we'll know what the others are planning. Then we investigate this our way."

"And by that, I assume you mean your way," Rowdy sighed.

"That's exactly what I mean," he focused on Skeet. "Can you live with that? It's my case. If we do this, we do it as an independent Chicago PD investigation into the abduction of Angela Perkins. We are not chasing a serial killer, are we clear?"

Subterfuge

"Call it what you want," Skeet decided. "Because when we succeed, the result will be the same."

"And by that, I'm going to assume you mean the suspect will be in custody, behind bars, awaiting a fair trial where he will be judged by a panel of his peers," Coop provided.

"Right," was all Skeet said.

"I'm going to head in, see if I can track down this Dumas guy before the meeting. I'd like to get a feel for what we're dealing with right away," Coop stood. "I've been advised the briefing is at zero-eight-hundred. Do we have everything we need on the case? Files, history, whatever?"

"I've got it," Skeet assured him. "I'll have to bring in the journal; but, I made a copy to keep here. If I can get through it, I might find a clue."

"What's the journal?" Coop asked.

"We found what he calls his workshop in Houston," Skeet told the brothers. "He always snatches the second victim before he's finished with the first. Always three in one city, then he vanishes. He was still working on the second girl when we located his hideout. He wasn't there, but Darla was. She was still alive, barely. As far as I know, she made it; but, her prognosis isn't good. Anyway, the lunatic was out abducting his third girl at the time. He got spooked, abandoned the van, and the girl. We rescued two girls that night; but, he disappeared into the wind."

"And, showed up here," Rowdy provided. "To kidnap your wife. You have his girls, he has yours. Now the note makes sense."

"Yes," Skeet swallowed hard. "Anyway, we caught him off guard. He had to leave everything. He wasn't prepared, probably never considered he might be discovered. We have a journal he used to document his experiments and we have his tools. He has to be scrambling. He needs a place to set up and he's going to have to restock the necessities."

"And, you copied every page of that journal?" Coop asked. "Because once your boss learns you have it, he's going to insist you return it."

"I'm ahead of you on that one," Skeet assured him. "That's exactly what he's going to do. There's one more thing. We've been at a loss this entire time, since the case started. He's careful, meticulous and has never left a single clue. I worked up a profile, early on when we found the first girl; but, until Houston, we had no idea who this guy was, what he looked like, or specifics about his process. We made an educated guess, and for the most part we were correct. But, the journal and a section of video we obtained in Houston puts us miles ahead of where we were. And, he doesn't know we have the video. He's operating under the mistaken belief we haven't seen him. We still haven't identified him; but, I'm working on that. At some point, we'll have to decide if releasing his picture to the media is beneficial or detrimental to the case."

"I'm not sure that will be our choice," Coop considered. "I mean, I expect that supervisor of yours will push for whatever he thinks is best."

"I may be benched; but, I still have Stan."

"Speaking of the executive director, assistant to the king, and mighty poohbah... you should probably call him. He was pretty worried last night when he left," Coop said with a grin. "Why do the feds feel the need to create important titles that run on for ten minutes?"

"Because we're the F...B...I," Skeet shrugged and sobered. "I'm going to grab a shower and head to the office, where I'll promptly be removed from the team. Then, I'm going to settle in at my desk to read through that journal."

"I could do that," Rowdy volunteered. He didn't think it was a good idea for Skeet to read through a sadistic killer's journal of torture techniques. Especially now that said killer had kidnapped Skeet's wife.

"Thanks, but it's something I have to do," Skeet sobered. "I profiled the guy; but, he's altered his MO significantly. I need to get into his head and try to anticipate his next move. It's the only way I'm going to save my wife."

"Alright then," Rowdy stood. "Let's go get kicked off the team."

Coop laughed, Skeet just shook his head, wondering what he had gotten himself into.

* * * *

Rowdy stepped into the large conference room and took a look around. No sign of Skeet. Apparently, his favorite fed already got the boot. He spotted Coop and settled into the chair next to his brother. "And, then there were two."

Coop gave a subtle nod of acknowledgment but didn't answer. He'd already had the pleasure of meeting SSA Frank Dumas and wasn't sure he'd survive working an entire case with the man. The guy was arrogant, condescending and subtly insulting. He just thought Coop, being a substandard local, wouldn't catch the sneering undertones.

Rowdy frowned but remained silent. Something had Coop fuming but now wasn't the time to get into it. He glanced up when a tall, lanky man walked briskly into the room and made his way to a small pulpit. Seriously, the guy was going to brief his men in the same way a college professor gave a lecture. *This ought to be fun.*

"Good morning," Dumas began. "I'd like to start this meeting by introducing myself." He proceeded to outline his entire career, his awards, and his major cases.

Rowdy couldn't take any more. Pretty soon, he'd have to endure a commentary on the man's favorite color and what he ate for breakfast. He pulled out his laptop and fired it up. He'd work while the important FBI guy continued his dissertation on every accomplishment he'd had in life. How that pertained to this case, or how it would help rescue a desperate woman from the clutches of a madman… Rowdy had no idea. This right here, was the reason he never participated in joint task forces that involved the feds.

Dumas spotted the computer and scowled. "Excuse me," he said moving up to the table where the man sat. He had no idea who he was, the guy was dressed for a briefing in jeans and a t-shirt. Clearly, he'd worn the black casual wear because it flaunted the emblem for the Chicago SWAT Team. That might impress some, but not Dumas.

Rowdy glanced up in acknowledgement.

"This is a federal facility and personal electronic devices are not permitted," Dumas scolded.

"Okay," Rowdy shrugged and refocused on the report he'd been reading.

"I must insist you shut that down immediately," Dumas pushed.

Subterfuge

"Huh," Rowdy straightened. "Oh, well you see, this isn't a personal device. It's my official CPD unit and it's been approved for use in this building. I have a receipt and everything." He grinned at the look the guy was giving him. Another two... three seconds tops and he might actually erupt.

"That may be," Dumas said, gritting his teeth. "But, it's rude to engage in... whatever, while a superior is speaking. If you want to be a member of this prestigious team, I expect you to respect my position as leader and pay attention when I am speaking."

"I can do that," Rowdy said cheerfully. "But, us locals, we're used to multi-tasking. Go ahead, finish explaining how you brought DeLuca down using his financials. I'll just work on... whatever, while you do it."

Dumas caught the challenge and the insult in the man's tone and decided now was not the time to engage in a pissing match. He would rise above it and just move on. "Now that you know a little about me, I'd like to take a minute to get to know each of you." He returned to the front of the room. "Mr. Cooper, why don't you start by introducing yourself?"

Rowdy and Coop looked at each other but both men remained silent.

"Mr. Cooper?" Dumas once again moved to stand in front of the table. He glared at Coop, fury radiating in his eyes. "We don't have all day."

"My mistake," Coop said sarcastically. "It's Detective Cooper, Andy Cooper. I'm with Chicago PD and the abduction of Angela Perkins is my case."

"I'm afraid you are mistaken," Dumas corrected. "That incident is a federal matter now and it falls under the jurisdiction of this task force.   I've agreed to your participation as long as it proves beneficial to the whole."

"I guess we'll just have to disagree on that point," Coop said flatly.

"Anything else?" Dumas asked.   "It would be advantageous to all of us if you would outline your credentials; length of service, relevant experience, awards, achievements… anything."

"I have eleven years on the job, five of that in my current assignment," Coop added.

"I see," Dumas said.   The entire room picked up on the condescension and blatant dismissal in those two words.

Rowdy fisted his hand and straightened in his chair.   He wouldn't sit by quietly while a guy that couldn't walk in Coop's shadow dissed him publicly.

Coop felt Rowdy's anger; and, as much as he appreciated it, he could stand for himself.   He gently pressed the heel of his foot onto the top of Rowdy's left foot.   "I'll handle it," he said softly so only his brother could hear.

"Coop's heads above the rest when it comes to investigating," Officer Dirk Bannon said without emotion.   "You're lucky to have him on this case.   And, the man has too much class to flaunt his accomplishments; but, we all know he'll be promoted to sergeant soon.   He's sitting number one on the list and we're down two.   I heard Cowley's leaving the first of next month.   You should take advantage of his expertise while you have the chance.   If that promotion comes through before you crack this case, we'll have to finish without him and that would be a shame."

"I wonder," Dumas pretended to ponder.   "Are all of the officers that work for the Chicago Police Department this disrespectful and disruptive?   I'm sure Mr. Cooper is grateful for your endorsement; but, I was speaking to him… not you." He glared at the man that had interrupted his inquiry.

"Detective Cooper," Bannon corrected. "And, I'm too old for this shit."

"On that, we wholeheartedly agree," Dumas mumbled. "As a seasoned officer, I suspect it's a little disheartening to work so many years and not advance to a position more… prestigious than patrol."

Coop scowled, he already had a headache and they hadn't even gotten though the first briefing.

"I'm outta' here," Bannon stood. "I hesitantly agreed to scope out the team. When the Sarge approached me and asked me to participate, I declined… vehemently. But, then, he told me we were looking for a cop's wife and I agreed to feel it out, see if I could tolerate another federal operation. I can't." He turned to the other members of the group. "I wish you luck, hope you find the sadistic SOB in time to save the woman; but, I've worked too long and too hard to put up with an arrogant bureaucrat like the one leading this team so late in my career." Then, he turned and strolled out the door without so much as a backward glance.

"You just made a huge mistake," Coop told Dumas.

"I'm sure you appreciate the endorsement from an associate, Mr. Cooper," Dumas said. "But, you need to get one thing clear. Right now, you're a big fish in a little pond. Executive Director Burns plucked you out of that watering hole and dropped you into the ocean. I suggest you focus on surviving."

"Sounds like someone doesn't appreciate local involvement in his precious operation," Rowdy said quietly. "It's too bad because Bannon would have been a valuable asset. Not that it would matter to you, but he retired from the NYPD as a lieutenant before moving out here to help care for his parents. You could have learned a ton from that man; but, hey... that's your loss."

"I doubt it. And yes, I believe local cooperation is essential," Dumas said in response. "But, I discovered recently, local departments don't play well with others. And, they seem to have a hard time understanding the pecking order. Don't make the same mistake the men in Houston made. I am in charge here and I won't hesitate to remove you if you get in my way. Now," he gave Rowdy a nod. "Introduce yourself."

"Cooper," Rowdy said. Several seconds of silence ticked by as Dumas and Rowdy stared at each other.

"Do you think that is amusing?" Dumas finally asked.

Rowdy pretended to consider. "I've never thought of my name as amusing."

"Your name?"

"Rowdy Cooper," he answered.

"I assume you are related to Mr. Cooper here," he pointed to Coop.

"Yes, Mr. Dumas," Rowdy said flatly. "We're brothers."

"And, what do you do? Other than SWAT?" he sneered.

Rowdy realized the man had some kind of issue with tactical operators. He'd have to ask Skeet about that later. "K9."

"Is that all, Mr. Cooper?"

"Yes, Mr. Dumas, it is," Rowdy responded. Two could play at this game.

Subterfuge

"I would appreciate it, if you would show me the respect I have earned and address me as SSA Dumas," the agent growled.

Rowdy didn't answer. He didn't think the request was worthy of a response.

Dumas moved on, questioning each member about their time on the force and demanding an explanation of why they were qualified to be on his team.

Rowdy couldn't take this any longer. He pulled his laptop back out and began reading another report. An entry caught his attention and he focused on the array of whiteboards displayed at the front of the room. Within seconds, he spotted the name he was looking for. The information was wrong. The date of the abduction was two days earlier than listed on the chart. Was that a current mistake or had they used the same data for months. It was a little thing; but, Rowdy knew sometimes little things led to big things that cracked the case wide open. He shifted and moved closer to Coop. "I need a picture of those boards. If I do it, he'll have a meltdown. See what you can do."

"Mr. Cooper," Dumas said without looking his way. "I must insist you remain silent while we complete this exercise. You have already disrespected the group by returning to your laptop, must you also engage in a personal conversation as well? The team members respectfully listened as you introduced yourself, it would be nice if you did the same. I expect members of this team to address one another by name as we try to work together. That will be difficult if you don't pay attention as they introduce themselves."

"Like I said," Rowdy answered. "I'm a multi-tasker." He pointed to the first table and began to rattle off names. "Then we have Fulmer, Krueger, Vance and Kirkwood."

"As I told the man who left us earlier," Dumas said, clearly furious Rowdy had proved him wrong once again. "I will not tolerate outbursts from members of this team. I'm afraid you are no longer welcome here. You are cocky, disrespectful and superfluous. I have no need for a dog cop on my homicide team. Get out."

Rowdy shrugged, closed the lid on the laptop and leaned to the side to put the computer in a bag. "Did you get it?" he whispered so only Coop could hear.

"Yep," Coop whispered.

Rowdy zipped the bag closed, flung it over his shoulder and cheerfully left the room.

* * * *

"Hey, slacker," Rowdy called as he approached Skeet's desk. "I'm surprised you don't have a time-out desk. You know, for federal agents that have been relegated to the doghouse."

Skeet glanced up in surprise. "You're out already?"

Rowdy shrugged and dropped into Skeet's visitor's chair. "The arrogant piss ant doesn't see the point in utilizing a dog cop."

"He said that?" Skeet said in wide-eyed shock. "Stan is not going to be happy. He went to a lot of trouble to get you on that team. Dumas made a serious mistake. I thought you'd last a full day, at least."

Rowdy cleared his throat and did his best Dumas impression. "Mr. Cooper, you are cocky, disrespectful and superfluous. Get out," he flung his arm out and pointed to the door.

Subterfuge

"No way," Skeet shook his head.

"Way," Rowdy shrugged again. "It's a talent. Now, enough about Agent Dumbass. What's your status? You stuck here for the duration or can we blow?"

"I have strict orders not to leave my desk until the briefing has concluded," Skeet frowned.

"Ouch," Rowdy said. "I'm afraid that might be awhile. They're still holding hands and singing Kumbaya in there…teamwork is about forming bonds and mutual respect, after all."

Skeet shook his head and ran a hand through his hair. "He does that every time. Needs the locals to know he's in charge and just how important he is."

"Yeah," Rowdy began. "I wanted to ask you about that. What's his beef with tactical cops?"

Skeet noticed Rowdy's shirt and grinned. "SWAT Commander in Houston told Dumas his Op was a cluster and refused to participate. Then, he got his own warrant and we served it on the real target; rescued the girls; and seized all the evidence — tools, notes… everything. Dumas wanted the accolades for that and blames the local Tac guys for interfering in his plan."

"I guess that explains the attitude," Rowdy decided.

"Sorry about that," Skeet said sincerely. "He's arrogant and pushy; but, he has no right to disrespect the locals."

"Agent Skeeter Perkins?" a man asked, stepping up to the desk

"I'm Perkins," Skeet told him.   The guy was young, sharply dressed in a well-tailored suit, close-cropped brown hair and immaculately shined shoes.

"I'm Agent Bryant Smith," he provided, holding out his FBI credentials.   "I was wondering if I could have a few minutes of your time."   He glanced at Rowdy, then focused on Skeet.   "I can wait until you're finished here.   I've got all day, just got in from Detroit."

"What is this about?" Skeet pressed.

Smith glanced at Rowdy again and hesitated.   "I think a case you've been working might link to one of mine.   I was hoping I could run it by you, get a few more details."

"What case of mine are we talking about?"

"It's... well, sensitive.   I can wait until you're finished here," Smith said again.

"If it's the serial killer, Rowdy's also assisting... locally," Skeet provided.   "This is Officer Rowdy Cooper, Chicago PD."

"Oh," Smith relaxed.   "It's nice to meet you."   He held out a hand in greeting.   "It is the serial case.   I have a situation, it's a little touchy and was hoping we could discuss it."

"We can do that," Skeet straightened.   "Normally, I'd move to a private room; but, I think we'll be fine here for now.   The rest of the men are in a briefing.   Grab that chair and show me what you've got."

Bryant Smith pulled out a file.   "I have one dead girl.   This one is a cold case.   We found the body almost a year ago.   She'd been dead for a couple weeks when the body was discovered. Local wildlife had gotten to her, so the body was a mess.   It's been cold ever since," he set out the crime scene photos.   "I discovered another one is missing," Smith provided.   "My SAC doesn't think they're related; but, I'm positive they are. Both girls disappeared about the same time."

"What makes you think they connect?" Skeet asked, already knowing they did. The girl's body was barely recognizable; but, the cuts and bruises matched his other victims. Skeet was sure he'd just found the location of three of his missing six girls.

"Timing mostly, and victimology," Smith answered. He dropped a detailed outline on the desk. "I have a third girl, a missing person that I think might also be connected. Her family said she was going through a phase, rebellious attitude, hanging with the wrong crowd, that sort of thing. But, it was a recent development. Before that, she was the perfect daughter, perfect student, perfect friend. Then suddenly, she vanished. Could be she ran; but, my gut says different."

"Your gut is probably right," Skeet told him. "I believe these are related to my case. I'm sure this girl," he pointed to the photo, "is one of his victims. And, if I'm right, there are two others. Two young, innocent girls you haven't found; but, who are also very much deceased. I'd start checking remote fields, areas with very little traffic. He likes trees, secluded areas where he can get in, hide his vehicle while he does the drop and get out. Stick within a thirty-mile radius of where those girls went missing. He doesn't go far, doesn't risk getting caught. And, if history is any indication, there won't be any evidence. He's thorough, cleans the body before he drops it. Not that it would matter at this point, a year is a long time to remain undiscovered."

"You just described my first scene to a tee," Smith told him. "Part of me was hoping I was wrong, my boss says I'm wrong but… well, the gut."

"Give me your supervisor's information," Skeet told him. "I'll send him an email and request his personal cooperation. We need to find those girls. There will be three of them. He always selects three, then moves on."

"There's no doubt?" Smith asked.

Skeet frowned. "You came here, all the way from Detroit because your gut told you it was connected. Why the hesitance now that I've confirmed it?"

"Because, that means I'll have to tell two sets of parents their daughter was killed in a slow, painful way that lasted days; and then, her body sat in some empty field or some other remote area for almost a year without being discovered. It's a lot to digest and no parent should have to face that," Smith said.

"I agree," Skeet's stomach was on fire. That's what his wife was enduring right now, and it was all his fault. "Let your boss know the timeline fits. I knew there were others and you just plugged a hole in my case. After all this time, you are looking for skeletal remains. There could be damage to the bones; but, the rest of the signs of what those girls endured is now gone. We'll have to rely on timing; we should be able to fit them into the timeline based on when they went missing. If I'm right, your victims are either ten, eleven and twelve or sixteen, seventeen and eighteen. He brands them — on their left hip — with a red tattoo prior to disposal. I'd appreciate it if you kept that information to yourself. It's something we haven't allowed the media to discover."

"I can tell you," Bryan pointed to the photo. "She's number eleven. We saw the tattoo. ME thought it was part of a bigger image; but, we couldn't reconstruct it because animals got to her before we did. There's enough to confirm, she's eleven." He fumbled through his paperwork and pulled out an eight-by-ten photo of the marking.

"I'm sorry," Skeet told him. "If you find the others, let me know. Are you catching grief from the boss on this?"

Subterfuge

"Not exactly," Bryant sighed. "He just doesn't believe me. He doesn't see the connection and has deemed the homicide a local issue… won't even touch the missing girls we didn't find. Until he changes his mind, I have no jurisdiction."

"I can help with that," Skeet assured him. "I'll call Executive Director Burns and fill him in. An email from the Director will have more impact than a request from me. Does he know you're here?"

"He knows," Bryant answered. "But, he said I had to do it on my own time at my own expense. He's expecting me to return disappointed and willing to put it all behind us."

"Then, I guess he's going to be disappointed," Rowdy said soberly as he studied the photos.

"Maybe," Bryant said. "Or angry. Either way, I know I did the right thing. I'll get out of your hair. You can keep that file, it's a duplicate. I figured if I was right, you'd want to add it to the others."

"Thanks," Skeet pulled out a business card and handed it to the agent. "Use the cellphone, call me if anything changes and I'll work on making contact with Burns." He watched as the young, idealistic agent walked away. "Guess I just ruined his day."

"Helped, though." Rowdy decided. "He'll be fine. He's got the cop gut, too bad he's a fed." Rowdy grinned and stood. "I'm heading home. Copy that new file and bring it to the loft. I spotted an issue with the data on the boards in the conference room. Is that something you've been working from this whole time?"

"Yeah," Skeet slid the new file into his briefcase. He'd pay Burns a visit in person and stop to get copies along the way somewhere. His mentor was hanging close to home these days.

He had promised to be available until Angela was found and this thing ended, just in case Skeet needed him for anything. "What kind of issue?"

"The dates are wrong," Rowdy said absently. "I want to go over your data again and make sure it's only the one."

Skeet frowned as Rowdy walked away. How had they missed something so obvious? And, was it important? The smallest thing could break a case, he wondered if this would change things. He'd give Dumas another hour. Then, he was leaving. Burns would cover for him, he was sure of it. And, his friend and mentor needed to know the SSA had already kicked Rowdy off the team. He also wanted Stan to send the official word to Detroit immediately. Bryant Smith had risked his career to come here, Skeet was going to make sure it paid off for the kid.

* * * *

Coop knocked twice then stepped into Rowdy's kitchen. He pulled one bottle from the six pack of beer he'd purchased, popped it open and headed upstairs. He entered the loft and took a look around. Rowdy and Skeet had the boards set up and the table was covered with files. He was frowning when he dropped into one of the uncomfortable chairs Rowdy had set up and took another long gulp of beer.

"That bad?" Rowdy said in sympathy.

"You need better chairs," Coop said in response.

"I've ordered a couple lounge chairs, should be delivered tomorrow afternoon."

Subterfuge

"I thought you were turning this into a home gym," Coop looked around. "What do you plan to do with the chairs when we're done?"

"Leave them," Rowdy shrugged. "There's room. I figured I'd set up the gym on that side of the room and add a little lounging area over here. Maybe mount a flat screen on the wall over there."

"Could work," Coop decided. "Did you get the images I sent you?"

"Yeah," Rowdy stood and moved to the board. "The feds have it wrong. I've spent the past several hours updating the information. I don't know who extracted the data from the report in Missouri; but, it was wrong. They had the abduction of Krissy Martin off by two days. They listed her as disappearing on the ninth; but, it was actually the seventh. That means he always takes the first girl during the first week of the month. Might be something to look at."

"Might not matter, could be a trigger only the killer understands. But, details," Coop stood and moved to the board. He glanced at Skeet. "There's something else we need to talk about."

"Sounds ominous," Skeet observed.

Just then the doorbell chimed.

"That might be Burns," Skeet warned. "He said he'd be stopping by."

Rowdy disappeared and returned with the high-ranking fed.

"Skeet," Burns said in greeting. "Looks like you guys have been busy."

"We have," Skeet nodded.

"Good," Burns told him.   "Now leave, I need to talk to the Cooper brothers alone."

Skeet frowned but left the room.

"If we're going to be a team," Rowdy began.   "We can't have secrets."

"This isn't about secrets," Burns settled into one of the chairs. "I want to say thank you; but, somehow, that just isn't enough. Words will never express how grateful I am for what you've done for Skeet.   He's a good man and he doesn't have any family... not the traditional kind.   But, he's mine and he's important.   I was impressed with his intelligence and his intuition the moment I met him.   As we got to know each other, I was even more impressed with his integrity.   It was nearly a year later when we discovered we had another connection.   Skeet's father was my best friend as a child.   We lost touch after we graduated.   Went our separate ways and I didn't even know he passed away.   That history made my connection with Skeeter Perkins even more important.   I consider him a sort of adopted son.   Yet, last night... I couldn't help him. You could, and you did.   I will always be indebted to you for that. You brought a stranger into your home, no strings, no questions, no expectations."

"Like I told Skeet," Rowdy shrugged that off.   "He's a cop, a brother, and he needed my help."

"I understand," Burns nodded.   "And, I also want to apologize for another of my men.   Dumas was out of line.   He's been reprimanded for his actions today and for the disrespect he showed both of you.   I wish I could say the problem has been resolved; unfortunately, I don't believe that is the case.   I'm afraid as long as you are on the task force, detective... he'll find little ways to insult you.   I just hope you understand he does not represent the Bureau, his attitude does not reflect our beliefs in any way."

Subterfuge

"No apology necessary," Coop said finishing off his beer. "You look like you could use one of these."

"I'd love one," Burns smiled. "It's been a hell of a day."

"More than dealing with Dumas?" Rowdy asked.

"Seems you two have a lot of friends... some powerful ones," Burns admitted. "Word spread pretty quickly about what happened in that briefing. My phone has been ringing off the hook ever since."

"I'm sorry you had to deal with that," Rowdy said sincerely. "And, I guess I should admit, part of it may have been my fault."

"My little brother tends to be over-protective, thinks he needs to defend my honor for some reason," Coop said handing a beer to Burns and another one to Rowdy. "Not everyone appreciates his... enthusiasm."

"The two of you are close," Burns stated. "I understand that, and I would never hold it against you. Now, I'm not sure if Skeet had a chance to discuss his status with you; but, I've placed him on administrative leave."

"What?" Rowdy protested. "That's not fair."

Burns smiled. "No, it probably isn't. But, I felt it was the best way to deal with the problem at hand. If I leave him active, Dumas is going to shackle him to his desk eight hours a day until this situation is resolved. If he's on leave, he can work from here, work the case without restraint, and find our dear Angela."

"What if he runs into trouble?" Coop asked. "Can he still utilize his weapon on leave?"

"I hope it won't come to that," Burns considered. "But, I'll protect Skeet, he has nothing to worry about."

"That will give him time to work the case while I'm tied up with Dumas and Rowdy works his regular shift," Coop decided.

"About that," Burns said with apprehension. "I uh... well, I called in a favor. Rowdy, you will continue to work the case rather than returning to your normal duties. It's been approved by Chief Griggs."

"By work the case, you mean?" Rowdy asked.

"I explained, in basic terms, how things didn't work out... having you on the task force that is. I requested your help on a special assignment," Burns explained. "I told Griggs you would be working directly with my best expert in an attempt to locate the man responsible and bring him to justice."

"So," Rowdy surmised. "I'll be working here with Skeet, rather than returning to my regular shift?"

"Yes," Burns agreed. "I'm told your sergeant isn't happy about it. Apparently, your unit is shorthanded; but, I convinced your chief I needed you on this. It is my belief that forcing you to work an eight-hour shift for Chicago PD; and then, expecting you to put in a long day coordinating with my profiler, would be detrimental to the case and your personal well-being. We both agreed, this case will be short term and it's a priority. You are cleared to work as many hours as necessary to assist Skeet until we locate his wife."

"Okay," Coop considered. "So, I'll put in time with Dumas and his team; and whenever possible, I'll hook up with these guys to work any fresh angles we agree on, which brings me back to the point I was about to make when you arrived. Mind if I bring Skeet back in so we can discuss it?"

"Not at all," Burns nodded. Once Coop left the room, Burns addressed Rowdy. "I meant what I said about being indebted. If there is ever anything you need, please don't hesitate to ask. I knew

Subterfuge

he wouldn't come home with me, and there was no way I'd leave him in that house alone. You solved that dilemma and I'll always be grateful. Like I said before, Skeet doesn't have any actual family. His parents were killed in a freak accident when he was seven. He grew up in foster care with families that did their best; but, they were always temporary. I am not; but, my position makes things a little more difficult. We have to be careful. Skeet is smart, he has natural talent; and because of that, he has enjoyed a level of career advancement others envy. It's a balancing act, I guess you could say."

"I understand," Rowdy said softly when Coop and Skeet entered the room.

"Okay," Coop began. "I'm going to preface this by saying I already explained my position to Dumas; who promptly brushed it off as nonsense. A harebrained theory developed by a local detective trying to make a name for himself."

"I'm sorry for that," Burns fumed.

"Its fine," Coop brushed it away. "I don't actually care what your man thinks of me or my ideas. My priority is finding Skeet's wife. I just felt I had a responsibility to share. I did, he shut me down — end of story."

"What's the theory?" Skeet asked.

"I think you have sent a lot of people on a wild goose chase," Coop said carefully. "One, that will not produce any results but is taking a lot of time and energy. They're wasting manpower that could be helpful elsewhere."

"How so?" Skeet asked.

"With the driver's license thing," Coop clarified. "You have multiple agencies running a photo of your suspect through their system, looking for a driver's license I do not believe exists."

"Why?" Burns asked.

"Timing," Coop began. "Our perp moves into a city and spends maybe three weeks in the state before moving on. He's not a resident, doesn't need a local driver's license, and probably couldn't get one if he wanted to."

"I hadn't thought of that," Skeet said in understanding. "I just thought... now we have a photo, let's search the largest database we have that contains pictures of average Americans."

"I see why you did it," Coop conceded. "I just disagree. There's a second reason I don't think he has a license in those states— Location. He doesn't take the girls to a place he owns. He finds a vacant house, building, or cabin. Somewhere remote where he has privacy and seclusion, but not a place of his own. In Houston, it was an old farmhouse that was tied up in the courts. In New Orleans, it was an apartment complex damaged by Hurricane Katrina that had been foreclosed on before the renovations were complete. It was also vacant and had been for a while. I could go through the six states we know of; and once we track down the new information from Detroit, I'm confident we'll see a clear pattern."

"I know the location," Skeet provided. "I've been studying the journal all day. I found the information, the documentation on the girls in Detroit. Proves Smith's gut was right, and they will eventually find three victims in that area. Unfortunately, our Scientist documents his experiments but not the disposal sites. It appears once the girl dies, the experiment is complete. Anyway, I have also determined the location of victims sixteen, seventeen and eighteen. They were abducted in Savanah, Georgia. I have agents in the area working on possible victims based on the timeline we've established. They would have disappeared sometime in April. We've now accounted for all the victims."

"Again," Coop said hesitantly. "I disagree."

"And again," Burns said flatly. "Why?"

"Because the kills are too clean," Coop provided. "Anyone that's worked homicide knows the first kill is sloppy. All of these are precise, meticulous and professional. He had at least one, probably more that he used for practice. He didn't bring attention to himself until he perfected his method. Number one is only number one for this project. He has priors, I'd bet my reputation on it."

"Then, I've completely messed up from the start," Skeet said with regret.

"No," Coop corrected, "you didn't. I read your case files, all of them. You insisted, rather adamantly in the beginning, that the body and the scene were too meticulous. You believed the killer had to have prior victims. You were shut down by pretty much everyone working the case. I can't prove my theory any more than you could. I understand why your assertion was set aside, I just believe you were right."

"I'm beginning to think leaving Dumas in charge of such an important unit was a mistake," Burns said with a sigh. "I didn't like the man, didn't want him there; but, I was new to the assignment and he has friends. It's time to correct the problem and transfer him to a different department. One less vital, where he can't bully his way through because his ego won't let him admit when he's wrong."

"I thought he was up for a promotion," Skeet frowned.

"He thinks he is," Burns shrugged. "His name was submitted for consideration. I considered it and dismissed him immediately.

He's not qualified for the job and the worst thing I could do is reward him for his bad behavior. He will be transferred; but, politics will get in my way no doubt. In all likelihood, the change won't occur until after this case has been closed. I don't think I can pull it off in time to help you resolve this."

"We'll work around it," Rowdy assured him.

"In the meantime," Burns stood. "I'll let you get back to it. I'm going to contact Dumas in the morning, order him to stop the runs for a driver's license in the target states. I think, if anything, those eight can be eliminated completely."

"I agree," Coop nodded. "And probably Hawaii. Travel is too restrictive and I'm also eliminating Alaska. He likes remote; but, he also likes his creature comforts. I doubt he'd be able to function in that environment."

"Well, there you go," Burns gave him an approving smile. "In one day, you've eliminated ten of the fifty states plus the good state of Illinois. You only have thirty-nine more to go before you narrow down his headquarters."

"I need air," Skeet said once his boss was gone. He jumped from his chair and headed out the door.

"He's feeling..." Rowdy paused. "Like a failure. I agree with you, one hundred percent. But, with me pointing out the error with the date and then you laying everything out like that... he's feeling responsible, not just for Angela, but for all of them."

"I know," Coop sighed. "But, I had to point it out. They were wasting time and we need to focus on other aspects of the investigation. In addition to the manpower at the local departments, Dumas assigned two members of the task force to check in regularly with each department and monitor their progress. I think the best thing for us to do right now, is go back to the beginning. You should read Skeet's first report, his first profile

Subterfuge

before he was basically ordered to alter it. He was shut down and shut down hard. I called Manchin, in Seattle. He told me Skeet wouldn't back down, the locals were convinced he was right but the feds... they hammered him — hard. Rumor has it, Skeet received a reprimand when he wouldn't drop it."

"So," Rowdy decided, "he dropped it. Tried to be a team player and now he's paying the price for it."

"Exactly," Coop ran a hand through his hair. "So, we go back to the beginning. I asked Lt. Manchin to start researching deaths in the area. I'm thinking he started in Seattle for a reason. Could be a connection to the area... a distant connection; but, I know it's there. I told him to go out two or three hundred miles. It's a big area, and that's going to cover several states and take a butt load of time; but, it has to be done."

"My gut says you're right," Rowdy agreed. "I think he has a place, Oregon, California, Idaho, Montana? I couldn't begin to narrow it down; but, it's there."

"So, we dig," Coop settled in for a long night of research.

Rowdy waited over two hours before he tracked down Skeet. The man was sitting outside on the porch, eyes closed, head leaned back, face full of agony. He settled into the chair a few feet away. "I had a case once," he began. "String of residential burglaries. High-end stuff, cash, diamonds, traveler's checks, anything the owners kept in a safe that was easy to transport."

"Rowdy," Skeet objected.

"After about a month, I made an arrest," Rowdy continued, undeterred. "The guy was a prominent businessman, he was friendly with some of the victims, always walked around in an expensive suit. He was wearing one when I booked him. My gut told me I'd caught the right guy. I was so confident I was right, I immediately started the process to get a warrant. I knew my evidence was in the briefcase he was carrying when I arrested him. The guy was actually stepping through the front gate of my latest target."

"What happened?"

"My sergeant at the time hammered me," Rowdy told him. "Pulled me into his office and railed on me, said I had made a huge mistake and my career would suffer because of it. Said the guy was an upstanding citizen and I didn't have anything that would prove otherwise. He ordered me to set the man free and write an official apology."

"Did you?" Skeet asked.

"Nope," Rowdy grinned. "I was right, maybe I couldn't prove it... not right then, but I was right. And, the sergeant couldn't force me to release a prisoner. He tried, even wrote me up for disobeying an order."

"The difference between what you did and what I did..." Skeet rubbed his face. "You stood up. You didn't let someone browbeat you into complying with something you didn't believe in."

"Actually," Rowdy disagreed. "I almost did. I started to doubt myself. Nobody believed the guy was really the burglar. No one but me. And, until I got that warrant, unless I caught him red-handed — my career was on the line."

"But you didn't," Skeet pressed.

"I did," Rowdy disagreed. "I typed up the paperwork to drop the charges and authorize his release. Then, I headed down to booking prepared to set my only suspect free. Fortunately, my dad stopped me. He insisted we had to talk before I did something I'd regret. We took a break, went to a little diner he preferred, and we

Subterfuge

talked through the case.   Then, he looked me in the eye and told me how disappointed he would be if I didn't stand my ground.   I tore up the paperwork right there, while we sat in that booth, and waited for the warrant."

"And?"

"And, once we got into the briefcase we found half a mil in cash and bonds," Rowdy smiled.   "Don't beat yourself up because you tried to be a team player.   You didn't have a father to intervene, to give you the courage to stand your ground.   We all make decisions and we have to live with them.   You wouldn't be the cop you are if you didn't make a few bad ones."

"But, so many girls have suffered… innocent kids have died needless deaths because I let myself get pressured into changing my mind," Skeet said softly.   "I'm not sure I can live with that."

"Hmm," Rowdy settled further into his chair.   "I didn't realize knowing Seattle wasn't the first would have made such a big difference.   I certainly didn't know it would have prevented the rest of the deaths.   In that case, I see your point.   Well, no I don't. Maybe you could tell me exactly how that little piece of information would have saved the girls in Denver?   And the ones in Kansas City, Detroit, Pittsburg, Savanah, New Orleans, and Houston.   I'm usually pretty perceptive and granted I'm not an ace at this detective work like you and Coop… but I'm not seeing how ruining your career, how creating even more hostility with your supervisor than there already is, would have saved those girls."

"Every detail matters," Skeet answered.

"You are absolutely correct," Rowdy agreed.   "Some of it matters during the investigation, some only matters at trial.   That little detail… it would matter at trial.   It will also matter to the victim's family and friends; but, it wouldn't have stopped the man before he killed again. We'll use it, see if we can track prior movement, maybe find a clue he didn't cover up early on. So, yeah, it matters. But, it doesn't change anything and unfortunately, it does nothing to help us find your wife. We'll do that by outsmarting the lunatic and working harder than he will."

"Is that your way of telling me to get back to work?"

"You're a smart man," Rowdy stood, "figure it out."

Skeet also stood. "I realized something a few minutes ago."

"What's that?" Rowdy asked as they made their way back to the loft.

"We always work with the locals," Skeet began. "There are a lot of reasons for that, but one is a fresh eye. Each time you start a new case, the locals have to look over the previous evidence and sometimes... like you did, they'll catch something we missed. Throughout this whole process, Dumas has shut them down. If they asked a question he didn't like, he ignored it. If they questioned a conclusion, he brushed them off as inexperienced. I think we need to go back and start at the beginning. We need to look at this as if we were just starting the case and see if there is anything we missed or could have done better."

"I'm glad you agree," Rowdy stepped into their new workspace. "Because that's what Coop and I have been doing for the past two hours. Makes it easier all around."

Chapter Four

The Scientist pulled up to the dilapidated structure and shut down his vehicle. He took a minute to look around before casually shoving open the door and moving to the side of the building. The woman two doors down was still watching his every move. He was now certain he had made the right decision when he decided to relocate. He had to find a new lab; this building would not do at all for his experiments. The crazy bat was sweeping her rocks as she continued to stick her nose where it didn't belong. He wished he could teach her a lesson, to demonstrate – using a very special technique – the meaning of the colloquialism *curiosity killed the cat*. But, he couldn't, he had to tamp down the desire to kill. He already had a test subject waiting. One he was going to enjoy working on more than the others. The nosey neighbor was safe — for now. He punched in a code, waited for the electronic lock to switch from red to green and stepped inside. He flipped on the pen light strapped around his neck and moved into the darkened room.

The woman hadn't moved an inch. He let his eyes adjust to the dim light and scanned the area for any sign of tampering. The boards were still secure on the windows and the locks were still in place. The air inside the building was cool, but not cold enough to pose a threat to his prisoner. He took a tentative step forward and kicked at the motionless form. She was still lying in the exact position she had been in when he left her on the old mattress; but, it could be a trick. After several seconds, he let out a relieved breath. Clearly, he had measured the chemicals correctly. He went to work, switching out the nearly empty IV bag and replacing it with a large, full bag of liquid. He tossed the empty bag aside, not in the least bit worried it would be discovered. He wouldn't be here long, anyway. Even if someone located the empty container, they'd never connect it to him... or his victim.

He focused on securing the new bag that contained his latest concoction. He had, once again, measured each item carefully as he prepared the new dosage. It was imperative he kept the woman deeply sedated while at the same time, providing the essential nutrients her body needed to survive. He dropped the wool blanket he'd found at his Aunt Elizabeth's house onto the unconscious body as an added precaution and smiled in relief. He still hadn't found a location for his work; but, he would. The situation wasn't ideal; but, he figured he could keep her here, undiscovered, for at least a week. He didn't like sedating his specimen's this way. If he miscalculated, he could ruin everything. But, he wouldn't miscalculate. And, there was no real threat in waiting. The cops had no idea who he was, where he was; or, what he was doing.

It still bothered him that Agent Perkins had found his last research facility; he'd been so careful and was at a loss as to what went wrong. No matter. He'd just make sure it didn't happen again. An even better reason to find an ideal, secluded work space and not settle for something that wasn't perfect. With the woman outside constantly watching his arrival and departure... this place was not perfect. Yes, he could keep this up for at least a week before he brought the fair Mrs. Perkins around and began experimenting. His body shook with anticipation. He couldn't wait to begin.

* * * *

Three days later, Coop stood in front of Clyde Barton's desk. He'd been waiting for the lab results, was counting on them to provide a new lead, and was annoyed at the delay. "Where are my results, Clyde?" he demanded.

"I'm afraid there's been a block placed on the blood work," Clyde said in dismissal. "I can't give it to you."

"It's my case, Barton," Coop gritted his teeth. "You can't block the primary on his own case."

"That case was reassigned to the FBI," Clyde glanced up. "And SSA Frank Dumas has issued strict orders in regard to all evidence pertaining to his case. He's dealing with a multiple homicide and the evidence must be protected."

"SSA Dumas?" Coop narrowed his eyes at the lab expert. "I wasn't aware you worked for the FBI, Barton. Somehow, I was under the impression you were employed by Chicago PD. I could swear I heard somewhere this facility is owned and operated by the local Police Department and the citizens of this community."

"I am," Clyde frowned. "But, if the FBI orders me to protect their evidence, I'm obligated to comply."

"If the FBI produces some evidence and then asks you to analyze it," Coop barked. "Feel free to comply all you want. Give me the results of MY evidence or you won't like the consequences."

"Don't threaten me, detective," Clyde glowered. "I'm just doing my job."

Coop leaned forward, pressing the palms of his hands on the top of Barton's desk as he invaded his personal space. "Unless you want me to physically remove you from this office and book you for interfering... you will produce the results of my evidence — immediately. I'll give you exactly thirty seconds, then you'll see what it's like to be strip searched and locked in a cage with Bubba for a few hours. I've heard he's taken a liking to.... scrawny lab techs with an attitude. And, Bubba? He's pretty inventive."

"SSA Dumas..." Clyde began.

Coop straightened and glanced at his watch.

Barton printed off the results and tossed them across the desk. "I'll be reporting this."

Coop snatched up the document and left the room. He was just pulling out of the lot when his phone rang. He glanced down, saw it was his division commander and sighed. "Detective Cooper."

"Coop," Captain Dave Mortens growled. "Did you tell Clyde Barton you would arrest him and lock him in a cell with some pedophile named Bubba?"

"Yep," Coop said as he entered the highway and headed for Rowdy's. "And if he ever tries to block me again, I'll follow through on the threat. SSA Dumas might be in charge of the serial killer fiasco, but that evidence was obtained in my abduction case. My case, sir. It was submitted to our lab and neither Dumas nor that piss ant Barton is going to block me — the primary investigator — from seeing those results."

Subterfuge

"I agree," Mortens said calmly. "He left that particular detail out of his complaint. I'll deal with Barton. Did you get what you needed?"

"I did," Coop also calmed.

"Then let me handle it," Mortens ordered. "And, I'll be having a second conversation with the chief. I expect a formal complaint to be submitted in regard to SSA Frank Dumas and his interference with a local investigation. If Griggs won't handle that, I'll submit the complaint myself."

"Are you sending the results over to the feds, or do you want me to handle that?" Coop asked.

"Let me think about it," Mortens decided. "I'll hash that out with Griggs as well."

"Let me know," Coop replied. "I'm off for the day; but, we have a briefing at zero-nine-hundred. I can provide a copy at that meeting if you want."

"Keep me posted on your progress," Mortens told him. "I'll get back to you. Right now, I'm going to remind Clyde Barton where he works and who he reports to."

"Good luck," Coop disconnected just as he was pulling into Rowdy's driveway. He took a minute to study the printout, shoved open the door, and headed for the loft. They had another lead to pursue.

Coop had barely stepped into the room when the doorbell chimed, and his cell phone began to ring. He glanced at the display, Mortens. "I have to take this."

"I'll get the door," Rowdy provided. Within seconds, he was back, and he wasn't alone. "Skeet," he said as he stepped into the room. "You have a visitor. Said he's not leaving until he talks to you. I thought about leaving him on the front porch for a couple hours; but, it seemed… rude. Not exactly in line with all that professional courtesy crap we try to adhere to, so I had a change of heart."

"Ryan," Skeet stood when Ryan Fulmer, long-time friend and favorite e-Man stepped forward.

Fulmer placed a supportive hand on Skeet's shoulder. "You holding up?"

"Mostly," Skeet said honestly as they settled back onto the chairs.

Fulmer took a minute to survey the room. "I want in."

"What?" Skeet asked, then shook his head. "I can't ask you to risk that. Dumas would have a coronary if he found out. I don't want you catching flak for this."

"Dumas is floundering," Fulmer sobered. "That task force is seriously FUBAR since you left. He doesn't have a clue what he's doing and we're all just chasing our tails."

"And, still…" Skeet persisted.

"I don't work for Dumas," Ryan pushed. "I have my own SSA and Jim approved the new assignment this morning. Said if you need anything, all you have to do is ask."

Skeet was surprised. "What about the task force? You've been officially assigned."

"Dumas brought in Cartwright," he sighed. "Said after Houston, I can't be trusted. I've been saddled with grunt work, he's wasting my time. The boss isn't happy about that, agrees I need a new assignment. Jim Whitaker is protective of his men. You know that. He was ready to pull me already. I asked for a

Subterfuge

favor, he granted it. He's behind me on this. He's behind you. If he says just ask, all you have to do is ask. In the meantime, bring me in. I need to help you get Angela back, Skeet. Don't shut me out."

Skeet looked at Rowdy then Coop. "It's up to them," he finally decided. "You have my vote, but this is Rowdy's house and Coop's case. They have the final say."

"I'm good with it," Rowdy shrugged. "I think we could use the help."

"I went over your work in Houston," Coop added. "I like the way you think; and, you found the van. Apparently, you have some skills."

"Some," Fulmer's mouth quirked, just slightly.

"If you cleared things on your end, I can use you." Coop moved to the table and pulled out the lab results. "I had some trouble getting this. Dumas ordered our lab guy to block it. Said it was only to be released to him."

"Dickhead Barton tried to block you?" Rowdy fumed. "I found that blood. He had no right…"

"And I told him that," Coop grinned. "He didn't appreciate my position on the matter; but, he relented. Chief Griggs will be filing a complaint with Burns sometime tomorrow regarding Dumas and his high-handed demands. I've been instructed to submit the findings at the briefing in the morning. That gives us a few hours head start. Let's see if we can identify our suspect before then.

"What blood?" Skeet asked, he had gone pale and concern was written all over his face.

"I kept that from you," Coop admitted. "I wanted answers before I filled you in. There were blood smears in the room where your wife paints. Not a lot, just a few smears and a couple small drops, but enough to analyze. Rowdy also found a rag saturated out back, near the trees along the back roadway."

"And what did you discover?"

Coop slid the findings over to Skeet. "The blood inside the house belonged to a female. There's no record on file so they couldn't identify it. I think we can assume it belonged to Angela. The blood on the rag was male. Barton also ran that through CODIS," Coop said, referring to the FBI's database that contained DNA information on criminals, employees and military personnel.

"Looks like he wasn't in the system," Skeet observed. "You had him run relatives?"

"I did," Coop nodded. "And, he got a hit from military records."

"Looks like a Grandfather Hill served in Vietnam," Skeet continued reading.

"I can work with that," Fulmer stepped up. "If we have grand-daddy, it's just a matter of following the line. I'll look for off-spring and then take it down one more generation. Could be dozens of names but it's a good place to start."

"Then it's all yours," Skeet handed Ryan the information. "While you work on that, I'll start running property records near Seattle. Focus on... let's say a three-hundred-mile radius and search for all records listed under Hill. It's a common last name; but, we might get lucky and find a hit."

"Or several hundred," Rowdy mumbled.

Subterfuge

* * * *

Angela slowly opened her eyes and tried to adjust to the darkness that surrounded her. There wasn't even a sliver of light anywhere. She forced her body into a sitting position and flinched at the pain. Her entire body ached, her muscles screamed, and she fell against a cold, concrete wall, exhausted. How long had she been out? There was no way to know. She remembered the needle, remembered fighting for her life when the man violently shoved it into her thigh, and she remembered the almost instant blackness as she succumbed to the poison.

She tried to shift, to find a more comfortable position, but was stopped by the short chain that secured her hands and legs to the wall. A shiver ran through her body and she began to shake uncontrollably. Not only from the cold, although that was an issue; but, an incapacitating wave of terror was starting to engulf her. She was going to die. Her chance of rescue was slim. She'd been captured by a madman. She knew that. She'd known the instant she glanced up and saw him standing a few feet away as she painted the beautiful ocean scene she'd been longing to start for days. That knowledge had solidified the instant she saw the envelope. The shocking, bold letters of her husband's name written in red and carefully displayed on their mantel.

That was the moment she knew. The serial killer Skeet had been chasing had found her. He had targeted her to punish her husband. It would work. Skeet would blame himself. She knew that meant he would work harder to find her, work harder to bring the man down, fight with everything he had to stop the predator responsible for so many innocent deaths. But, if he didn't make it in time, if he couldn't save her… she was afraid it would destroy him. It would break him to the point he would never recover. She tried to gather her resolve, to force away the fear and concentrate on survival. She'd do everything in her power to make sure she lived through this. For her, of course, but also for her husband.

Despair and need threatened to overcome her. She needed her husband, needed to see his face, to feel his strong arms wrapped around her, needed to tell him she was sorry. She'd been stupid and selfish; and, right now, she couldn't regret that more. Skeet wanted to visit her. Wanted to fly out to New Orleans and spend some time together; just a couple days to break up the long absence — but she'd refused. She insisted on the time apart, had told him she couldn't be distracted, that she had to focus on work... she was always focused on work. She told him he was smothering her and neither one of them could afford the interruption to their schedule. Her main focus was on her exhibits, on the upcoming shows. She had wanted to be available for last-minute changes, additions, menial tasks that she realized now; didn't matter. Plus, Skeet had to catch a killer. She'd been so sure she would see him when she got home. Now, she might never see him again. Three and a half weeks of loneliness... for what? That time away would only make it harder on him.

Angela began to cry. Hot tears slid down her cold cheeks. It was so cold inside this dark, concrete room they cooled by the time they reached her trembling chin. Within seconds, she was sobbing. Ugly, uncontrollable sobs that wracked her body so violently she fell back onto the floor in defeat. Her head was pounding now as despair replaced resolve. Pain shot through her temple; but, she couldn't stop. She was going to die and her amazing, loving, selfless husband's life was going to be destroyed... shattered beyond repair. And, she wouldn't even have the chance to say goodbye.

* * * *

Subterfuge

"Winfred Scott Hill had two sons," Ryan Fulmer announced. It was seven o'clock in the morning, the group had called it a night just after three then gathered for a quick breakfast at six. They were now back to work, anxious to find something that would provide answers. Angela was starting her fifth day in captivity. Nobody wanted to guess what condition she was in; but, they knew time was running out. "He survived the war and inherited a fortune from his grandfather on his mother's side," Fulmer continued. "Apparently, the man was an inventor and created some fancy doodad that's still used in scientific labs all over the world. Winfred has since died. The rights to the invention was split down the middle between his two sons. One of the sons, Charles Hill, is currently alive and enjoying the lavish life of luxury. He hasn't worked a day in his life and clearly enjoys the fruits of his great grand-daddy's labor. The second son, Henry, was a gambler. He lost most of his inheritance early on and was killed in a back alley in New Jersey just over ten years ago."

"Either one have any children?" Coop asked.

"I'm still tracking that down," Fulmer provided. "Looks like Charles and his wife, Piper, may have had a kid; but, there's not a lot of information."

"And Henry?" Skeet asked.

"Henry was a gambler and a player," Fulmer said in frustration. "Lots of newspaper articles and personal accounts of his dastardly deeds readily available. Sounds like a real peach of a guy, that one. Anyway, he lost his money the instant he got it. Lost women nearly as quickly. I'm working on the ancestry sites, trying to piece it all together. I'm finding several sons and daughters that might belong to him. All illegitimate which makes it harder."

"You keep working on Henry," Rowdy suggested. "I'll take Charles, see if I can track down the possible kid and go from there."

"Send me the information you have on both Charles and Henry," Skeet added. "I'll start working on property and see if I can track down the current location of Charles and Piper. Maybe we can pay them a visit and find out from the source what happened to the kid."

"While you guys work on that," Coop stood. "I have to check in with Dumas. Briefing is at nine. It's going to be interesting to see how he handles the new information. He was very adamant the results go to him and only him. I'm guessing he won't be happy when I steal his thunder."

"I doubt he'll give you any grief," Skeet glanced up. "I talked to Stan last night. Griggs already called to complain. Burns planned to have a one-on-one this morning, before the briefing. Dumas probably already knows the results are in and you have them."

"That makes things easier," Coop decided as he left the room.

* * * *

Angela set the large bolt cutters on the ground against the wall where she could find it later. She had to get the screw out before the man returned, but her fingers were raw and two of them were bleeding from the effort. Failure was too terrifying to consider. Her mind was running wild, considering what that monster might have in store for her with this hideous weapon. Skeet had been chasing this guy for over a year. He had refused to discuss the details no matter how many times she'd asked. He told her she didn't need to know just how sadistic and demented the man was. That made everything so much worse. She was afraid she

Subterfuge

just might find out first hand; and, she wasn't looking forward to it. Skeet called him the Mad Scientist and admitted he tortured his victims to death. Angie had been curious but didn't press too hard. She was glad she hadn't, glad she didn't know what was coming. Fear of the unknown was a little terrifying; but, she was certain the details would be much worse; and, they would most likely render her unable to function.

From what she saw the previous day, the man was batshit crazy, not simply mad. And, she understood with every fiber of her being just how imperative it was to disable those bolt cutters. She couldn't paint without her fingers and she was pretty fond of her toes as well. Skeet would find her, she was counting on that. But, she had to do everything in her power to be in one piece when he did. She couldn't do anything about the other tools he'd dropped off. The hammer was probably to break her bones. The additional electrical wire worried her; but, unless she could get free, there was nothing she could do about that particular horror. She would focus on one problem at a time. Right now, she'd remove the screw and drop it down the grate she'd accidentally located less than a foot away.

The chains attached to the leather manacles he'd fastened to her ankles and wrists were short and didn't allow much mobility. Plus, she had to be careful because she'd already been shocked by the things three times. If she wasn't worried it would electrocute her, she'd just use the stupid bolt cutters and cut the chain. But, the links were too large and she was too weak. Would the metal on metal serve as a conductor and increase the intensity? She had no idea; and, that meant she couldn't risk it. She'd have to disable the tool and hope Skeet found her before it was too late. Her options were limited, so she just hoped the hole was deep and the screw would be lost forever. If she could just get rid of the screw, the tool would be useless. It wouldn't stop him; but, it might delay the inevitable long enough. "Skeet, I'm counting on you," she whispered into the darkness. "Save me. Please, save me." Angela picked up the cold metal bolt cutters in one hand, the hammer in the other, and once again, began to pound at the nut.

* * * *

Coop stepped into the loft after his shift and paused. Fulmer was the only one inside the room. "Where is Rowdy?"

"He went to find Skeet," Fulmer frowned. "He's in bad shape. It's getting to him. We're moving too slow and he knows... with the others, he knows what condition they were in by now. I think he's lost hope, convinced himself she's gone, and he failed. I tried to pull him back, but... well, he wouldn't listen. Rowdy's seeing what he can do."

Coop nodded and left the room. He found Rowdy in the kitchen. "Skeet?"

"Outside," Rowdy sighed. "Maybe, you can knock some sense into him. So far, Fulmer and I have both failed. He's given up, decided she's gone, and he's shattered. He's a mess, Coop, and I don't know how to help him."

"Any progress?" Coop leaned against the counter and took a sip of Rowdy's beer.

"Some," Rowdy turned, grabbed a second beer from the fridge and handed it to his brother. "Fulmer's confident he's located a daughter and a son that belonged to Henry. I'm not having as much luck tracking the kid Charles and Piper had. I've tried hospitals; but, I get that whole HIPAA thing and patient rights. Vital Records probably has the info; but, I had to submit a request and they'll let me know — when and if."

"Did Skeet find anything on the property?" Coop pushed.

Subterfuge

"No idea," Rowdy shrugged. "He's been working on it; but, then he just had a breakdown. Threw his pen across the room, got up and left."

"I'll talk to him," Coop straightened. "You go see if you can get anywhere with his notes. I think the property is going to be key. If we can track down this Charles and Piper, we might be able to eliminate their kid. That leaves Henry and his forty thieves... but, it's all we have."

"Let me know if you need anything," Rowdy headed back to the loft and Coop headed out the door.

Coop stepped onto the back porch and studied his new friend. Rowdy was right, the man was shattered. Skeet was lying in a lounge chair, his eyes closed, his face taut, misery radiated from every inch of his body. Coop moved forward and settled into a chair a few feet away. "I heard we're giving up."

"Don't start," Skeet said softly. It was his only reaction. He didn't move an inch or even open his eyes as he spoke.

"I'm not arguing with you," Coop said casually. "If we're giving up, I can spend more time with my wife. I'm not looking forward to breaking the news to Mags, though. She'll be a lot less understanding and probably confused. I mean, she's a cop's wife. An amazing wife. She lives with the stress, the fear, and the uncertainty every single day... year after year. I'm not sure she's going to understand your position. I mean, giving up that is... that's not even a possibility for my Maggie.

But then, she has more experience dealing with the stress of the unknown — the stress created by the job we both do. The stress experienced by those left behind, those left to wonder and worry every second we're away. She even stood by me when I told her I wanted to join SWAT. Didn't bat an eye even though I knew it made her panic —just a little. I think she was relieved when I became a marksman rather than an operator. I mean, it kept me out of the line of fire; but, she had a different set of worries. She always knows when I'm on an Op; and, she waits at home hoping that next incident isn't the one. Hoping that I'm not forced to take a life. She knows I'd struggle with that; but, she's still there... waiting, worrying and supporting what I do. Anyway, she's on her way over. Maybe, you could explain why we're just walking away; because, to be honest, I don't really get it myself."

Skeet suddenly sat up and jumped to his feet, moving away from Coop to lean against a large post. "We all know she's gone. I know she's gone. I know his pattern, how long he keeps each woman. She's the first here in Chicago. That means he started immediately and not one of his victims lasted more than three days. She's been gone for five. Five long, horrible days of torture and for what? Because I got a little too close and he wanted revenge. My career killed the only woman I will ever love."

"Unlike you," Coop moved to stand on the other side of the post. "I don't believe Angela is dead."

"Based on what?" Skeet asked scornfully. "The infallible Cooper gut?"

"There is that," Coop said undeterred. "But, there's also the fact that you took his tools. He has to replace them. Then, there's the fact he didn't have a full month to prepare. He had to find a hide-out...somewhere he could be isolated and absolutely confident nobody would see him enter or leave each day. The entire city knows we're looking for a cop's wife. He made a mistake taking Angela; he just doesn't know it yet."

"Still doesn't mean she's alive," Skeet pressed. "I mean, it's been five days. He could have found a place that first day... before he snatched her. That gives him four days to come up with tools. I agree they wouldn't be as elaborate as the ones he lost; but, any hardware store has what he needs. There is no reason to believe he didn't start in immediately and she's gone."

"Actually, there are plenty of them. And, there's no reason to believe he did," Coop argued. "But, there is one reason that is indisputable and, in my opinion, it's the most powerful one. Angela is not dead because we haven't found her body."

"You do remember Detroit," Skeet argued. "Those girls were taken nearly a year ago and Smith has only located two of the bodies. They may never find the third." Agent Bryant Smith had called earlier that day to notify Skeet they were making progress. His people had located the remains of one of the two missing girls. So far, his instincts were right. Dental records had confirmed the skeletal remains belonged to one of Smith's original missing girls. They were now scouring every remote area in the city in hopes of finding the third. Bryant still believed it was Tanya Stewart and Skeet was pretty sure he was right.

"Detroit wasn't about revenge," Coop countered. "This time is different. I wish I could get you to understand that. Throw your profile away. It's irrelevant and it's distracting you. Stop looking at this as if your wife is the next first victim in a new city. Angela doesn't fit his MO, doesn't fit the specific requirements of his other victims. She's not an experiment, Skeet. She's payback. That means, if we don't get there in time... we are going to find her body proudly displayed on his favorite landmark... like freakin' Millennium Park in front of Cloud Gate."

"Okay," Skeet said after several silent moments. "Let's say I agree. How does that help?"

"Because, now is not the time to give up hope," Coop said softly. "It's the time to work harder. She's alive, I know she is. Every cop instinct I have tells me your wife is alive. And, because she's a cop's wife... she's fighting. I can't promise he hasn't hurt her; but, I can promise she's fighting and she's got something none of those other girls had."

"What?" Skeet studied Coop, truly curious.

"Us," Coop said with a shrug. "You know this guy better than anyone. Rowdy found DNA that is going to lead us to his true identity. You have a photo. We're close, Skeet. And, we're motivated... more so than ever before. Don't give up on your wife because I guarantee... she hasn't given up on you."

"Sometimes, I'm so afraid of what she's enduring, I can't breathe," Skeet admitted. "I do know who I'm dealing with and he's a monster. Knowing Angela is..." he stopped. "Knowing what is happening to her, right now. Knowing I put her there, I'm not sure I can live with that. It gets in the way. Every time I sit down to work, it takes over... the pain, the grief, the guilt."

"That's because you are letting your emotions drive you," Coop said softly. "Nobody could function that way. You're letting your fear and the guilt interfere with the job. Tuck it away, Skeet. I'm not saying ignore it. I'm not saying you should stop feeling. I'm saying push it back, don't let it consume you. The love you have for Angela shows through every second I'm around you. Use that love, channel it. Push the fear and the guilt aside because there's no place for it. Start using your mind. You're smarter than he is and that's how we are going to stop this maniac. It's how we're going to reunite you with the woman you love. And, when we do, the love is what will get you through the rest. We will find her, there's no other option."

"My profile," Skeet began.

"Is crap," Coop interrupted. "Throw it out, Skeet. You work serial cases, I get that. I work homicides. We need to approach this the same way I work all my cases; assault, abduction, homicide —doesn't matter. They get worked the same way. Stop looking for patterns, stop trying to guess his next move based on history. None of that matters. What matters is what we're doing, what we have been doing. Tracing his family, finding people to interview, and searching the city for vacant homes and apartments... that is how we will locate his hideout."

Skeet looked up in surprise. "We haven't even started that search."

"Yes," Coop said. "We have. Vance got his girlfriend, Amy I think it is, involved. She's working with Miles, Josie and Carter; whoever that is. They say they're making good progress and should have a list of buildings for us to check in the morning. Unless we're giving up, that is."

"No," Skeet pushed away from the post. "I'm never giving up. And uh... thanks."

"Always happy to kick a guy when he's down," Coop grinned as he followed Skeet into the house.

* * * *

Skeet stepped into the loft and spotted a petite blond huddled in the corner with Rowdy. The instant they walked in, she was up on her feet, across the room, and launched herself into Coop's arms.

"Skeet," Coop laughed, set Maggie back on the ground and turned her to face the group. "I'd like you to meet my wife, Maggie Cooper."

"It's a pleasure," Skeet held out a hand and was surprised when she brushed it aside and pulled him into a big hug. "Uh, wow. Um, sorry I've been keeping your husband occupied the last few days."

Maggie frowned. "It's not your fault and this is where he needs to be."

"Thanks for that," Skeet said softly, liking Coop's wife immediately. He could see the good detective was smitten and he understood why now that he'd met the strong, spunky woman in person. "Will you be staying?" He glanced around the room not sure he wanted her to see the evidence of what they were facing.

"Bryan, that's our son, he left earlier today to spend some time with his grandparents," she settled into a chair. "My parents have a little farm in Iowa and Bry loves it there. Without the munchkin under foot, I'm free to help out here. And, don't say this is police work. I know that. I also know the wife of a cop is missing and that makes her family. I'm going to help my family."

Coop picked her up and settled into the closest chair, placing Maggie securely on his lap. "I don't normally let my wife assist with cases, if that's what you're wondering," Coop glanced at Skeet. "But, as you can see, she's determined to help. And, I kind of figured we have a lot of ground to cover. Plus, Mags has helped her mother do their family's genealogy. I was thinking she might be a good resource in tracking down the children. Legitimate and illegitimate."

"I'd take the help," Fulmer spoke up before Skeet could object. "I haven't done a lot of genealogy and I'm stumped. If you're willing, I'll show you what I've been working on today."

"More than willing," Maggie stood and moved to a chair next to Ryan Fulmer. "Hi, I'm Maggie."

Fulmer smiled. "Agent Ryan Fulmer. It's a pleasure to meet you."

The group worked for several hours before Maggie insisted she had to have food before she collapsed. Rowdy ordered Chinese and they talked about the case while they ate. Once they finished, everyone returned to the individual tasks they were working on.

"I've located three properties owned by Charles and Piper Hill," Skeet announced. "One in the Hamptons, one in Paris and one in Oregon."

"Where in Oregon?" Rowdy asked. "Is it within the parameters we set outside of Seattle?"

"Actually," Skeet studied his map. "It is. They have a large home near Lake Oswego. In fact, it looks like it's right on the lake."

"Give me the information," Rowdy dropped down next to him. "I'll start running deaths in the area."

"You think the killer would pee in his own pool, so to speak," Skeet asked.

"I think his first kill wasn't nearly as organized as the twenty-two he's proud of," Rowdy countered. "I think it's possible the first one was an accident, or he may have made a mistake. So, yeah. I think he might have peed in his own pool, realized it was bad business and hit Seattle. The first gave him a taste for it, Seattle was his coming out party. He was proud of his accomplishments in Seattle and was obviously happy with the results; otherwise, she wouldn't have been number one."

"How does that help us find Angela?" Maggie asked.

"Maybe it doesn't," Rowdy admitted. "But, maybe it will tell us something about our killer. Like, how he reacts when his plans are foiled. If he panics under pressure. If he has a temper."

"Nothing in the profile suggests he has a temper," Fulmer disagreed. "He's controlled, meticulous and disciplined."

"We're ignoring the profile," Skeet said, still studying the map. "And Rowdy is right, the first kill might help us understand him on a different level. It might give us insight into where he would go when he's desperate. So far, with the others, he's had plenty of time to plan. This time, he left Houston, flew to Chicago, and abducted Ange the following night. It was impulsive, not controlled. He left evidence, hers and his. He's thrown out the rulebook and he's working one day at a time. Maybe that's what happened with his first kill. Anything helps."

"Do you want help?" Fulmer asked.

"No," Skeet said absently. "Keep working on identifying Charles and Henry's kids."

It was just past midnight when Maggie stood and stretched her arms over her head. "I think I have five names for you," she began to twist and turn, unrolling the kinks as she spoke. Her back immediately started to make soft popping noises. Coop jumped up and moved behind her, gently pressing his fingers into the knots in her shoulder blades. "Thanks, babe."

"You think or you're sure?" Skeet asked for clarification.

"Right," Maggie slid a piece of paper closer, so she could read it. "First, I found a name; nothing else. Just an entry on another tree that mentions an Eddie Hill as the son of Charles and Piper. There aren't any other details and if he's still living, I'm not going to find much. That one comes under the category of 'I think' right now."

Rowdy jotted down the name. "And, the others?"

"Right," Maggie continued. "Henry's kids are all illegitimate. I can't find any marriages in his records and he's easier because he's dead and he was so active — not in a good way. These fall under the 'I know' category. He has a kid that is forty-

Subterfuge

two, lives in Norfolk, Nebraska... where ever that is. His name is Spencer."

"Okay," Rowdy signaled for her to continue. "The mother's name is Connie, still living. The second one is a daughter. I have the info if you want it, but..."

"Yeah," Rowdy nodded. "Let's just stick with the men for now."

"Okay, there are three. All of them have different mothers. Spencer was first, then Ian. His mother is Nancy Freeman. She resides in New Mexico and I think he's there, too; but, I'm not positive on that one. Since he's still living, the law enforcement databases will provide better information on him. Finally, there is Darrell Stowe. His mother was Scarlett. She passed away last year. Last known for Darrell was Canada. Again, he's living so I can't get much more in here."

"I'll check the records," Fulmer decided. "But, I think we can eliminate Darrell. Unless of course, he's entered the US and never left."

"I agree," Skeet nodded. "Maggie, you're tired. Why don't you and Coop call it a night? I appreciate all your help, but I don't feel right keeping you up so long."

"I can keep going," she focused on Coop.

"Naw," Coop stood. "Let's head home. I think we've done all we can tonight, anyway."

The others worked to track property and locate Henry's kids for another hour before reluctantly taking a break to get a couple hours downtime. Rowdy set Fulmer up in a second guest room. It was only sparsely furnished and mainly used by fellow LEO's who dropped by to catch a game and consumed one too many in the process. As cops, they were all extra careful about impaired driving and tended to error on the side of safety. Rowdy was ready and willing to accommodate when the need arose. Ryan didn't care, the bed was all he needed. The instant his head hit the pillow, he was out cold.

* * * *

Skeet headed downstairs for coffee. He knew it was early and the others would still be resting; but, he couldn't sleep. Until Angela was found, he'd push himself until he dropped. They were running out of time. He stepped into the loft and froze; surprised Rowdy was already up and working. The guy was only a couple years younger than Skeet; but, his stamina was amazing. He moved forward and settled into the second lounge chair to wait, realizing Rowdy was on the phone.

"Hey," Rowdy said, slipping the phone into his pocket.

"Do you ever sleep?" Skeet asked, taking another sip of the coffee and wishing he was more alert. "You want a cup?"

"Naw," Rowdy settled back. "I already had three."

"Seriously?" Skeet stared in shock. "How long have you been up?"

"Awhile," Rowdy evaded. "I couldn't sleep. My mind kept circling back around to this Eddie guy, the son of Charles and Piper. I think he's our man."

"Why?" Skeet considered. "I mean, one of Henry's kids would fit the profile a lot better than the son of Charles and Piper. Two-parent home, money and privilege compared to single mother, no father; mom was probably in control and demanded perfection."

Subterfuge

"I get it," Rowdy shrugged. "And, I don't have an answer for you. It's just… well, I'm a street cop, not an investigator like you and Coop. I'm not a profiler. I survive by following my gut. Let me explain it this way. I'm chasing a suspect, have a specific description and I come around a corner where I encounter a group of people loitering. I have to either stop them or dismiss them within a matter of seconds. If my suspect is a guy, out go the women. If he's tall, I'll just walk by the short guys. If he's slim, I skip the body builders and the overweight fatty's."

"How does that pertain to our situation?" Skeet asked.

"None of Henry's children fit," Rowdy insisted. "One guy is in his forties. No way is your guy that old. That is a recent photo and he's thirty, tops. The next one lives in Canada. There are too many reasons to state for him to be eliminated. The girls are out. That leaves the guy in New Mexico. He's a possibility; but, I did a little digging. Ian Hill doesn't have a record, he's thirty-two, spent eight years in the military and left with honors. It just feels like we're plugging a round peg in a square hole with him. I found an old photo, seems he's gone off the radar since he got out. Which, I admit is odd; but, he could have dealt with some seriously bad shit over there and just wants to be left alone. Anyway, there's a resemblance… I'll give you that. But, I still think he's too old to be our man.

Then, there's this Eddie guy. No record, very little mention that Charles and Piper even have a kid. Why? Was he deformed? Mentally deficient? The fact that we can't find anything pushes all my buttons on this. I can't find a driver's license for the guy in any of the fifty states. Tell me that's not odd."

"You think you're not an investigator; but, the process you just described is exactly what an investigator does to narrow his options."

"Maybe," Rowdy conceded. "But, I'm used to doing it in real time, I'm an action guy... not a sit around and scour through documents to find a single clue kind of guy. I'm struggling here, and I had to act."

"And, by that you mean?"

"I put something together," Rowdy stood and retrieved a stack of papers, settled back in his chair and handed them to Skeet. "I was going to send that over to our local prosecutor an hour ago; but, decided I should run it by you before I go there."

Skeet read through the application for a warrant, impressed. Rowdy outlined his probable cause for requesting the financial data on Charles and Piper Hill in such a way, no judge would deny it. "We could send this to the local prosecutor; but, I think we might have better success if we went through the A.G.'s office. We want everything, and that couple has property on both sides of the continent."

"Okay," Rowdy shrugged. "Do you have a contact you want to use or how should we handle it?"

"Email this document to me and I'll take it from there," Skeet decided.

"Already did," Rowdy smiled. "There's one other thing and I didn't wait to ask on that one."

"Okay," Skeet moved to retrieve his laptop and returned to the chair.

"I called in the locals," Rowdy watched Skeet for a reaction. When he didn't get anything, he decided to elaborate. "In Oregon and the Hamptons, I mean. I asked them to pay a visit to each of the homes."

"That could tip him off if we're getting close," Skeet warned.

Subterfuge

"I thought of that," Rowdy told him. "I asked them to send out a couple patrol guys. Men in uniform to hit the target and a couple neighbors just in case. They're going to make up a fake emergency. Hamptons said they'd claim a rash of burglaries had occurred over the past week. They are questioning all the residents to see if they noticed any strange vehicles in the area. Then, they'll ask about the owners. Are they home, will they be staying in the home over the next few weeks, who are they... names and vehicle descriptions. Hampton PD values their residents and they don't want to hassle or inconvenience anyone unnecessarily. Are the owners expecting company? How about adult children that drive, will they be visiting in the next few weeks? You get the idea."

"That might work," Skeet told him. "Why not detectives? Or, I could have Stan send a couple of our guys."

"Wouldn't work," Rowdy shook his head. "Feds would raise all kinds of red flags and the staff would block. People like that... big money, they hire staff that will remain loyal. You send out the feds or even a couple of cops in suits and they'll shut down. You send in uniforms with a crisis, they'll be more than willing to help."

"Okay, and Oregon?"

"Same instructions," Rowdy told him. "They didn't say how they'd handle it; but, I'm sure they'll come up with something. We should have an answer before the end of the day."

Skeet's computer beeped. "Request has been received. We'll know about the warrant in a few hours, tops."

Several hours later, Skeet, Rowdy and Fulmer were scouring through the records that had started to filter in from the warrant while they impatiently waited for the rest of the documents to arrive.

Rowdy's phone buzzed, and he gladly snatched it up, ready for a break from the tedium.

"Any chance you can skip out for a few hours," Coop asked. "Dumas assigned me, Mike, and Gunny to do property checks. We have an odd man out. Either he expected me to sit out while the patrol guys did all the work, or he figured we'd waste the extra man and stay together. No matter how you slice it, that dude doesn't make sense. I was thinking you could bring Knight. You and Mike can take the dog and clear a couple vacant apartment complexes while I take Gunny and handle the single-family homes."

"I could do that," Rowdy decided. "Skeet and Fulmer can hang out here and work on the data coming in on the money. Why don't you head out, divide up the list, and do the first search while you wait? I'll meet you there and we can each take our portion of the list and knock out as many as we can before dark."

Coop rattled off the first address. "See you when you get here."

* * * *

"Agent Smith," Bryant said in greeting. He didn't recognize the number and hoped it wasn't another case that would take him away from his current project.

"Detective Mark Lee," came the reply. "I saw your alert this morning and I have something I think you might want to check out."

"What did you find?"

"A human skull," Lee said soberly. "I'm not saying it's yours... the girl you're looking for, but... it could be."

"Female?"

Subterfuge

"No idea," Mark Lee admitted. He rattled off the address. "I think you should just head out — take a look for yourself."

"I'm on my way," Smith disconnected and headed for his car. He had mixed feelings about the discovery. On one hand, nobody wanted to find the skeletal remains of anyone. It meant another family was going to be destroyed. On the other, if they had located Tanya, his search would be over; and, other than notification, that case could be turned over to the experts. If anyone could identify and locate the killer, it was Skeeter Perkins. He could at least give the grieving parents that much when he destroyed their entire world.

Smith headed to the address just outside of town, turned up the dilapidated drive that led to a remote agricultural development and pulled in behind the marked patrol units. It still surprised him that he could find farming pockets intermingled amongst the industrial backdrop of Detroit. He shoved open his door and moved forward to greet a no-nonsense detective walking his way.

"Smith?" Detective Lee asked. "You made good time."

"Timing was just right to miss the bulk of our end of day rush," he glanced toward the large group of men standing around what looked like a large pile of dirt. "She in there?"

"The remains are in there," Lee corrected. "At this point, the skull hasn't provided many answers. It could be male or female."

"What brought you out in the first place?"

"Owner decided to do some clean-up," Detective Lee turned and headed for the area he had designated a crime scene. "We had that heavy rain, nearly a year ago, and that hill couldn't take the added weight. He erected those barriers over there — wanted to ensure the mud didn't wipe out his crop. It wasn't as devastating as predicted. The damage is restricted to this area. It's remote, used to be a stand of trees over here. As you can see, the mud wiped those out and created quite a mess out here. The owners name is Bob Newberry. He had a little extra time, decided he could take a couple days and deal with this. So, he brought out the backhoe and dove in. He'd been out here nearly an hour when he pulled up the skull. Stopped immediately and called us. Based on the timing and your alert... well, I thought it might be the girl you're trying to locate."

"What are they doing?" Bryant was referring to a group of — he didn't know what. They were crouched down, sifting through the debris. He just hoped they weren't compromising his crime scene. Not that they would find anything that was even close to a clue. The killer, if this was Tracy and they were uncovering his third victim in the Detroit area, the killer was careful.

"Forensic anthropologists," Lee advised. "We've used them in the past. They're professionals and they're thorough. Our department contracts with them on the rare occasion we have skeletal remains that need to be unearthed. I called them in early, wanted the experience and the careful exhumation if we are dealing with that killer of yours. If there's a clue in there, that group will find it."

"There won't be," Bryant sighed. "But calling in a crew of experts was the right call. Where did you send the skull?"

"State lab," Lee continued to watch as the crew pulled what looked like a leg bone from the rubble. "They promised to rush it. We'll at least know the gender by the end of the day. I sent it over before these guys arrived, or they could have given us the basics."

"Why didn't you wait?"

"Supervisor over at the lab said if I didn't get the thing to him within the hour, he'd start on something else. I didn't want to wait in line for another opening."

Subterfuge

"Makes sense," Smith decided. "You have a log you want me to sign before I head down?" Smith asked.

"Yeah," Detective Lee pointed to a rarely traveled pathway. "Let's take that route, it's easier; and, I've got Babcock stopping anyone that doesn't need to be here. You can sign the log over there."

Bryant followed what was clearly an experienced detective to the scene, knowing it was going to turn out to be a very long day.

* * * *

Rowdy was clearing the third floor of a vacant apartment building. Well, to be honest, Knight was doing most of the work and Rowdy was following. Mike had started at the other end of the hall and was working his way back toward the dog team. So far, the place was a bust; so, Rowdy decided it was a perfect time to update Skeet. "Hey," he said when the fed answered the line.

"Anything new?" Skeet asked.

"A couple things," Rowdy turned a corner and recognized the signs immediately. Knight was alert and on the hunt. He opened the door to the next apartment and followed the dog inside. Knight immediately disappeared around a corner and started to growl. "I need a minute," Rowdy told Skeet, slipping the phone into his pocket. Knight started to bark, moved closer to a small closet, then started to growl; a low, menacing sound that Rowdy recognized. They had a rat cornered behind door number one. He slipped his gun from the holster and slowly slid the door open.

A man was huddled on the floor, eyes wide, his large frame frozen in place. Knight repositioned his body and leaned forward slightly, ready to pounce if he saw something he didn't like.

"Smartest thing you ever did," Rowdy stepped forward and glanced around the tiny enclosure for a weapon. "No sudden moves just put your hands in the air... do it slowly. Don't make any aggressive movements and you'll be fine."

The man slowly raised both hands in the air, never diverting his attention from the dog.

Rowdy glanced back when he heard a noise. Mike was just holstering his weapon as he stepped into the room. "Heard the dog, thought maybe you found trouble."

"I'll call off the dog, you cuff him," Rowdy suggested.

"Sounds like a plan," Mike waited for Rowdy to give the order. He'd done this before.

"Knight, out," Rowdy commanded. Knight immediately stood and moved across the room to stand at Rowdy's side. "Stay." The dog was still posed to lunge at the slightest provocation; but, he obeyed the command.

Mike stepped forward and yanked the man to his feet. In seconds, the guy was cuffed and secure. "You want him booked?"

Rowdy motioned to the large amount of drugs that were hidden behind the prisoner. "Turn him over to Narcs and let them decide. I don't really care if they lock him up or use him as long as he gets out of my way. We don't have time for a low-level dealer that decided to move his operation inside hoping out-of-sight meant out-of-mind," Rowdy said. "If they decide to book him, make sure they know about the B&E."

"I didn't break in nowhere," the guy objected. Mike gave him a shove and marched him out the door.

Subterfuge

"I'll finish up here and meet you outside," Rowdy decided. This wasn't their target and they both knew it. "You still there?" he asked Skeet as he pulled out his phone.

"Trouble?" Skeet asked.

"Not really," Rowdy said, moving into the next apartment. "Drug dealer, Mike will turn him over to the Narcotics Unit and they can decide what do with him."

"You said you had something," Skeet reminded him.

"Right," Rowdy pulled open a closet and let Knight sniff inside. "I got a call from the Hamptons. The butler, a guy named Dalton Forester, confirmed the place is owned by Charles and Piper. He said they're on some annual excursion. Apparently, the couple takes a few months each year to sail on their fancy yacht and escape reality. He doesn't know where they are, somewhere in the middle of the ocean is all they could get. It's going to be difficult to track them down if the butler's information is accurate."

"I agree," Skeet sighed. "I was hoping we could send someone out to interview them about their son. If they're out in the middle of nowhere, that will be difficult. We can hold that in reserve for later if we need it."

"Right," Rowdy stepped from the apartment and moved across the hall. "Jeeves confirmed they do have a son named Edgar, but the family calls him Eddie."

"Jeeves?"

"The butler," Rowdy shook his head. "Eddie is somewhat of a recluse. Comes around unannounced now and again but never stays long and as far as they know, he doesn't drive. They didn't dare press more than that, thought it might come across as suspicious. I'm thinking it might be time to send out the feds, see if they can break lose any more details on the kid."

"Let me call Stan and see if he can swing that," Skeet decided.

"Before you do, I want to cover Oregon," Rowdy said as he stepped into the hallway. One more apartment and the entire building would be cleared. "Our guys out there spoke to the groundskeeper. Eddie used to spend a lot of time in Oregon. In fact, the guy said up until about two years ago, Eddie was there more than his parents. Seems the Oregon place is somewhat of a vacation spot for Charles and Piper. They might spend a week out there during the winter but not much longer. Eddie, however, would drop by unexpected and spend up to a month before he disappeared again. Nobody really knows where he goes, or if he even has a permanent residence. He's a loner. Even when he was at the lake house, he spent his time in a special room he setup in the attic. The door is always locked and even the maid isn't allowed inside."

"Interesting," Skeet sat back. "What happened two years ago to send him packing?"

"They don't know," Rowdy admitted. "Said he was acting a little weird, locked himself in the attic for several weeks at a time. Then one day, he got up and left the house. Leaving became part of his routine. The staff saw that as an improvement. They worried some, knowing he rarely left the house and none of them think he had any friends. Then suddenly, poof. He vanished in the middle of the night and hasn't returned. They don't expect him to show up and they also confirmed the parents are in the middle of their annual yachting trip."

"I want a couple men to follow up in the Hamptons," Skeet decided. "We can send someone to Oregon if we need to; but, it doesn't sound like he's going back there. Maybe, because those

Subterfuge

mysterious outings led to the first kill. It's more likely he'll crash out east once he leaves Chicago. Unless he has another location in mind and he just slides back into his regular pattern. I'd like to know if he returns to the Hampton's for that month when he disappears between jobs, though."

"I'd like to know what he has in that room in Oregon," Rowdy countered.

"I agree, but we need more," Skeet said thoughtfully. "We can't get a warrant to search the place on what we have. I'm still working my way through the money. I've found a place in Paris and they have another long-term lease on a place in Mexico. The yacht makes sense, accounts for a monthly fee I found. Probably a slip fee if I had to guess. Let me call Stan and I'll get back to you. Any idea when you and Coop will be finished with the property searches?"

Rowdy stepped outside and glanced around for Mike. "I'm done. I'll tag Coop and see how many he has to go but unless he needs help, I'm heading in."

* * * *

Angela pushed her body as far against the wall as she could manage. She'd finally gotten the screw unhooked and threw it down the hole beneath the grate late the previous evening. Her hands were raw; but, at least her fingers had stopped bleeding. Now, she'd have to face the consequences. The man she'd come to fear more than anyone or anything she'd ever imagined, was walking towards her. She knew the instant he spotted the broken and useless tool. Maybe he should have been more careful the last time he visited her concrete prison. Anger filled his eyes and a red flush started on his neck and slowly spread upwards covering his chin, his cheeks, and finally his ears. She was in trouble and she had no way to fight.

"You stupid, stupid woman," he screamed. "Where is the screw?"

Angie didn't say a word. Telling him wouldn't help now and her mouth was so dry, she wasn't sure she could form the words.

The man dropped a gallon jug that contained some kind of liquid on the ground next to his prisoner and slapped her across the face. "I can't start my experiment yet; but, you are going to pay for the destruction. You may have delayed your punishment; but, you did not prevent it." Fury surrounded him like a cloud as he began to kick at the lump huddled on the floor.

Angie whimpered and sucked in a breath. Was he going to beat her to death over the damage to his tools? She hoped not, he said her punishment would be delayed but would she survive the damage he was inflicting right now? Pain radiated through her entire body as he kicked again and again. She sucked in a breath, trying to work through a blow to her ribs, then another, he moved to her shin, her shoulder... he was ruthless and relentless. If he didn't stop, he was going to damage her internally and she was pretty sure she would never survive that.

Anger flowed through him pushing him to lash out over and over, he kicked the woman harder and harder. He couldn't stop, couldn't control his rage, didn't even want to. This family was going to pay. First her husband had taken everything - now this. The woman was more trouble than she was worth, but Agent Perkins had to suffer. His wife had to suffer. She'd broken his nose during her capture, had kicked him so hard in the stomach he'd been

Subterfuge

nauseous for hours, now she had damaged his tools. He raised his leg for one more blow and stopped. If he kept this up, he'd kill her for sure. That wouldn't do, it wouldn't do at all. He had to know, would the feisty, aggravating woman last longer than the rest? Or would she succumb easily in a matter of hours? He'd never taken anyone this old before. His subjects were always young, vibrant, full of life, and innocent. He couldn't wait to see how an older, mature specimen would compare.

He took a step back, studied the woman for several seconds, then left. He'd inflicted more damage than he had intended. Lost his temper and now, the experiment would have to wait even longer. No harm done, he could wait. The clueless police and the FBI were mindless social servants. They had no idea who or where he was. Agent Perkins would never find his wife alive. She would be discarded just as the rest, in a vacant field somewhere. A place he hadn't selected yet; but, he would... eventually. He'd locate the perfect dumping ground and the irritating family would finally learn their place. The Perkins were nothing but peasants and they should have remembered that. Instead, they got in his way. Ultimately, the infuriating couple would understand what happened to people who interfered with his mission. Maybe, he'd select a location sure to attract attention. Some place more populated; that would send a strong message to his enemies, wouldn't it? He'd have to think about that. No worries, he had plenty of time... and he was going to make this one count. Oh, he was going to enjoy this; and, while their fair Mrs. Perkins begged him to stop, he'd make sure she knew it was Agent Skeeter Perkins' fault she was chosen — her adoring husband's fault she would be subjected to all kinds of pain and suffering before she ultimately succumbed to her injuries. She would hate the man she currently loved before he was through... and Agent Perkins would hear her say it, over and over again as he laughed in the background. Yes, this experiment was going to be special and he could hardly wait to get started.

* * * *

Rowdy was just pulling into his driveway when his cellphone began to ring. He glanced at the display and realized it was the office. Shifting into park, he snatched the device off the passenger seat and answered mere seconds before it clicked over to voicemail. "Cooper."

"Hey, Rowdy," came a familiar female voice. "Sorry to bother you, but are you still with Mike?"

"Sorry, we split up," Rowdy frowned at the hesitance and the obvious tension in Jade's voice. Mike's wife was also a dispatcher, and Rowdy knew she was still on-duty. "We caught a low-level dealer at that last apartment. Mike's hooking up with the Narc guys so they can deal with the problem. What's going on?"

"Ummm..." she hesitated.

Rowdy heard muffled speaking and realized she was talking to someone in the background.

"Let me call you back on my cellphone."

Rowdy's frown intensified when the call disconnected. He waited – impatiently – for the phone to ring again. When it finally did, he answered on the first ring. "Jade, what's going on?"

"Sorry," she realized she'd put him on alert. "Nothing bad. It's just... well, I didn't think I should explain on a recorded line. I had to take a break and go outside."

"Okay," Rowdy relaxed a little. "That makes sense. Mike might be tied up for a while, can I help you with something?"

"I know Mike was supposed to keep the photo of that monster a secret," Jade began. "But... well, you know Mike. He worries. That guy's a serial killer and he already abducted a cop's wife..."

Subterfuge

"I know Mike showed you that picture," Rowdy admitted. "He told me. I don't have a problem with it and neither did Coop; once I explained it. I don't think you're in danger from this; but, I understand Mike's reasoning. You probably shouldn't broadcast that information though. So, getting off the recorded line was smart. Just keep it between us, but don't stress over it."

"Thanks," Jade said sincerely. "That's a relief."

"So," Rowdy pressed. "I'm guessing that's not the reason you called."

"Right," Jade took a deep breath. "I got a call a few minutes ago. Well, more like fifteen now. The lady came across as a little crazy — just a nuisance at first with a mild dose of nutty on top. You know what I mean, we get those type of calls all the time. But, by the time I hung up with her; I wasn't so sure. I really think someone needs to check it out and I thought maybe Mike could swing by and just see. I was actually hoping you'd go with him."

"You lost me," Rowdy admitted. "How is this connected with Mike showing you the photo?"

"Sorry," Jade realized she wasn't making sense. "This lady, she calls in and starts yelling at the call-taker. Says she called three days ago and nobody ever came out. The call-taker doesn't really know what to do, so she tags me. It was my area, so I said to go ahead and transfer her. We weren't that busy and I thought I could calm her down, you know."

"Okay," Rowdy was still wondering what this had to do with their case.

"So, I answer, and she immediately starts up again. Laying into me, the same as she did with Anna. She's going on and on about this creepy guy that was hanging around and how she pays taxes and why is it so hard to just drive by and check it out. I figure, sure... she has a point. But, deep down, I'm also thinking whoever gets the call is going to give me some flak over it on account the woman is seriously out there."

Rowdy smiled, she wasn't wrong.

"Anyway," Jade continued. "That's when she starts talking about this warehouse and how she knows the owner and this creepy guy is not the owner; so, how did he get access? Of course, I have no idea, so I just let her talk a little. That's when she starts to describe the man, says he can't be related because the property owner is Irish and this guy; he's got blonde hair. Not surfer blonde, but a dark blonde on bottom with lighter blonde on the tips. I swear, Rowdy, my heart nearly jumped out of my chest. Maybe because Mike's been so crazy about safety and watching out for the guy. He made me look at that sadistic prick every night since he got that photo. Said he wanted to make sure I'd recognize him if I ever saw him."

Rowdy's cop senses had just jumped into high alert. "Did she tell you anything else?"

"Yeah," Jade admitted. "She said he scared her. She was outside, kind of watching... If you ask me, she was snooping. But, she said when he looked at her, it was like he looked right through her. And, get this... she'll never forget how cold those clear blue eyes were. She said that. Said she always thought of blue eyes as kind; but now, she doesn't think she can ever look at a man with that color of eyes again and not think ...evil."

"Don't get mad," Rowdy said slowly. "But, I'm just wondering why you didn't dispatch a couple cars that way immediately."

"Shelly," Jade answered in a tone that meant the one-word response should be enough.

Subterfuge

"She stopped you?" Shelly Cobourn was a mid-level supervisor whose authority had gone to her head. All the dispatcher's hated the woman and if just half of the stories were true, he couldn't blame them.

"She got involved when she heard how the lady treated Anna," Jade explained. "Shelly was standing over me, watching over my shoulder, waiting as I talked to the caller. The instant I hung up, she ordered me to short-form the call and move on. I tried to talk her into sending out a car, but she shut me down completely. I didn't dare tell her I saw the photo, but I did tell her about the van. Oh! I forgot to tell you about the van."

"The guy drove a van?" Another red flag.

"Yes!" Jade practically yelled. "A blue one and get this... it was stolen. Glenda, that was the caller, she has a photo of the van with a clear shot of the plate. I ran it, stolen from the east side a week ago. It has to be followed up on, Rowdy. You know, if Mike wasn't busy dealing with your doper, he'd head over there immediately."

"Can you get me the details, from the call, without suffering the wrath of Helly? I mean Shelly?"

Jade laughed. "I'll send it to your computer. We both know if she tries to discipline me, Lt. Ridens will back me. She could write me up for sending a car when she very clearly ordered me not to; but, providing one of the investigators a lead... she wouldn't dare try to cause a stink over that. Plus... I'm golden with the boss. Ridens likes me and he's usually fair."

"Shoot me the info," Rowdy told her as he laughed. She was golden, but she was one of the best dispatcher's they had; so, as far as Rowdy was concerned — she'd earned it. "Coop just pulled in behind me, I'll make him back me on this. Don't bother Mike with it. He had court this morning and then we kept him out late. He needs the break."

"I'll wait until I get home to break the news," Jade agreed. "And, I'm pretty sure you will be backing Coop on this one. I know it's not exactly protocol; but, will you tell me if you find anything? I'm beyond curious and I can tell you're having the same warm tingly's that I had when I heard the description. And, the van... then, there's the fact it's an abandoned warehouse."

"I'll let you know," Rowdy promised. "But, for the record... I never tingle. Now, I have to go break the news to Coop. From the look on his face, he thought he was done for the night."

"Better you than me," Jade said before she disconnected.

Chapter Five

Rowdy and Coop pulled into the crumbling parking lot that led to the old warehouse. To say there were potholes would be a drastic understatement. Clearly, the building had stood vacant for years. Just another red flag that made Glenda's complaint legitimate. They had just left the house of the tenacious neighbor. Jade wasn't exaggerating, the woman was a little goofy. But, she was also compelling and very persistent. After just a few minutes with the woman, the brothers were convinced she had a valid complaint. The instant they approached the door, they were on high alert.

Rowdy reached for his mic. "Kilo-3," he said into his walkie.

"Kilo-3," came the familiar voice of Jade Laser.

"I'll be out with Car 201 on a suspicious activity complaint," he rattled off the address to the warehouse and asked Jade to update the official information. "We'll need a case number and the complainant will be Glenda LeForge; use the address of the warehouse on the call. Also, can you locate a number for the property owner or a business manager? We need permission to enter the premises."

Within seconds Jade was back. She provided the name and a phone number for the current owner of the industrial property.

"Donald Huesman?" Rowdy asked. "I thought you said he was Irish."

"Beats me," Jade replied. "Maybe she thinks all red-heads are Irish."

"I'll call," Coop pulled out his phone and dialed the number Jade had provided. "I'm looking for Donald Huesman."

"This is Donald," came a hesitant voice.

"Mr. Huesman, this is Detective Cooper with the Chicago Police Department. Are you still the legal owner..."?

Rowdy stepped away and continued down the side of the building. He didn't need to hear Coop's conversation and he wanted to see if the other locks had been switched out as well. The state-of-the-art digital combo-lock on the side door was enough for him to know something was off here. The thing was so new it still had that out of the box shine. If Jade was right and the owner lived out of town, who had recently installed that expensive locking system? And why? He was afraid he knew; and, he just hoped they weren't too late. They needed to get inside — immediately. Rowdy had made it halfway down the side of the building when he heard Coop call his name. He turned and headed in the opposite direction.

"Owner doesn't know anything about new locks," Coop said, once the brothers were only a few feet away from each other. "In fact, he said he's in the final stages of negotiations. He should have the place sold by the end of the year. If everything goes through, the new owners are going to tear the place down and start over. There'd be no reason to put a new, expensive locking system on the building. Looks like he switched out the old locks on every door."

"Looks like it," Rowdy focused on the door Glenda said their unknown intruder used. "So, how do you want to handle this?"

"Huesman gave me verbal permission to break in the door," Coop said absently. "But, he said there is a maintenance entrance on the other side of the building. He'd prefer we try to get in through there before we damage one of these. Apparently, he received notice from the city a few months back. They said the building was being used by squatters. He was given thirty days to restrict access or they'd levy a stiff penalty. He's hesitant to say we can just break down the door."

"He's hesitant to deal with the city again; especially, if he's trying to off-load the property," Rowdy corrected. "If we have to break it in, I'll board it up. We'll make sure the local vagabonds can't get inside. Unless it's an active crime scene," he added hesitantly.

"We'll deal with that, when and if," Coop decided as he started for the other side of the building. "Huesman said the maintenance entrance is boarded up already. He doesn't think a stranger would know there's even an entrance there. If Creepy Van Guy switched out all the locks, there's a good chance he missed that one."

Rowdy smiled. Glenda LaForge was the one to dub the name Creepy Van Guy. Apparently, it stuck. If they were dealing with Skeet's Mad Scientist, he probably wouldn't appreciate the moniker. As far as Rowdy was concerned, that was even more reason to use it. "Hey," Rowdy called out to Coop. "I'm going to stop at my truck, grab a crowbar and a flashlight. Do you need me to notify dispatch and let them know we have the verbal okay to enter?"

"Sure," Coop said over his shoulder as he continued around the building.

Rowdy shook his head, half jogged to his truck and snatched up the tools he thought he'd need to get inside. He used his walkie to update dispatch and made it to the boarded-up entry in a matter of minutes.

"Give me the crowbar," Coop said the instant Rowdy stepped in beside him. "I think if we pry off this board and maybe that one..." he pointed to the left side of the barrier, "we may be able to nail them back up when we're finished."

Rowdy passed over the tools and waited while Coop cleared the way. Once the boards were gone, they could see the original lock on the door was busted and the mysterious lock fairy hadn't realized this opening was here. "What are you going to tell Agent Arrogant about this?"

"Nothing to tell," Coop grinned. "Why do you think I'm having you relay everything to dispatch? This is your call, brother. Just a routine patrol detail. I'm only here to provide a back — since I was available and in the area."

"That might work," Rowdy smiled. "Until he finds out it was my call."

Coop shrugged and maneuvered his large body through the small space, disappearing into the darkness. Rowdy followed, pulling his flashlight from his pocket before stepping over the aged, slightly damp, wooden planks.

The two men silently made their way through the building, clearing each room meticulously before they moved on to the next. Years in SWAT and the fact they were brothers, helped them to

Subterfuge

work as a cohesive unit. They didn't need words to telegraph their next moves. Hand signals, and years of hushed mischief guided their way. The building was large; but, it was vacant. Garbage, old mattresses, and various items of useless clothing were scattered throughout the entire place. Here and there, graffiti littered the walls; indicating the local street gangs had tagged the structure, claiming it as their territory before the building was properly secured.

They had nearly finished going through the entire building when they spotted the mattress, the IV pole, and the fresh plastic bags that laid empty on the concrete floor. Neither one said a word, they didn't have to. Both of them realized what the discovery meant immediately. Angela Perkins had spent several days locked up in this drafty, smelly prison —drugged and maybe alone. If only... there were so many possibilities that could end that sentence. So many things that could have fallen into place days ago. So many opportunities to rescue a scared, possibly injured, woman.

"Don't go there," Rowdy whispered. "It won't help."

Coop turned, fury radiated from his entire body. Glenda saw something and said something. She took action and the local department failed her; had failed their victim; had failed Agent Skeeter Perkins. How was he going to break the news to Skeet? Suddenly, he couldn't breathe. He needed air, he needed space... what he didn't need was a lecture from his brother on why it wasn't their fault.

Rowdy watched as Coop walked briskly from the room. He wasn't sure how to handle things at the moment. Wasn't sure he could relate; knew he couldn't empathize. Not really. Coop had a connection with Skeet that Rowdy would never understand. Every time something happened, or in this case didn't happen, Coop imagined how it would feel if Maggie were the one missing.

Something as simple as messing up a tip frustrated Rowdy; but, it seemed to derail Coop. He knew it was going to derail Skeet. He also knew they had to deal with it — soon. Because, Rowdy knew Skeet would forgive them for missing the clue; but, he wouldn't forgive them if he thought they were trying to hide it. He decided to take a minute to go over the evidence alone, then he'd round up his brother and deal with the rest.

Coop spotted the large cardboard box that had once contained a refrigerator, then served as a make-shift home for the desperate — and completely lost it. He took two steps forward and began to kick the offensive container over and over again. Anger, frustration, sorrow... so many emotions were flowing through him. The box toppled to the side; but, he continued to kick, didn't stop when it slid several feet across the cement floor, didn't stop when it split down one side then the other. He didn't stop until the box was lying flat and he couldn't continue even if he wanted to. He turned, breathless and a little embarrassed. That's when he spotted his brother casually leaning against the wall, waiting for him to finish. "Don't start."

"We need to call Skeet," Rowdy said in answer. "And, we need to notify dispatch. They should log our progress, log the time this place was cleared, and we need Forensics to process everything that was left. The IV lines probably have DNA. We also need at least one other officer to secure the area until we're done."

Coop sighed and studied his brother for several seconds. "After that..." he pointed to the box that was now completely destroyed. "Your response is we need to get back to work? Why?"

Now, Rowdy sighed. "Coop," *how to continue?* "I can see the toll this is taking on you. I think that may have been just what you needed. I mean, what you and I felt when we realized Angela Perkins was here — recently? Times that by about two- hundred percent and it might come close to the devastation Skeet will

Subterfuge

experience when we tell him about this. But, the same pain, the same raw desperation, the same sorrow and frustration I see in his eyes; every time I look at him..." Rowdy shook his head. "It's the same that I see in yours, on a smaller scale; but, it's there. You have Maggie and I know you worry about her. You empathize with Perkins, put yourself in his shoes, and you struggle to deal with it all. I can't understand that, not completely. I can't begin to relate to that. So, I've got nothing. Nothing but, let's get back to work."

Coop didn't know how to respond. He thought the worry and the fear he was feeling over this case had been hidden inside, deep inside where his wife and his brother wouldn't see it. Apparently, he wasn't as good at shielding his family as he believed he was. But, Rowdy was right... it was time to get back to work. "So, let me guess," Coop forced a smile. "You're going to use this situation to justify your fear of commitment?"

Rowdy was silent for several seconds. "I don't fear commitment, not really. I'm just not sure a cop has a right to fall in love and subject any woman to that kind of... uncertainty."

"You're wrong," Coop disagreed. "If I thought of it that way; sure, I would have thought twice about marrying Mags. But, she's my salvation and I'm not sure I'd survive this career without her. I hope, when the right girl comes along, you'll remember that."

Rowdy smiled. "The right girl comes around every weekend. Then, she rides off into the sunset never to be seen again."

"Nice," Coop shook his head. Clearly, he wasn't going to get anywhere with his brother on this topic.

"Seriously," Rowdy sobered. "I hope you're right; and, if I did find someone like your feisty Magpie, I might consider the white-picket fence. But, I wonder; that's all. I wonder if it's fair to them. And, this case has forced those questions to the forefront." He shrugged and gave his brother a cocky grin. "Not that I have to worry about that. Bachelorhood agrees with me."

"Did you find anything else that I missed?" Coop changed the subject. "Before you call dispatch and bring in the Calvary — Anything I should know?"

"No," Rowdy moved toward the door. "Reception's bad in here. Give me a minute, I'll call this in and see if Gunny's available. He can watch the door while we deal with Skeet. You, on the other hand, get to deal with the feds."

"Lucky me," Coop mumbled as he moved to the old mattress to look for clues.

* * * *

Skeet took the news in stride. He didn't blame anyone for the misstep. Rowdy was watching him closely; but, there wasn't any sign of anger or resentment. That confused him, to the point he decided to ask why.

"Several reasons," Skeet was crouched over the old mattress. He scanned the area one more time before he slowly stood and faced Rowdy. "It's nobody's fault; not yours, not Coop's, not even the dispatcher who believed the complainant was a nuisance." He studied Rowdy and realized that wasn't explanation enough. "Coop keeps telling me to throw out what I know, trash my profile and look at this with fresh eyes because our guy is not following pattern with Angela. This..." he waved his hand around the room. "It validates Coop's theory; and, in a way, it gives me hope. My suspect has never done this before. He abducted Ange, brought her to this warehouse and drugged her, probably for several days. That goes against his MO. Seeing what he did here, tells me he's floundering. His actions are frantic, desperate even. He's never frantic and desperate. He's organized, careful, and in control."

"So," Rowdy considered. "He's off his game. The evidence he left here proves it. I guess I get that, but still..."

"It's not your fault," Skeet insisted. "The Scientist is careful. And, as much as I need to throw out the playbook and come at this from a different angle, the past is still relevant. I've been here before with this guy. I've interviewed witnesses, missed capturing our guy by a matter of minutes. Completely missed him in Houston while he watched us from a few hundred yards away. He slipped through our fingers and flew to Chicago while we chased our tails in Texas. Something like this comes with the territory when you work serial cases. I'm disappointed, sure. But, I'm not mad — I'm hopeful. This means he didn't start the experiments on Angela right away. You have no idea how reassuring it is to know that."

"I'm glad," Rowdy decided. "I completely missed the mark on that one, and I'm relieved I did. So, did you find anything we missed?"

"No," Skeet motioned toward the door. "But, I'm betting Ryan did. He should be able to get all kinds of new leads from the security system that was recently installed on this building. Our Mad Scientist made a mistake this time, and he doesn't even know it."

The group had just settled back at Rowdy's loft when Skeet's phone rang. "Perkins"

"Hey, Skeet," came a familiar voice. "It's Vance. Burns sent me and Kirkwood up here to the Hamptons to see about interviewing the hired help. They're not inclined to answer our questions. Any ideas on how we should handle it?"

Skeet paused when he spotted Maggie step through the door. She slowly made her way across the room and settled into a chair next to her husband. "I'm putting you on speaker, so you can explain the situation to all of us." Skeet pressed a button on his phone, set it gently on the large table, and settled into a chair. "Okay, tell me everything. Start at the beginning."

"Not much to tell," Vance sighed. "We got here a short time ago and asked the butler if we could speak with him for a minute. He initially said no, then had a change of heart when I threatened to sit in the driveway all night. I sort of suggested the neighbors might talk. He let us in, escorted us to some kind of sitting room and hasn't said much since. He's not talking. Kirkwood threatened to arrest him if he didn't go get the maid, so we could question her. He finally complied but she's not saying anything, either. We're at a standstill. Our options are pretty much leave or arrest them both for obstruction."

"Describe the situation for me," Coop requested. "Are they live-in help or do they commute to the house every day? What is their interaction like? Friendly? Contentious? Can you split them up and get them to talk?"

"They both live here," Vance considered. "They seem to get along fine; and, I'm guessing if they didn't, one of them wouldn't reside here full-time. The one answer we did get from the girl was confirmation the owners are rarely here."

"They get along?" Rowdy questioned. "Or, they've had a bounce or two in the guest room before the maid changed the sheets?"

"I'm not asking," Vance insisted. "These two are looking for any excuse to complain. I guarantee even the hint of something that personal would set off a hornets' nest — no matter how I approached it."

"He doesn't need to ask," Maggie whispered.

"What are you thinking, Maggie?" Skeet asked.

"Who is Maggie?" Vance demanded.

"Doesn't matter," Skeet countered. "Go ahead, Maggie. Do you have an idea?"

"Well," Maggie began. "I was just thinking about Coop and Rowdy. Or, Mike with Jade. They are so protective. If the two people at the house are involved, I think all you would have to do is separate them to get answers. If the butler still didn't cooperate, threaten to arrest the girl."

Skeet smiled, she was right. "Do it, Vance. Separate them and try to question them individually. If they still resist, tell them you are taking the girl down to the local precinct for a formal interview. The butler will insist on going, don't let him. Tell him you're finished with him for the evening but not to go anywhere. If there's something going on between those two, he'll suddenly become cooperative — I guarantee it."

"Where do we take the girl?" Vance considered. "We can't take her to the precinct, Burns wants this a little more covert than that — at least for now. Dumas doesn't even know we're here. He just knows we're on an assignment for the boss and it will take all day."

"I don't think it will come to that," Skeet decided. "But, if it does, just take her for a ride and question her in the car. She might be more open without the butler, anyway. Especially, if she thinks she's being hauled in for an official interrogation. Loyalty only goes so far."

"I'll let you know," Vance said before clicking off.

* * * *

Several hours later the group was still gathered in Rowdy's loft. Vance had called back; but, they were stumped by the information he had obtained. According to the maid, Charles Hill had an illegitimate sister. One, they were having a difficult time locating. Nellie, the maid, was fond of Charles and Piper but she admitted they were not what you would call loving parents. After the birth of their only child, they hired a nanny and never looked back. Edgar, or Eddie as everyone called him, was a difficult child. He was spoiled, selfish and insisted on perfection.

Nellie recalled one summer when Charles and Piper were setting off for their annual trip and the nanny fell deathly ill. Nellie couldn't remember what the illness was, just that Ms. Tamarisk quit her job and never returned. Charles and Piper were beside themselves, Eddie needed a place to stay while they were away. Nellie offered to care for the teen; but, the Hills told her that wasn't her job and they had already found another solution. It's the only reason Nellie knew there was a distant aunt; one they never discussed. That summer Eddie went to stay with the secret relatives; and, when his parents returned, they had a new nanny in tow. Nellie didn't know anything about the mysterious sister and the couple never mentioned the relative again. Nellie thought maybe the staff in Oregon might have more details; but, she couldn't be sure.

Fulmer and Maggie were scouring the sites for any mention of another sister. So far, they hadn't found a thing. Rowdy was running the information through the law enforcement databases; but, he too was coming up empty. Coop decided he'd make a few calls. He knew a guy that worked in Oregon and Mike had a friend

Subterfuge

in the Hamptons. They were working those angles as well. Skeet was focused on the money. At the moment, he was trying to get access to the details on Winfred Scott Hill's account. The one he used to transfer the funds to his two boys. So far, the prosecutor wasn't helping. He insisted they needed more before a judge would sign off. They didn't have more; and, Skeet knew he was running out of time. He had been honest with Rowdy earlier that day, seeing the setup in the warehouse did give him hope. But, that didn't mean he was any less worried. If the maniac hadn't started torturing his wife already... he was going to start, soon. Time was running out and to him it seemed like they had all just hit another brick wall.

* * * *

Angela looked up when the man stepped into the room and wondered if he came to finish her off. The jug of water he had left yesterday, before the beating, was salt water. Once she could move again, she'd been so thirsty she had to try. But, she didn't trust him; so, she just dipped her finger in to taste it before she actually drank any. She was glad she had. It took all her willpower; but, she'd left it alone knowing if she drank even the slightest bit, she'd become even more dehydrated. Now he was back, and he was carrying another container of liquid and a bowl. She silently watched as he set the items within reach, studied her for several seconds and left the room. Angela heard the click of a lock being secured as she was once again engulfed in darkness. What was he up to now?

She forced her body into a sitting position, careful to protect her ribs and removed the lid from the small bottle. She dipped a tentative finger inside and raised it to her tongue. Relief flooded her when she realized it was nothing but water... fresh water. She took a small sip then removed the lid from the bowl. She didn't trust the man, wondered if it was a trick, but moaned at the mouth-watering aroma of the fresh, hot soup that filled the air. Maybe he was playing mind games, keeping her on edge never knowing if the small offerings were tainted or harmless. At the moment, she didn't care. Other than two granola bars that he'd left that first night, the man hadn't given her a bit of food. It might be tainted; but, she was starving. She would just eat a little and wait, if she was okay after an hour she could finish it off. She gulped another swallow of water, lifted the bowl to her lips and sipped. It tasted like heaven; and in that moment, she didn't care if he had drugged the soup. She was going to savor it, anyway.

* * * *

The Scientist was whistling happily as he left his hide-out and headed for his car. His prisoner was making good progress. A few more days and her injuries should be healed enough to finally start experimenting. He paused when he heard a noise behind him, glanced backward, and spotted three large men in their mid-twenties headed his way. They wore baggie jeans, tight t-shirts and bandanas around their heads. He recognized them as members of a local street gang immediately. The look on their faces screamed trouble and he knew they were just looking for an unsuspecting target they could intimidate, frighten and terrorize. The social deviants were obviously bored and looking to set an example; one, that would satisfy their perverted need for fun. He picked up the pace, desperate to reach his car before they caught up to him.

"Pyro," the largest of the men sneered.

"Yeah, man," Pyro answered absently.

Subterfuge

"What do we do to horribly dressed white boys that trespass on our turf?"

"They get dead?" Pyro guessed.

"Naw," Creeper shrugged. "They just wish they were dead when we're finished."

All three men laughed and continued their steady march toward their target.

The Scientist picked up the pace. By the time he reached his car, he was practically running. His heart was beating so fast he thought it might jump out of his chest. He pulled the keys from his pocket and tried to press the button to unlock the door. It took him two attempts; his hands were shaking so badly he completely missed the button the first time. He slid behind the wheel and locked the door behind him. When he glanced up, he realized the three men were now standing directly in front of his vehicle and one of them had a large bat. *Where did that come from?* The Scientist swallowed hard, wondering what they planned to do. He didn't have to wait long.

"You can run, but you can't hide," the one the Scientist assumed was Pyro called out.

"This is our territory," the guy with the bat, Creeper, growled. "Nobody invades our territory without asking." He lifted the bat and let it drop into the palm of his hand, then did it again.

The Scientist's hands were still shaking as he tried to slide the key into place on the side of the steering wheel. This time, it took him three attempts before the metal object finally slid into the tiny hole. He twisted his wrist with so much force he worried he may have broken the thin metal key in half before the engine finally roared to life. He let out a relieved breath, shifted into drive and stomped on the accelerator. The rear tires squealed and spun before they caught, and the car lunged forward. The three men barely had enough time to dive out of the way before the small compact car flew by them. The Scientist heard a loud thump as he passed by and figured the one with the bat got in one good swing in retaliation. He'd have to pull over in a couple blocks and make sure the taillight still worked. He couldn't risk being pulled over by a cop; he didn't have a driver's license. Never had, and most likely never would.

He was still shaking when he pulled into the driveway and shut down the car. He just sat there, considering his options for several seconds. Then, a solution came to him. He remembered the summer he spent here years ago. Remembered his uncle had a gun. And, he was pretty sure he knew where it was. Hopefully, his bimbo aunt didn't get rid of it when the blithering idiot was transferred to the care center. He was pretty sure he wouldn't even have to use it; the three thugs would pee their pants if they brandished a bat, and he pulled a gun. He was still smiling when he stepped through the front door. The moment he entered, his smile faded as he was confronted by his aunt.

"How did the job hunt go today?" Anticipation evident in the woman's voice.

The Scientist stopped and glared at the woman. He was not in the mood for this right now. And, really? Did she seriously believe he was going to get a common job? He'd put her off for days, avoided her, simply ignored her inquiries; but, her persistence was getting on his already frayed nerves. He could just pay the annoying freeloader, which would shut her up – temporarily. But, he was philosophically opposed to giving the illegitimate parasite another dime of his family's fortune. His father had already given her enough.

"I'm sorry," Elizabeth added. "I hate to bring it up again but with Stanton's condition, the expense of his care..." she trailed off.

Subterfuge

The Scientist sighed and pulled out his money clip. He passed her two hundred-dollar bills, turned, and made his way to the guest room. He could not wait to get out of this place. The instant he shut the door, his mind started to ponder the possibilities. He hated his Aunt Elizabeth, nearly as much as he'd hated her husband. Stanton was a common laborer, a peasant who had worked in the gutter... literally. The summer he'd been forced to live with the disgusting couple had been the worst of his life. He had vowed never to step foot in Chicago again, just another thing Agent Perkins was going to pay for.

He settled into the comfortable chair by the window and considered. He normally conducted his experiments in batches of three. Should he deviate? He originally planned to get his revenge on the interfering federal agent then leave. But, what if... he paused to measure the inherent pitfalls. He didn't like altering his routine. The idea of only testing one subject left him feeling empty, as if he was leaving something incomplete. He was afraid that feeling would haunt him forever. But, if he gave in to his inner craving and worked on his aunt, she would have to be the last. And, he'd have to make sure there was nothing in this house that would lead back to him — or his identity. The authorities could not know he was connected to the irritating woman in any way. Then, there was the question of the third... or, second subject. He began to smile when he thought of the perfect woman. He'd go back to the warehouse and capture the nosey, rock sweeping, busy-body that had foiled his plans in the first place. If she had minded her own business, he wouldn't have been confronted by the three thugs today. Yes, he had the perfect target for his second experiment. She deserved to die, and he was just the man to make it happen. He began to hum as he stared out the window, formulating his next move.

Once his aunt went to bed, he'd sneak into his uncle's office and see if the old man's gun was still safely hidden in the bottom drawer. It was just dumb luck that the man had tried to use the thing to bond all those years ago. At the time, he'd had no interest in the dangerous weapon. Now, it just might keep him safe from the lowlife scum that trolled the streets looking for trouble. In fact, he might just keep it when he moved on. It could come in handy while he roamed the next city searching for a new crop of girls. You could never be too careful, today demonstrated that fact in spades. He glanced at the door in anticipation and scowled. He hated waiting, didn't have the patience for it, and never had. But, tonight, it couldn't be helped. He focused on the upcoming mission and tried to push the weapon out of his mind... for a little while.

* * * *

Rowdy was in the kitchen, preparing another pot of coffee for the tired, but dedicated group. They'd pulled an all-nighter and it was starting to show. Skeet hadn't been able to pull off a warrant for grandpa's financials; but, they still had the info on Charles and Piper. Fulmer was helping Skeet trace that back as far as they could. Unfortunately, once they got a few years back, the electronic records became scarce. He was just stepping back into the loft when his phone began to ring. He glanced at the display wondering who would be calling this early. "Cooper."

"Rowdy," came a male voice. "It's Greg Whitman and please don't destroy my morning by saying you don't remember me."

"Greg, wow," Rowdy tried to remember the last time he'd spoken to the fellow lawman. "You left the department..."

"Six years ago," Greg confirmed. "Seems like a lifetime."

Subterfuge

"Yeah, I hear ya," Rowdy set the coffee on the table and moved to the lounge chair. "So, to what do I owe this walk down memory lane?"

"I'm guessing you didn't hear," Greg began. "But, I moved out west. My wife's mother was ill, and we tried to do the Arizona thing for a while; but, it was just too hot for all of us — especially Peggy, that's my mother-in-law."

"Yeah," Rowdy grinned. "I remember giving you a rough time about that when you left."

"Well, we now live in Oregon. Near Lake Oswego to be exact," Greg provided. "The climate fits us perfectly so I image this is where I'll call home from now on."

"Please tell me you are calling about our case," Rowdy said, excited.

Coop stood and moved to sit next to his brother. Rowdy had something new. Coop could hear it in his voice.

"Knew you'd catch onto that," Greg grinned. "I got a call this morning, first thing. Apparently, the groundskeeper at the Hill estate started thinking about that time a couple years back when he last saw the owner's son, Eddie. He remembered something and called us back at zero-six-hundred."

"That is early," Rowdy agreed. "Let me put you on speaker. The team working the case here are buzzing around like vultures and that way I won't have to relay the story later on." He hit the button to switch to speaker and turned the volume up as loud as it would go. "Okay, go ahead. This is Greg Whitman, he works in Oregon now, and he was called back to the Hill estate this morning."

"Hey, Greg. It's Andy Cooper," Coop began. "The case out here is mine; so, I might have some questions as you go along."

"Hey, Coop," Greg greeted. "I'd love to catch up; but, I think you need the Intel first."

"I appreciate that," Coop said in answer. "This case is a priority for us. I also have a couple feds in the house; so, if you hear a voice you don't recognize it's probably one of them."

"Yeah, no problem," Greg acknowledged. "Anyway, like I was explaining to Rowdy, I got called back by the groundskeeper. Ever since the visit a couple days back, he's been thinking about that time... when Eddie left unexpectedly. He remembered the bicycle and wondered if it was important."

"What bicycle" Coop asked.

"Pete, that's the gardener, landscaper, groundskeeper, handyman; you name it, I think this guy does it. Anyway, Pete said he remembered finding a strange bicycle the day Eddie left. He thought it was odd because Eddie rarely left the house; and, when he did, he drove the car. That day, Eddie headed out early in the morning and was gone most of the day. Pete isn't sure what time Eddie returned home; but, he thinks it was late afternoon or maybe early evening. He said Eddie did the usual, came straight into the house, went up to the attic and locked himself inside. Pete had to go out to the garage for something and that's when he spotted the bicycle leaning against the far wall. It was out of place and he said Piper Hill is obsessive about the garage being tidy and free of clutter. He was worried, if she saw the bike, she'd get upset. So, he locked it in a shed out back, thinking someone would claim it in the coming days. They never did. Then, Eddie took off and he completely forgot about it... until yesterday. I have now secured the bicycle and booked it into evidence."

"Why?" Skeet asked, perplexed. They couldn't link the bike to a crime.

"Because Pete asked me to take it," Greg provided. "He said the staff had talked it over and they all agreed it couldn't belong to anyone in the household. It just suddenly appeared that last day Eddie stayed in the home."

"I don't understand..." Skeet began.

"Just wait for it," Rowdy answered. "Greg's a good cop. He didn't call to inform us he has a lost bicycle. If we just let him explain, I have no doubt he'll tell us the reason for this call."

"Thanks," Greg said, humbled. "That means a lot coming from you, Rowdy. And, you're right. This isn't about a lost bicycle. It's about a bicycle a fifteen-year-old girl was riding when she went missing just over two years ago. It's about a cold case... a brutal murder where the poor, innocent teen was snatched off the street, mutilated almost beyond recognition, and dumped in a remote area by the lake."

"It might be about our suspect's first kill," Coop practically whispered. "You can tie the bike to the girl?"

"There's no doubt," Greg affirmed. "The parents had the thing licensed with the local PD. The information is still in the system, the Homicide Dick retained it, flagged it in case it ever turned up. He wanted to make sure if the bike ever was discovered, he could prove it belonged to the missing girl. She was only fifteen, didn't have a driver's license; so, she rode that bike everywhere she went. There were other distinguishing marks as well; a couple stickers and some red twine wrapped around one of the handlebars. There's no question it's hers. Plus, the primary investigator has several witness statements that put Roslyn Tanner on her bike that morning prior to her disappearance."

"What chance do we have of getting the complete file from the Cold Case Detective?" Coop asked Whitman.

"He's ready and waiting for your call," Greg advised. "But, he has one request."

"Of course, he does," Skeet mumbled.

"Nothing too difficult, I wouldn't think," Greg added. "He just wants to be a part of this. He was a rookie investigator at the time of the homicide and it was his first case in the division. He wasn't the primary, just backup, but it was pretty horrible — what was done to that girl. He said the images have lived with him ever since and he just wants to be sure you won't swoop in and steal the case away. You can have it, he's not getting territorial. He just wants in, wants to be a part of it in some way, mostly he wants to help get justice for that girl's family."

"I can do one better," Skeet decided. "He will remain primary; but, he'll have to work with a couple agents from the local bureau. I'll call Stan and set it up. Give Rowdy your contact info and I'll work on this from my end," Skeet turned to leave then thought of something. "You said Eddie frequently drove the car. What happened to it? Is it used by the help to run errands? Does Charles or Piper use it when they visit?"

"Oh," Greg said. "I forgot to add that in. No, the help never uses that particular car. It's a Rolls Royce and they have a minivan they use for shopping or landscaping needs. Pete said the car has been parked in the garage since Eddie left that summer. Normally, Charles and Piper use the limo service when they stay in the residence. Neither one of them likes to drive, which is why they never bothered to get Eddie a license."

"Are you telling me Eddie is the last person that can be put behind the wheel of that car?" Skeet asked.

"Sounds that way," Greg said immediately.

"Can you get back in touch with Pete and confirm that? If so, I want that car included in the warrant," Skeet instructed.

Subterfuge

"Probable cause is weak; but, with the bike, I think we have enough to search any place in that house that Eddie called his. You will most likely be limited to the attic and his bedroom but make sure the judge knows the bike was left next to the car and Eddie was the last person to drive it. If we get lucky and the judge is feeling generous…"

"We might be able to swing the car as well," Greg finished. "I'll call Monroe, so we can get started on this. I'll also give him the good news that he's still in charge. Give me the info where you want him to send the file and a contact number where he should call if he has questions."

Rowdy took the phone off speaker and provided the information. When he hung up, he turned to the group. "The file should be here within the hour."

"Can we project a map up on that television?" Skeet asked Fulmer.

"Sure," Ryan answered and started checking connections on the back of the computers. "I think I have a cable in my car that will work with these. Give me ten minutes and I'll have you set up."

"Rowdy?" Coop said as he stared out the large window and methodically pondered the new information. "Can you call Greg back? Ask him, since he's going to talk to this Pete guy again, to ask if they know anything about Charles' illegitimate sister."

"Right," Rowdy pulled out his phone. "I can't believe I forgot about that."

* * * *

An hour later, the group was still gathered in the loft.   Coop and Rowdy were skimming through the old homicide report from Oregon.   Fulmer was tapping away on his computer, only he knew exactly what he was doing and why.   Skeet had Google Maps displayed on the big screen television mounted to the wall and he was placing electronic pins on various locations throughout the city.

"What are you doing?" Maggie asked when she stepped into the room and spotted the map.

"Marking the places we know our suspect has visited," Skeet said absently as he placed a marker on the old warehouse.

Fulmer pushed back from his chair and moved to the map. "You can add one here…" he pointed to an area on the map near a shopping center.

"What's there?" Rowdy asked, moving to study the large map.

"That is where our guy purchased the new locks for that abandoned building," Fulmer provided.   "I need to head over, see if I can find anything from the security system.   The owner said our guy picked up the merchandise in person but paid cash.   There's no record that will help — no address, no phone number, nothing. He's pulling the original paperwork to see if there was anything else that might help us.   One more thing, he purchased two extra locks. Two additional devices that were not attached to that warehouse."

"I guess that's something," Coop decided.   "At least, we know we're focused on the right family."

"Are you guys any closer to finding Angela?" Maggie asked.

"Everything brings us closer," Coop moved to his wife and pulled her into a tight hug.   "It's slow going; but, we're making progress."

"Not nearly enough," Skeet said in frustration.

Subterfuge

"Greg and Detective Monroe are going over the car and the house as we speak," Rowdy provided. "If there's something to find, Greg will find it."

"You seem to have a lot of confidence in this Greg Whitman," Fulmer observed.

"Like I said before," Rowdy shrugged, "he's a good cop."

Skeet sighed and stood. "Come on, Ryan. I'll go with you to the electronics store. I need to get out of here for a while, anyway."

Rowdy watched as Perkins left the room. "The hope he felt when we found that stuff at the warehouse is wearing off again."

"I know," Coop settled into a chair. "I'm feeling a little depressed about the whole thing myself. If we don't find his wife soon..." he trailed off, remembering Maggie was in the room.

"Don't hold back because of me," Maggie insisted. "What can I do to help?"

"With the information Greg brought us from Oregon," Coop pondered. "I'm comfortable focusing on Eddie Hill. I'm confident he's our guy. Once they get into that room, we'll know more; but, let's focus on him for now."

"Maggie," Rowdy decided. "Use that computer and find anything you can on Eddie. His legal name is Edgar Hill. Search social media sites, blogs, just Google his name. We might get lucky and find a newspaper article about the family or something. Go back a ways for me. See if he was ever a witness in a crime, anything. We need something that tells us where this guy lands when he's not killing."

Rowdy pulled out his laptop and started to do the same through the law enforcement databases and court systems. He was going to thoroughly search every system he had access to. If they could just find the guy's residence, they might find the guy.

Chapter Six

Angela woke with a start and realized her captor had tricked her again. She'd been so hungry she hadn't cared if the soup was safe or not. It wasn't. How long had she been out? What had he used to drug her? Whatever it was, she hoped it wouldn't cause permanent damage. She struggled to push her body into a sitting position and realized she wasn't as sore as she had been before she passed out. How many days had passed by without her knowing it? Skeet must be frantic by now. She wished there was a way to help him. Wished there was a way to get free, or at least to get word to her husband that she was still alive.

She knew that didn't matter. Skeet would not stop looking until he found her. But, would it be too late? Would he find her before this maniac did even more damage? Her question was answered a short time later.

The Scientist stepped into the make-shift lab, anticipation was making him giddy. He couldn't delve into his work completely; but, he could get a taste.   The woman was still healing from her injuries.   He'd caused too much damage; but, it was time to see how she reacted to pain.   He moved forward, careful to remain a safe distance away as he shot her with his favorite tool. He'd developed it himself, perfected it over time, and immensely enjoyed watching the results of his labor.   It was an electronic device similar to a Taser unit the police carried.   It worked the same way.   He could shoot tiny wires from the tip and incapacitate his subjects instantly.   He watched as the woman's body instantly curled into a ball and she silently endured the intense shock to her nervous system.

He couldn't decide if he was thrilled with the results, or disappointed.   Normally, his specimens would scream and carry-on when he used this tool to control them.   Not Mrs. Perkins.   She seemed to withdraw into herself.   Her body reacted, it didn't have a choice; but, she remained completely silent.   Her response unnerved him, and he stood there watching, amazed and transfixed for several seconds before he shook himself and got to work.   Once the camera system was installed, he focused on setting up the platform.   It wasn't as good as the one he'd abandoned in Houston; but, it would have to do.

Angela forced her mind to focus on Skeet.   Her husband would rescue her.   She would be saved, all she had to do was survive a little longer.   She ground her teeth and tried to ignore the pain.   It didn't work; instead, the electrical current caused them to chatter uncontrollably.   So, she closed her eyes and forced her mind to remember her favorite vacation.   Skeet was between cases and they'd spent two long, relaxing weeks in Hawaii.   She loved lounging on the beach, swimming just under the surface of the clear blue water as they snorkeled all afternoon, and sunning under the huge umbrella.   The nights were the best, midnight picnics on the beach, making love in the moonlight, and talking like they had never talked before.   Her eyes flew open when she realized the monster was humming; and, he had moved in closer.   He was directly in

Subterfuge

front of her now. She watched in horror as he bent slowly and began lifting her incapacitated body onto some kind of platform. She wanted to fight, desperately wanted to remain on the cold, hard, concrete floor; but, whatever he had shocked her with had disabled her nervous system completely. She couldn't fight, she couldn't even move.

There was about an inch of liquid that covered the slightly curved interior of the platform. She didn't know what it was; but, something told her to avoid it. She glanced up and saw the disgusting, malicious animal grinning. That was all she needed to know, things were about to get worse — much worse. She just hoped she had the fortitude to survive. And, she prayed with every fiber of her being, that her husband would hurry and find her. She needed him now more than she'd ever needed him before. Angela closed her eyes and waited. She didn't want to know what the man had planned, or what he was going to do with the large knife he just pulled from the pocket of his white lab coat.

* * * *

It was after ten in the evening when the call from Oregon finally came through. They were getting desperate. Internet and social media was a bust when it came to the elusive Eddie Hill. Skeet and Ryan Fulmer had returned nearly an hour earlier and went straight to the computer to analyze the video. The merchant that sold the locking system to Hill had cameras inside the store, but nothing outside. The image was clear, and it confirmed their findings from Houston. The same man that had driven the white van and disposed of Amanda's body had purchased the new, fancy locking mechanisms installed on the abandoned warehouse here in Chicago. But, that was all they had. The man paid in cash and never provided any personal data to the store. The arrogant SOB even reserved the items for pickup under the name Stephen Hawking. The bigger surprise was that the clerk didn't recognize it as a fake. Skeet wondered, if Eddie claimed to be Bill Gates, would the clueless teen recognize that as fraud? Probably not.

Skeet had called Coop to break the bad news but was directed next door and to a second business in the area. It was a large strip mall and Coop had dealt with two of the owners in the past. He knew, for a fact, at least those shops had cameras that covered a section of the parking lot. Fulmer and Skeet had stopped in at every establishment in the area and gathered up hours of footage in hopes of capturing the man's vehicle. They were pretty sure he wouldn't drive around in a stolen van more than necessary. They were hoping to find a rental car or maybe one he borrowed from family or friends in the area. They needed another clue, desperately.

"Tell me you have something," Rowdy answered his ringing phone, thinking it was his old friend, Greg Whitman.

"Officer Cooper, I presume," Detective Monroe responded.

"Who is this?" Rowdy asked.

"I borrowed Greg's phone," Monroe provided. "He had your contact info stored already, so I thought it would be easier. This is Detective Doug Monroe, the primary on the Roslyn Tanner case. First, before I get into the warrant; I want to say thank you. My case was beyond cold before you got in touch. It's not much; but, at least, I'll be able to give her parents the comfort of knowing who killed their little girl. Hopefully, when this is all over... they'll also have the pleasure of knowing the man is behind bars. This case demonstrates our need for the death penalty. Sometimes, even that isn't punishment enough."

Subterfuge

"I'm glad we could connect the dots," Rowdy said in answer. "Is there anything you guys found out there in Oregon that will help us up here in Chicago?"

"Not sure," Monroe admitted. "The staff affirmed your guy is my guy. That picture you provided is definitely Eddie Hill and he left evidence all over the place out here. Our case is a slam dunk. The monster followed that girl for nearly a week before he grabbed her. The idiot kept a detailed journal. Laid out the entire plan from start to finish, even described how he felt as he bashed that poor girl's skull in. We are dealing with one sick SOB."

"Yeah," Rowdy sighed. "We know."

"Anyway," Monroe continued. "The judge included the car in the warrant; and we can put the girl in the trunk, my victim that is. We found hair, fibers, blood, the works. We're still processing the attic. That place was set up as a scientific lab of sorts."

"Wait," Rowdy stopped him "I'm going to put you on speaker. The rest of my team needs to hear this." Rowdy fumbled with the buttons on the phone then set it on the coffee table in front of him. "Okay, go ahead"

"The attic," Monroe repeated. "It had all kinds of glass jars and tons of electronic stuff. I'd guess he thought of himself as an inventor slash chemist of some sort. There are old motors, electrical wires; you name it, he has it up there. Then, he had shelves full of chemicals. It looks like he was experimenting with some pretty toxic stuff."

"He was probably developing the acid he uses on his victims," Skeet said softly.

"Acid?" Monroe asked in shock. "Roslyn's body didn't show any evidence of that."

"He probably hadn't perfected it back then," Skeet supplied.

"What else?" Rowdy pushed. "Anything that will help us find him?"

"Like I said, I'm not sure," Monroe admitted. "The Little Shop of Horrors helps us in our case; but, the only thing I found that might help you is an entry in his journal. When the kid was around fourteen, he had to go stay the summer with a distant relative. He never says where he was going; but, he wasn't happy about it. He filled several pages describing just how unhappy he was with the arrangement. He did say he was going to stay with Aunt Elizabeth and he had a lot of disdain for her husband, Stanton. No last name and he obviously thought of them as beneath him."

"That might help. We haven't found any link to an Elizabeth or a Stanton; but, a maid in the Hamptons said Charles had a secret sister," Coop considered. "Can you scan that journal and send us the entire thing?"

"Sure," Monroe decided. "I don't see any conflict with that. The two agents the feds sent over already looked at everything I have. Nothing seemed to jump out at them as helpful, either. I'm sorry, I can't tell you much more. If anything surfaces as we go through the attic, I'll ring back. His bedroom was a bust. Looked more like a guest room than an actual bedroom. Anyway, I'll have my secretary scan the journal before I book it. I'll also tell her to send you all the reports we've completed on this case to date. My packet will take a few days before it's ready to take to the DA for screening. Once it's complete, I can send that to you as well. We'll give you all we have, I just don't think it's going to be much help."

"You never know," Coop disagreed. "Something that didn't mean anything out there could link up with something we have here. Send us what you can immediately and then the rest as soon as it's available."

"Will do," Monroe agreed before disconnecting.

The room was silent for several seconds.

"I think I found something," Fulmer finally said.

"What do you have?" Coop moved to stand behind the electronic guru.

"This car," he froze a frame in the video he had been scanning. "And here, again. That's the best I can do as far as clarity; their system is substandard and grainy."

Skeet moved to the chair next to Fulmer. "That's definitely our guy," he pointed to the screen. "See, his hairline is the same and you can just barely see that same shirt under the jacket. That's the guy that purchased the door locks."

"I agree," Ryan nodded. "I'm going to back this up and see if we can get a plate off that car. You were right, he's not risking detection in the stolen van."

"Not that it helps," Skeet retorted. "We've still got nothing."

"Actually," Coop disagreed. "We have too much."

* * * *

It was just after four in the morning when Ryan shook Skeet awake. He hated to disturb his friend but knew Perkins would need to know what he found.

"Huh?" Skeet's body jerked awake. His initial reaction was surprise; but, it was immediately replaced by anger and annoyance

— at himself. He had fallen asleep again, in spite of his best efforts to work through the fatigue. Sure, he was trying to function on no sleep. All of them had been up for nearly forty-eight hours straight. But, that was no excuse. Angela needed him, and he had dozed off as he read through the documents Oregon had sent over.

"Table that," Ryan whispered. "I have to show you something." He pressed one finger to his lips as he glanced at the two lounge chairs that contained the Cooper brothers. "They went down twenty minutes ago. I don't want to disturb them with this yet."

Skeet stood and followed his friend to the end of the desk where the computer was running a complicated scan that only Ryan understood.

Fulmer settled back in his chair and pulled up the newspaper article. "Just read it and tell me if I'm onto something here. It seems too…"

Skeet started to scan the report and frowned. "Coincidental?" he whispered. He moved closer and settled into the chair. The article was a human-interest piece about a guy named Stanton Proctor. He was the manager of operations in the Sewer Department for the city of Chicago. Stanton was working the tunnels below the city when an entire section collapsed. He suffered brain damage from the incident and a colleague was killed. The story outlined the difficulties Stanton's family had suffered since the tragic incident and reported the man was being transferred to a care center for treatment. They were asking the community for donations to help with the relocation costs and the high price of on-going care the man would need for the rest of his life. Skeet scanned the article three times searching for the name of the wife. They had left that out completely, just referred to her as Mrs. Procter when they commended her selfless dedication the past four years as she did her best to care for her handicapped husband.

Subterfuge

"Do you really think it could be them?" Ryan asked after several minutes.

"I don't know," Skeet said honestly. "I mean, what are the odds?"

"Exactly," Ryan whispered. "That was my first reaction as well. I mean, a kid from Oregon… a rich kid at that, and a city worker. It fits with the anger and the disgust. A spoiled rich brat wouldn't be happy if he were shipped to Chicago to stay with a man that worked for the Sewer Department."

"We need more information," Skeet decided. "I'm going to shower and head over to the city offices. If I get lucky, I might find a supervisor or a secretary that can tell me about that family."

"Should I wake the sleeping duo?" Ryan glanced at the brothers.

"Naw," Skeet decided. "In fact, why don't you take the couch? Get a couple hours down while I shower and look into this. I'll wake all of you when I get back. How did you find that, anyway? That article was written…" Skeet glanced at the date, "ten years ago."

"I programmed a deep internet scan when we got the names from Oregon," Ryan said absently. "It's been running for hours and I hit on about a hundred possibles. Still checking some of them out but when I saw this one, it was just too weird to keep to myself."

"I'm serious, Ryan," Skeet stood. "You should crash for a while."

"I'm good," Ryan shook his head. "I didn't last as long as the rest of you. I snagged a nap yesterday at around two. Don't worry about me. I'll grab a couple hours when I need them. Right now, I want to see what I can find on the initial incident. This article says four years earlier. I might be able to find some details on the initial collapse."

"Alright," Skeet relented. "But, let those two sleep. I'm also going to call Stan. He may have been working in the area when the tunnel was destroyed. That's before my time; but, Burns was an agent out here years ago."

"I would have been working overseas during this time period," Ryan provided. "Stan might be a decent resource, good call."

Skeet left the room and Ryan went back to work.

* * * *

Angela was pressed up against the far edge of the platform. She knew if she moved even an inch, she'd fall over the edge and never be able to climb back up. The chains were too short to allow escape. She'd tried that already, tried to climb from the hideous thing back onto the ground. It didn't work and all she had to show for her efforts were deep burn marks on her arms where the acid had penetrated the skin. The only thing that had neutralized the burning was her saliva, and that had been difficult. Her mouth was so dry, and she felt weak and nauseated from the pain her capture had inflicted. She had slices all over her body. And, as if that wasn't bad enough, the prick had doused her completely in salt water. He used a huge bucket and dumped the painful liquid over her head while the cuts were still bleeding. Her entire body stung, and it took all her willpower not to scream. She somehow knew that was what he wanted. She might not be able to escape this hellish prison on her own; but, she would not accommodate his sick perversion. Denying him that satisfaction made her feel like she was doing something.

Subterfuge

She let one tiny tear escape from the corner of her right eye when the man stepped back into her dark prison. She was in for another round of torture and she wasn't ready for it. She wasn't emotionally prepared to block out the pain. But, she would, she would survive... for herself and for her husband. She had to survive for Skeet. He was looking for her. He was doing everything in his power to find her. She knew that with every fiber of her being. She would do the same. She would do everything in her power to stay alive until he got here.

She watched as her sadistic capturer took a long drink of water; to torture her mentally, of course. She continued to watch as he set the large, insulated water jug on the lip of the platform. Angie realized he wasn't paying attention to what he was doing. The container was a fair distance away from her; but, she knew she could reach it. She'd tested her bindings, knew exactly how far she could get before the taught line prevented her movement and the huge bottle was within her reach. Was this a test? A trick? She didn't care, she had to try. She'd located a loose slat on the base of the platform earlier that morning while trying to find a way to get free. She knew it would be the perfect hiding place. Now, she just had to get it without him seeing her.

As the man turned to select one of his atrocious tools, she saw the glee and anticipation in his eyes just before he turned his back completely. She waited a few seconds, hoping she was right. She was pretty sure the man was so focused on selecting his next hideous tool that he wouldn't notice the slight movement behind him. She had to try. Angela held her breath and put her plan in motion. Once she snatched up the fresh water, it only took a few seconds to slide her fingernail beneath the slat and slip the jug inside — thankfully it fit. Task complete, she quickly settled back into the exact position she'd been in prior to her theft. She barely made it before he swung around, smiled that evil smile she hated, and took a step forward. That's when he realized his water was gone. At first, he seemed confused. He glanced back at the table that contained his tools, searched around on the ground then glared at her.

"Where is it?" he demanded.

Angela remained perfectly still. She had an idea. It was going to be painful and her timing had to be perfect; but, it would be worth it — if it worked.

The Scientist took another step forward, anger growing stronger with each passing second. He couldn't allow her to have the water. It was imperative for the experiment that she be denied. Everything had to be exactly the same as the others. She had to suffer, had to beg for him to give her the tiniest morsel. He wanted to record the precise moment she realized he wouldn't show mercy. She was ruining everything. He picked up the pace and marched to the side of the platform, raising the large cattle prod he held in his right hand high above his head. She was going to get the full force of the instrument right in the stomach. She was going to pay dearly for this little stunt. Then, he would take the water back and move on to the next test.

Angela held her breath, one more step and he would be close enough. She forced her face to remain neutral, refused to give him the slightest hint she was up to something, and waited. Finally, he took another step forward. He was now in range, this was going to work. She was sure of it. The instant he raised his right arm, she put her plan in motion. She cupped her left hand and dipped it into the pool of acid, holding tight to the side of the platform with her right hand so she didn't accidentally fall in. Then, using as much force as she could muster through the pain and agony as the toxic liquid began to eat through her flesh, she flung the liquid into the face of the man she had come to hate. She watched as his expression changed from a mixture of fury and gleeful anticipation, to shock, and finally turned to pain. She continued to watch as he dropped the cattle prod and flung his hands over his face. She

177

Subterfuge

could barely hear the clank, clank, clank of the metal bouncing on concrete through her enemy's high-pitched, agonized screams. He continued to screech and cry; sobbing uncontrollably as he made his way to the door.

The instant the large metal trap was shut, Angela reached down and snatched up the water jug. She was so thirsty and realized she could take care of two problems at once. She flipped up the spout and took a large gulp of water, swished it around to moisten the inside of her mouth, then spit it onto the palm of her hand. The cool liquid covered her palm and neutralized the burning instantly. Angela realized the large water jug contained ice water. That was even better. It took a few minutes; but, she was finally able to twist the top off and take another long sip. An ice cube fell onto her tongue and she gripped it in her teeth, secured the lid and placed the container back in her hiding place. With her right hand, she gripped the ice cube and began running it gently over her burned palm, then the sides of her aching hand, cleaning between her fingers and all the way up to her wrist. It only took a few minutes before she was sure the acid was no longer a threat. Now, she'd just have to deal with the raw, tender wound left behind. She settled onto the edge of her prison and tried to relax, knowing the killer would not be back for the rest of the day. She had bought herself a few more hours. Now, she just needed Skeet to do his part and this nightmare would be over. "Baby, I need you. Please, find me soon."

* * * *

Skeet stepped into the loft and took a look around. The place was empty, except for Ryan Fulmer. He was pounding away on

178

the computer, completely focused on his work. "Where are the Coopers?"

Fulmer looked up in surprise, he hadn't even heard his friend come in. "Uh… Rowdy got called away. Something about an intruder at the warehouse and they wanted a dog. Coop got a call from Dumas; the guy was beyond livid. Said Coop is hiding you and he better produce you immediately. He was summoned to the office to answer for his crimes."

"I'm calling Stan," Skeet pulled out his phone.

"Maybe, you'll have better luck than I did," Ryan sat back with a sigh. "I wasn't sure how long you would be, and I tried calling; but, it went straight to the recording."

Skeet dialed the number; but, it went straight to voicemail. He clicked off, he'd leave a message later. It wasn't like his friend and mentor to be offline for so long, he just hoped nothing was wrong.

Fulmer pulled his attention from the computer and focused on Skeet. "I thought you were just stopping in at the city offices. At least, tell me you found someone that knew our guy."

"Yeah," Skeet dropped into a chair and rubbed his face. "But, it was a cluster. The secretary only knew one guy that still remembered Stanton. Apparently, they had quite the turnover after the accident. The men didn't believe the tunnels were safe and they didn't like the way Stanton was treated by the city. Most of them just walked out, moved away or found jobs in the private sector. Anyway, she sent me forty minutes out of town to track the elusive colleague down. He was deep in the tunnel system trying to fix some kind of electrical glitch."

"Was it worth it?" Ryan asked. "Did you get anything that will help?"

Subterfuge

"Stanton was married to a woman everyone called Beth," Skeet began. "Could be short for Elizabeth."

"Fits," Ryan agreed.

"He said Beth is quiet but likable. She didn't raise a fuss when her husband was hurt," Skeet continued. "In fact, all she wanted was the medical bills paid in full and for the city to help with on-going expenses. They turned her down, which is why so many guys split. They paid the initial bills, said that was on the job stuff. But, with the head injury, the brain damage, he couldn't go back. He had to quit and that's when the city cut them off. Beth now works just to pay the bills. A local attorney sued the city on her behalf and she won enough to pay for the care center but that's it. She had to get a job to cover everyday living expenses. And, Earl, that's the guy I talked to," Skeet continued. "Earl said Beth still goes to the care center every single day to see Stanton and make sure he's okay. He's basically a vegetable, doesn't even know she's there, but she goes anyway, never misses a day."

"They must have had the kind of love that lasts," Ryan surmised. "I mean, that kind of dedication is rare and it's kind of sad, you know?"

"I know," Skeet sighed. "Anyway, I got directions to the house. Where Beth lives that is. He didn't know the address but gave pretty detailed instructions on how to get there. I was hoping one of the brothers could join me while I scope out the area. We could look for that car you spotted in the video. By the way, any luck on a plate?"

"Only a partial," Ryan admitted. "But, I did run Stanton and Elizabeth Proctor through the system. I was hoping the car would come back to one of them. They don't have any vehicles registered in their names. I didn't find a driver's license for Elizabeth either. Not in the state of Illinois."

"Keep looking," Skeet decided. "See if you can find any kind of marriage license with a maiden name. She might be using that instead of Proctor."

"That doesn't make sense to me," Ryan shook his head. "If she visits her husband religiously, why would she change her name?"

"Earl said she is very private," Skeet provided. "I'm just thinking she may have gone back to her maiden name to make sure nobody made the connection. I'm told the incident was big news around here at the time. Reporters were everywhere. That must have been difficult for a woman who was worried about her husband and just trying to survive; especially, one that was so private. Her full name is never mentioned, not once, never — in any newspaper. I'm thinking maybe she did that on purpose and she changed her name to make sure outsiders never found her."

"I guess you could be right," Ryan relented. "I'll see what I can find. It's going to be difficult with both of them being alive and us not having a warrant to pry."

"Just see what you can do," Skeet stood.

"Now where are you going?" Ryan asked.

"To save Coop," Skeet shrugged. "Stan's not answering for me either; and until I stop in and see what Dumas wants, he's going to be a constant annoyance. He's already left me a dozen messages today alone. That's excessive, even for him."

"He wants to know what we have so he can take credit for our work," Ryan surmised. "And, I hope you leave him in the dark where he belongs."

Skeet was about to answer when his phone started to ring. "Perkins."

Subterfuge

"Hey," Rowdy said in answer. "I just cleared the warehouse, did Fulmer tell you I got called on a suspicious person in the building?"

"Did you find anything?" Skeet asked.

"I located a guy," Rowdy pulled into a park a few doors down and across the street from his target. "Not much there, he has some issues. I'd say he's about thirty; but, he only operates on a twelve-or-thirteen-year-old level."

"Okay," Skeet frowned. Another dead-end.

"But, here's the thing," Rowdy continued. "He had a necklace in his possession that matched the one you said your wife never took off. Tiny gold chain with an engraved heart pendant."

"Could have fallen off while she was at the warehouse," Skeet countered. "That doesn't necessarily mean anything."

"True," Rowdy agreed. "Except he said he got it from Miss Beth's garbage can."

Skeet straightened. "He knows Beth?"

"Apparently, he does. And, I'm currently sitting at the park near her home," Rowdy supplied. "There's no sign of the woman, yet. And, the driveway is empty... no car. I'm going to wait here, walk the dog and try to blend in a bit. Hopefully, if this Mad Scientist of yours is staying here, he won't think anything of a local cop stopping in at the park to give his dog a break. I'll tag you if anything comes of it."

"I was just thinking of going out there myself," Skeet admitted. He relayed his morning to Rowdy and made sure his partner was at the same residence Earl had described. He was. Then, he decided to head to the office and save Coop. Rowdy could handle the house and if the Scientist saw Skeet anywhere near the area... he'd bolt for sure.

"I'll do my best to make sure Knight does his job well," Rowdy promised before disconnecting. "If we're lucky, maybe he'll get a staph infection at the hospital while he's getting a dozen or so stitches before he's transferred to a cage."

"Hope springs eternal," Skeet smiled as he disconnected the call. "If you need me, I'm heading in to hook up with Coop. Let me know if Burns calls. I need to talk to him, immediately."

"Understood," Ryan said without taking his eyes off the screen. "Good luck, I think you might need it."

* * * *

Stanley Burns had finally made it through security at the White House. He still had no idea why he was here. What kind of emergency bypassed the Director and landed on the Investigative Assistant Director? Hopefully, he'd have the answer to that question soon. He didn't like leaving Chicago with Angela still missing and Dumas out to destroy Skeet. He had promised Perkins he would remain close just in case he needed him. Burns sighed inwardly, it couldn't be helped. When the White House called, you jumped. He just wished the timing could have been better. He paused to check in at the desk he'd been directed to and was escorted to an empty office he happened to know was next to the Oval Office. Things were getting more intriguing by the minute. He fished out his cellphone and shut it off, the last thing he wanted to do was get a call in the middle of a meeting with the President. Was he meeting with the President? Nobody had said for sure.

Stan practically jumped to his feet when a man he recognized as the President's Chief of Staff entered the room.

Subterfuge

"Stanley Burns," John Harris held out a hand in greeting. "I'm sorry to call you here on such short notice. Thank you for your willingness to accommodate our request."

"I'm happy to assist in any way I can," Stan said honestly.

"The President is ready for you," John motioned to a side door. "Let's not keep him waiting." Harris moved forward, opened the door and motioned for Stan to proceed him.

Stan stepped into the oval office and tried to appear calm. He'd never been privileged enough to step inside this room before. Actually, he'd never met a sitting president before now. He wasn't entirely sure what the protocol was for such a meeting.

"Relax," President Hollander stood to greet his visitor. "We're all friends here."

"Thank you, sir," Burns moved forward and gripped the hand the most powerful leader in the world offered him. "I'm sorry," he smiled and shook his head. "I'm just a little caught off guard by all of this. It's quite a surprise to put it mildly."

Hollander motioned to the couch and moved to settle into a comfortable looking chair. "I'm sorry for all the intrigue, the cloak and dagger style request, but it was necessary."

"I understand," Stan settled onto the couch.

"I'm not sure you do," Hollander picked up a steaming cup of liquid and sipped. "Coffee?" he asked before setting his cup back on the small table.

"No, thanks," Stan answered immediately.

"I received some unexpected and, to be honest, devastating news two days ago," Hollander began. "Director Steven Thatcher is ill. I'm afraid I'm going to have to deem this conversation

184

private, exercise executive privilege so to speak. Steven would like his condition to remain... well, it's a personal matter. His family knows, I know, John knows and now you know. Let's keep it among us for now."

"I'm sorry to hear that," Stanley sobered. "Is it serious?" He brushed that aside with his hand. "Of course, it's serious, otherwise we wouldn't be having this conversation. What can I do?"

"I'm glad you asked," Hollander settled further into his chair. "I'm in the market for a new Director... for the FBI. Your name has come up multiple times over the past two days. It seems Stanley Burns, you are somewhat of a superstar within the Bureau. Based on recent conversations, I'm surprised we haven't met... previously."

Stan wasn't sure how to respond to that. He was humbled for sure, and he wondered who the President had been speaking to. "I'm fairly confident the superstar comments were greatly overstated. I do, however, take my job seriously and always try to lead my men with honor."

"And apparently, you have succeeded," Hollander recognized the humility and decided to move on. So far, Stanley Burns the man was living up to his reputation. "Now, I have a few questions before I consider you for nomination."

Stan swallowed, shocked, humbled and incredibly terrified. The President of the United States had him on the short list for consideration. He could be nominated to succeed Steven Thatcher as Director of the FBI? It was just a little surreal.

"Shall we proceed?"

"Yes, sir," Stan said as he tried his best to prepare for the most important interview of his life.

Subterfuge

* * * *

The Scientist maneuvered his vehicle into the residential neighborhood he hated more than anything. These were common people with common lives and modest homes. He longed for a comfortable bed, room service and an expensive meal. For the first time since he left Houston, he wondered if he had made a mistake. Agent Perkin's wife was a vicious, troublesome woman that had brought him more pain than he'd ever experienced in his life. Working on her was supposed to be satisfying; he expected to experience a level of euphoria he'd never achieved before. But, instead of pleasure, instead of revenge... he was the one in pain. Somehow, one woman had turned the tables on him and he didn't know how to regain control. The only reason he'd come here was to take something away from the man who had spoiled his work and stolen everything he held dear. But, at the moment, he didn't feel Agent Perkins was paying the price. It felt like he was, and that was unacceptable. He needed to regroup, to formulate a better plan. It was going to be difficult in that ugly, flowery guest room his aunt loved so much. At least, she would be working when he arrived. He wouldn't have to come up with a lie to explain his injury.

As he rounded the last corner and pulled onto the road that led to his aunt's one-story rambler, he spotted the marked police truck at the park. He slowed and cautiously glanced around for the officer. The instant he spotted the guy with the dog, he knew he found his mark. The man wasn't in uniform, so he couldn't be on duty but he practically screamed cop. Was it possible the police were here for him? He dismissed that concern immediately. He was too smart for some local public servant to find him. Anyway, he'd been careful. Nothing led to him, he made sure of that. It was the reason he tolerated the pesky woman that claimed to be family. The reason he wasn't currently relaxing in a lush hotel with fine silk sheets and room service.   But, why then was a cop loitering in the park just down the street from his hide-out?   He nearly brushed his concern aside, but hesitated.   Agent Perkins had found him in Houston.   He couldn't risk it, even if the risk was minimal. He'd head to the other side of town and find a motel that would accept cash and a fake name, regroup, and formulate a new plan. His current specimen was going to pay for the damage she inflicted today.   She was going to pay dearly for that little stunt.   Eddie continued on past the house, knowing he'd have to return and eliminate all evidence he'd been there.   The cops couldn't connect him with dear Aunt Elizabeth.   Hiding his true identity was essential to his mission.   He wasn't worried, not really; but, he learned early on to cover his tracks and never leave a trace the blithering buffoons could follow.   He wasn't going to change his habits now, they had protected him and his work far too long to get sloppy.

* * * *

"Agent Perkins," Dumas said the instant Skeet appeared in the doorway.   "Nice of you to join us.   I assume you lost your cell phone somewhere.   It's the only explanation for the dereliction of duty."

"No," Skeet shrugged.   "I assume you got the memo.   The one from Assistant Director Stanley Burns placing me on admin leave.   I believe he made it clear, I only answer to him until that status changes.   I'm under orders from your boss, Dumas.   But, since I couldn't reach Burns, I thought I'd stop in and see what has you calling me more than a dozen times today."

"Burns is out of town," Dumas was pleased to know something Perkins didn't.   "He was called to Washington and will be unavailable for at least two days.   You do answer to me and I need you here first thing for a briefing. Conference room, zero-eight-hundred."

"Sure," Skeet shrugged. "I can do that, as soon as Burns gives the order."

"I just gave the order, Perkins," Dumas fumed. "And, if you don't show, I'm recommending termination."

Skeet shrugged and turned to Coop. "You done here?"

"Apparently," Coop stood. "I've just been informed my services are no longer needed. Funny, I'm off the team the same day he wants to put you back on. Wonder if there's a method to his madness."

"Careful Mr. Cooper," Dumas warned. "I still might make that phone call. You are up for a promotion, aren't you? A complaint from the FBI just might make that Chief of yours reconsider and promote someone else."

Coop laughed out loud. A complaint from Dumas would probably prompt Chief Griggs to promote him immediately. He was still grinning as he exited the exterior doors and turned toward the parking garage.

"Why now?" Skeet pondered. "Did he give you a reason?"

"Not exactly," Coop sighed. "He's got nothing and he's counting on this case to earn him that promotion Burns said he's not getting."

"So, he kicked you off? How does that get him closer to arresting a killer?" Skeet still couldn't figure the angle.

"He's been trying to get information from me for the past two hours," Coop admitted. "He was looking for anything, the slightest lead he could follow. When he didn't break me, he decided I was no good to him.   Said he didn't need a local cop that wasn't contributing to the team."

"He thinks having you on the team will encourage me to go rogue," Skeet surmised. "I did that already, in Houston, with the locals out there.   He's worried I'll do the same thing again out here and he won't get credit for the bust.   What he doesn't understand is that I won't be attending his briefing tomorrow.   Burns was afraid Dumas would flounder and try to bring me back in.   I was advised, in no uncertain terms, that I was not to return to regular duty until I receive written notification from the one and only Stanley Burns. Dumas can recommend termination if he wants.   He's going to lose this one and if he continues down the road he's traveling, he'll lose big time."

"I'm surprised he's even going there," Coop considered. "Doesn't he know how close you and Stan are?"

"I guess not," Skeet shrugged.   "I don't know how he missed it, but it's not something I advertise.   Plus, you know how he acts. He doesn't really pay attention to those beneath him.   It's all about impressing the brass.   He views me as one of the little people.   One that needs to be reined back in because I'm out of control."

"So," Coop reached his car.   "Are we meeting back at Rowdy's or did you find something to follow-up on?"

"Rowdy's sitting on the house," Skeet advised.   "He'll call if anything changes.   I'd like to go out and interview this Beth woman, see if there's anything she can tell us about Eddie."   He proceeded to fill Coop in on the details, assuming he hadn't been briefed since he was tied up with Dumas all morning.

"I want to ask her if he's been staying there the past few days and if she's noticed anything out of the ordinary.   Or, if she loaned him her car," Coop added.

Subterfuge

"Oh," Skeet affirmed. "She did. She changed her name after the accident —officially. Ryan called just as I was entering the building. Rowdy provided the exact address of the residence and the property is owned by Elizabeth Proctor Newman. The car is registered under Elizabeth P. Newman and it fits the description of the blue compact he drove to purchase the locks."

"Maiden name?" Coop surmised.

"Probably," Skeet agreed. "Ryan's trying to run it down, see if they own any other property in the area where he might be hiding Angie. I know we're closing in; but, I can't help feeling like we're moving too slow. We have to save her, Coop. I don't think I can handle a recovery mission."

"I'm holding out hope and you should, too," Coop climbed into his car and started the engine. "Let's get back home, maybe Ryan has something for us and I'll tag Rowdy for an update. We'll regroup and go from there."

Skeet gave a nod and made his way to his own vehicle. He was having a difficult time fighting the depression. Angie had been missing far too long. The possibilities... he shuddered. There were so many things that madman could have done to her already. If he could just find his wife, he'd make sure she never endured one moment of pain again. He'd be there for her, never leave her alone again. He'd protect his wife with his life until the day they both died. Then, he'd protect her in the next life. She just had to hold on a little longer. "I'm coming, baby. Hold on for me, I'm coming."

"Rowdy thinks he may have spotted the car near the residence," Coop said as he stepped into the door. "Ryan, any luck on Beth? We need to know where she works. I want to talk to her, now."

190

Ryan glanced up and saw Skeet join them. "I'm working on it. I've tracked the name, Newton is her mother's maiden name. Now, I'm running that through E-Verify to see if we have a record of an employment transaction. It's slow going, I have to filter through millions of names. Do you have any idea how many people apply for work in just one week throughout this country?"

"Why are you running the entire country?" Skeet asked as he moved forward and took a seat. "Can't you apply a filter that narrows it to Illinois?"

"I have," Ryan said impatiently. "But, it's all in the same system. Just give it time. We'll find her."

"Time is something my wife doesn't have," Skeet grumbled.

"Anyway," Coop continued. "I told Rowdy to wait. Eddie may have been spooked when he saw the marked unit; but, he doesn't know we were there for him. He might swing by later to check the area and make sure it's clear before he turns in for the night. Rowdy's moving the truck to the other side of the park. He says he can use a nearby building to block the view of anyone that drives by looking. The downside, he won't be anywhere near his truck if the guy returns and spooks again. Plus, the car slowed near the park but drove right by the residence without hesitation. It might be a coincidence, not even the right car at all. We're really waiting on Beth. She has to come home sometime."

It was three hours later when Rowdy called with an update. Elizabeth Newton exited the city bus and casually made her way three blocks north to her home. Rowdy watched as the woman entered the residence and appeared to settle in for the evening.

Chapter Seven

"Mrs. Newton?" Skeet asked the moment the woman answered the door. They decided it would be best if Coop joined Perkins for the interrogation. Rowdy was relieved to head home, feed the dog, and give him some down time. Knight was always on high alert when he was in the K9 truck. He needed a break and at least a few hours to play in the back yard and just be a regular dog. After hours loitering in the park, Eddie hadn't returned... if that was Eddie that Rowdy had spotted earlier. There was no way to really know. It was time to move on to Plan B.

Beth stood just inside her home with the flimsy screen shielding her from the two men looming over her on the front porch. "Who are you?" She'd been able to shield herself from trouble by changing her name. Were these two men reporters out for a story or con men, thinking they could scam a helpless woman out of what little she still had?

Skeet pulled out his credentials. "I'm Agent Perkins with the FBI. This is my friend, Detective Cooper from the Chicago Police Department. I'm hoping we can have just a few minutes of your time."

Coop held out his badge, so the skittish woman could inspect it. "If you want to verify further," Coop offered. "Just call the non-emergency number in the phone book and the dispatcher can verify my employment."

Beth considered. It could be a trap; but, the identification looked real enough. "No, come on in." She pushed open the screen door, moved to the side, and indicated they should come inside. "Feel free to have a seat," she motioned to a couch. "It's modest but comfortable."

"Thank you, ma'am," Coop moved forward and settled into a large, rose covered lounge chair. Skeet followed and settled onto the couch.

Beth moved slowly forward and lowered her body onto the edge of a second chair. "Can you tell me what this is about?"

"We are actually here to ask you about your nephew," Skeet took the lead. "We were wondering if you've seen him lately."

Beth frowned. "Has Eddie done something wrong? I mean, if you're the police he must have done something bad. He's supposed to be out looking for a job."

"So," Coop asked. "He is visiting you, then?"

"Um... yes," Beth said slowly. "He stopped in just over a week ago and asked if he could stay with me for a few days. I was happy to help, I mean, he's family. But, when he seemed to settle in for the long haul... I had to ask him to help out. I insisted he had to find a job, to pay some rent. I hated to do it, but I... well, I needed the money."

Subterfuge

"We are aware of the situation Mrs. Proctor," Skeet used her married name to make it clear they knew who she was. "I'm sorry things have been so difficult the past fourteen years."

"How did you…" Beth paused. "I guess you're the police so that's how." She let out a long, deep sigh. "Well, then you know why I couldn't carry a grown man while he wandered the city doing who knows what all day."

"We understand," Coop pushed. "So, did Eddie get a job?"

"I don't think he did," Beth admitted. "But, when I asked, told him I needed the money, he pulled out two one-hundred-dollar bills and handed them to me. I know his family has money; but, if he's carrying that kind of cash around, why in the world did he need to flop here?"

"I assume he's not home," Skeet asked casually.

"No," Beth shook her head. "He was supposed to be. He promised he would be here when the repairman arrived. That was two hours ago. He didn't show. The company called and said I had to reschedule because nobody was home. Said if I was a no-show again, they'd fine me for the inconvenience."

"Is there any chance we could check out Eddie's room," Skeet asked.

Beth hesitated. "I suppose that would be okay. But, can you tell me what he did? I mean, should I be worried? I think that boy has a temper. He hasn't done anything to me… not yet; but, sometimes, when he looks at me… well, I'm sure I'm just a paranoid old woman but he makes me uncomfortable sometimes."

"I think Eddie can be dangerous," Coop answered. "When he has a mind to be. I'd suggest you call us if he returns. I'm not saying he'd hurt you or anything but just to be safe, I think it would

194

best if we had a talk with him. You never know, maybe he's not involved in our case and we can clear things up and get out of your hair."

"Oh, that would be nice," Beth stood and made her way to the guest room where Eddie had been sleeping. "I don't think he has much in here, but you're welcome to look around."

The two investigators conducted a cursory search of the room. They were careful not to invade the privacy of the occupant, not wanting anything they found to be thrown out by a good lawyer. They hit the jackpot almost immediately. A nearly empty journal laid open on the small table next to the window. The handwriting matched the other two journals they already had in custody. That was enough to get a warrant for a more thorough search. Coop secured the area while Skeet headed to the car to make a call.

"Excuse me," Beth stepped back into the doorway. "I'm just wondering, well that officer seemed to be in a hurry. Did you find something I should be concerned about? I mean, well... I live alone and I..."

"Mrs. Proctor," Coop began.

"Oh, you can call me Beth," the woman interrupted.

Coop smiled. "Beth it is. Do you have a friend or a relative close by? Somewhere you could spend the evening? I don't want you to worry; but, I think it would be better if you went to visit a friend for a few days."

"Then he did do something bad?" Beth whispered. "Okay, I'll call Dottie and see if I can bunk at her place for a while. Um... well, should I stay there until you arrest Eddie? Is it safe to come back if I forget something? Oh, this is just awful." Beth put her hand to her throat, clearly distressed.

Subterfuge

"There's nothing to indicate he will hurt you," Coop tried to reassure her. "I don't want to scare you; but, we think Eddie can be dangerous. This is just a precaution. Here, this card has my cellphone number on it. If you forget something and you don't feel safe coming back here alone, you call me. I'll be right over to meet you and I'll wait while you retrieve anything you want. You've been through so much turmoil already. We just want to make sure you don't have to endure anything else. Okay?"

"Alright," Beth nodded. "I'm going to go call Dottie. You do whatever you need to in here, it's my house and I give you permission."

"I'm afraid when Eddie gave you money to stay here, it muddied the waters a bit," Coop supplied. "Agent Perkins is getting a warrant just to make sure it's legal. We're fine here, you go call Dottie and pack a bag. Everything is going to be okay, I promise."

"I guess I should have said no," Beth decided. "When he showed up on my doorstep and asked for a place to stay for a few days, I should have just made an excuse and said no."

"He's family," Coop was cringing inwardly at the suggestion. Knowing Eddie Hill, if Elizabeth had said no, she'd probably be dead right now. She'd made the right decision and he'd explain that to her, once they had Eddie in custody. He'd explain everything once Eddie was no longer a threat.

* * * *

The search of the guest room took less than an hour. The warrant on the other hand took nearly two before a judge would sign off. They were all frustrated at the lack of progress. Skeet called

196

in a forensics team to go over every inch of the room. He was hoping they might find a few particles that would help Krueger narrow down a location, the same as he did in Houston. The downside of that, Dumas now knew about Elizabeth Newton. Skeet worried his boss would interfere with his progress; but, there was no getting around it. And this way, nobody could say Skeet wasn't cooperating with the Bureau or accuse him of withholding information. If Burns would just call back, Skeet would be in the clear on all of it. Where was Stan, anyway?

It was late in the evening when Skeet and Coop made their way back to the loft. They were both dragging from lack of sleep; but, neither man was willing to rest yet. Angela needed them, they could catch up later — once she was located.

"Any luck?" Rowdy asked the instant they entered the room.

"Not really," Skeet admitted. "I had Krueger and his team gather up a few particles. If we're lucky, they're unique; but, I think that's asking a bit too much at this point. He came through for us in Houston. Two in a row… that's unlikely."

"We'll hope for a miracle," Fulmer said groggily. "I'm not finding anything in the system as far as property. Clearly, the Proctors didn't have the funds to afford more than their house."

"Yeah," Coop settled into one of Rowdy's lounge chairs. "And, Beth wasn't happy Eddie took her car. She rarely drives it because she can't afford another one. She rides the bus to and from work to save on mileage and wear and tear. She's really regretting her kindness where that guy is concerned."

"She's lucky she was kind," Skeet added. "If she'd rejected him, she'd be dead. I have no doubt about that."

"I agree," Coop sighed. "It hit me the instant she said she should have turned him away. I realized, if she crossed him, she would be dead. It helped me to accept the stress I was causing her

Subterfuge

by forcing her out of the house. She's probably okay; but, now that we've been there, I couldn't take the chance."

"I don't think he's going back there," Skeet said defeated.

"Why?" Rowdy asked.

"Because I think he saw your truck, passed by the house and found a new hole to hide in. He might even be staying in the same place he's holding Ange. That's what he usually does. So far, Chicago has been different; but, that's only because he had Aunt Beth to fall back on."

"Sorry," Rowdy frowned. Had he just scared away their only chance of catching this guy?

"Not your fault," Skeet assured him. "It would have happened, eventually. This guy spooks easily. Something as simple as passing a squad car on the roadway would have sent him packing."

"So," Fulmer asked. "What do we do now?"

"I'm going to go through the new diary," Skeet decided. "Maybe there's a clue in there somewhere. It's a lot shorter than the others; but, he tends to document everything."

"Monroe sent his final report over while you guys were dealing with Beth," Rowdy added. "I'm still going through it; but, so far, I haven't found anything that will help us out here."

"I'll keep looking for property," Fulmer decided. "But, I'm going to focus on abandoned places within this area." He punched a few buttons and the map they'd been working from popped onto the television. It was the same, all the previous markers were still there, but Ryan had color coded it and highlighted a circle that covered a two-mile radius.

"Why that area?" Skeet stood and moved to get a better look.

"Because, that hits every place we know he's been," Fulmer explained. "Here's the warehouse," he moved the mouse to point at a marker. "Here is Beth's house, the electronics store where he bought the locks." He continued to move the mouse around the screen.

"What is this?" Skeet asked.

"That is something I've been working on while you guys were gone today," Ryan stood and moved to the screen. "This line here," he pointed to a yellow line that ran through the city. "That's the route the kid took, the one you found inside the warehouse. He said he got that necklace out of Beth's garbage; but, she disputes that."

"But, Eddie could have placed it in there without her knowing about it," Rowdy challenged.

"Could have," Ryan agreed. "And, it's even likely he did," Fulmer consented. "But, what if he got it somewhere else?"

"Okay," Coop nodded. "So, you mapped out his regular route. The one he described to Rowdy."

"Yeah," Ryan nodded. "And, that spot right there jumped out at me."

"Because?" Skeet said impatiently.

"Because, that's the only place in this area that sells caramel mocha cappuccinos."

"Good call," Skeet commended his friend.

"Why is that significant?" Rowdy asked.

"Because when we located his lab in New Orleans, our suspect left several insulated cups behind. We had all of them

Subterfuge

tested and every one had remnants of the same drink it in. The same in Houston. We interrupted him there; but, he had tossed the empty cups in the corner and forgot them."

"So," Coop considered. "Our guy is addicted to a very specific drink. Why not clean up after he's done? It was sloppy to leave something that specific behind."

"Because he's rich," Rowdy decided.

"Meaning?" Coop asked.

"He doesn't clean up after himself," Rowdy rolled his eyes. "He has servants to do that. Plus, he never believed anyone would find his labs. He probably doesn't even know they found that one in Louisiana. He only knows about Houston because he wasn't finished. Every vacant building he's set up in probably has that same discarded garbage in the corner."

"Okay," Skeet decided. "So, we go with Ryan's map for now. Let's figure out which of these empty buildings you guys didn't search and we'll narrow it down from there."

The group went to work, trying to find a needle in a haystack.

* * * *

Eddie Hill, the man the media had dubbed "The Scientist," made his way through the dark tunnel with ease. It was early, he'd left his motel at four that morning. Anticipation was flowing through him and he couldn't wait to get started. He could admit the previous evening was difficult. Once he reached the motel; bribed the clerk for a room; and settled in; he headed straight for the bathroom. The moment he saw the damage to his face, he had lost it. What once had been beautiful, flawless skin was now distorted. His entire face was bright red, raw and hideous. Large blisters had already begun to form on his nose and his chin. He was in so much pain, he could barely function. For over an hour; he didn't. He just dropped onto the bed and sobbed. Fury soon replaced sorrow; and rather than feeling sorry for himself, he began to plot his revenge. It was nearly midnight when he finally finished his new tool and settled into bed. He needed to be rested when he started his next experiment.

Anticipation and excitement had him up at three. He carefully showered, lowered his new tool into the trunk of the car and headed out of the lot just after four. It was time to show Mrs. Perkins just who was in charge here. It was time to make her pay for the pain and the agony she had caused him. He patted his pocket and grinned. He was going to tape this session. Then, when he finished, he'd mail the recording to Agent Perkins. He wished he could be there, to see the grief and the horror on his enemy's face when he heard the agonizing screams of his wife. But, that was impossible. He'd settle for the screams, and the knowledge it was his actions that would cause the interfering couple unspeakable misery. They were helpless specimens in his universe. He was in control now and he was going to enjoy testing out his fancy new instrument.

He parked the car up the road in the abandoned church parking lot and made his way to the entrance of his private sanctum. So far, the gangsters hadn't returned. He subconsciously ran his hand over the jacket pocket that contained his uncle's pistol. His pistol now. Parking his vehicle up the road, instead of here out in the open seemed to hide the fact he was still working in the area. Hopefully, his luck would hold, and he could finish his experiments without interruption. He smiled, anxious to begin. He was so excited for the day's work he could hardly contain himself. Agent Perkins' wife was going to regret the trouble she had caused. She would pay for injuring him yesterday; but, she was also going to pay

Subterfuge

for the rest. She'd been nothing but trouble since the moment he laid eyes on her. Agent Perkins was going to rue the day he got in the way of progress.

Eddie made his way carefully through the secluded wilderness. When he reached the outer door to his temporary lab, he shifted the cheap backpack that contained his new tools and punched in his secret code to release the lock. The bag was inexpensive and embarrassing, but necessary. He had purchased it at a rundown store next to the revolting hotel he'd been forced to stay in. Just another thing Angela Perkins was going to pay for today. He tried to push his irritation aside and focus on his upcoming experiment. He couldn't wait to get started. With the sturdy lock firmly attached, he wouldn't have to worry about intruders. He could savor the moment, enjoy her agony and revel in the knowledge he was once again in control. He slid the door open a few inches, just enough to silently maneuver his body inside. Darkness surrounded him the instant he heard the soft click. He was safe now; he thought as he started down the long corridor that led to his lab.

He missed his equipment, missed the toys he'd assembled over the past couple years; but, watching the effects of the creative new implement he'd developed the previous evening would make up for the loss... at least a little. He found himself walking just a little bit faster in anticipation of what was coming. When he finally stepped into the room and spotted the woman on the platform, he was disappointed. She was still wide awake and so far, she'd been able to avoid the pool of acid just inches away from her perch. With a sigh, he set the large backpack on the ground and moved toward the camera system. The thing had stopped working and he couldn't figure out why. The electricity in this section of the tunnel was spotty at best. After fiddling with two of the devices for several minutes, he finally gave up. He could have his fun without them. As he turned to face his research specimen, he grinned and rubbed his hands together. "Let the fun begin," he said softly and unzipped the pack.

Angela watched, terrified as the man pulled one item after another out of his backpack. She knew she was in trouble, knew she'd be lucky to survive whatever he had in store for her, knew Skeet was going to be devastated when he finally located her lifeless body. Her time had run out she didn't have any more tricks up her sleeve. But, by the look on her captor's face —a face that was mangled and raw because of her — it was clear he had a few tricks up his. Whatever he had in store for her, Angela knew it was going to be awful.

Eddie pulled the last item from the bag and frowned. Where was the connector? His new tool wouldn't work without it. He paused to carefully remember every move he'd made since he got out of bed. That's when he realized he left the mechanism in the backseat of his car. *Stupid, stupid, stupid.* He'd have to risk going back out there. It was dangerous, the thugs could be waiting; but, it couldn't be helped. He didn't have the means to make the tool work without it.

He turned and focused on his prisoner, considering his options. The woman was wily and unpredictable. She should be out of reach, unable to sabotage the rest of the parts... but he wasn't willing to trust that. She had surprised him before, accessed areas she shouldn't be able to access. He still hadn't found his water bottle and that fact infuriated him. He smiled as the solution came to him. Reveling silently at just how clever he was, he searched in his bag for the solution. He found it in the outer pocket of the backpack. It was a tiny tool he had crafted months ago. The long tube provided a means to incapacitate his victims from a distance. He liked to con his women into his waiting van; but, when that didn't work, he'd just shoot them with a tainted dart and accomplish the same thing. It was quick and easy, and best of all... there was no risk involved.

Subterfuge

Eddie carefully slipped one tiny dart with an exceptionally sharp point from his metal case. He'd designed that as well, a seemingly innocuous container that held a collection of darts, color coded based on dosage. To the casual observer, it just looked like an expensive set of recreational darts. To him, it was a carefully arranged cornucopia of poisons; another tool he could utilize to accomplish his objective. He smiled as he twisted off the top and slid the small, tainted tip into the hollow tube. Inhaling a deep breath, he lifted the system to his lips and blew — hard. The dart flew across the expanse and lodged securely in the woman's upper arm. Not a bullseye by any means, but it would still do the trick. Now, he waited. It took less than a minute and the woman was paralyzed.

Eddie moved quickly, knowing the dosage was low and the effects wouldn't last long. He rolled his subject onto her back and grinned. The woman was in a state of panic, her pupils were frantically moving from side to side and her skin felt clammy and cold. She couldn't move; but, her body's natural response to fear was obvious. He just wished the woman would scream. It was unfair... the fact that she was able to deny him that pleasure. He shrugged, unconcerned. That would change — once he got started, the woman wouldn't be able to stop herself. And, he planned to catch every blood curdling sound on tape. He wanted Agent Skeeter Perkins to hear, loud and clear, every terrified shriek, every painful moan, every curse. He wanted Perkins to suffer; he wanted Perkins to pay.

He was humming as he gathered up the pieces of his new toy. He continued to hum as he slid one thin strip of tubing up the woman's left nostril. He actually started to sing as he worked on securing another strip inside her right nostril. Once that was complete, he wrapped a thick rubber brace around her neck and fastened each end to the platform. It wasn't as tight as he had hoped; but, it should still work. It would confine her movement enough to make it impossible to escape. Now, he just needed the connector that attached the tubes to electricity. After glancing around the large open space one last time, he slipped out the door and headed for his car. He felt like a kid on Christmas; giddy, anxious and more than ready to begin. He'd have to start with a mild shock and see how she coped with the jolt to her nervous system. Once he reached the perfect level, he'd be vindicated. Mrs. Perkins would finally give him what he craved, she'd scream and scream and scream. He was practically skipping as he made his way down the long corridor to a junction that led to a shorter tunnel. The passageway would eventually take him back to the exterior door that led outside. He started to open the first door and froze.

* * * *

It was five in the morning when Coop jolted awake. An idea had surfaced in his sleep and he wanted to check it out. He silently made his way to his brother and gave his shoulder a slight nudge. Rowdy bolted upright and looked around in a panic. When he spotted his brother, he relaxed. Coop was holding his finger over his lips and motioning for him to join him in the hallway.

"What's up?" Rowdy asked immediately.

"I had an idea and I want to check something out," Coop whispered. "Grab your jacket and let's go."

"Shouldn't we wake up Skeet?"

"Not yet," Coop glanced back and knew he was making the right decision. Skeet hadn't slept in days and this could be a wild goose chase. "If it pans out, I'll call."

Subterfuge

Rowdy frowned but decided to follow his brother's lead on this one. Once they were in Coop's car, flying down the highway he demanded answers.

"I want to check out the old tunnel," Coop admitted. "The one where Stanton was injured, and that other man was killed. I realized that incident happened the same summer Eddie was sent to Chicago to stay with his secret relatives. He was here when it all happened. What if he was in the tunnel with his uncle when it happened? It could have been the trigger that started all of this."

"At fourteen," Rowdy realized. "That kind of carnage might have fascinated a sociopath."

"Exactly," Coop nodded. "Beth didn't say anything about that, but we didn't really talk about Stanton or the incident. I thought it would be too difficult for her."

"But isn't that kind of a long shot?" Rowdy wondered. "I mean, he wasn't close to the uncle. He may not have cared about the accident."

"That's what I thought at first," Coop told him. "The idea hit in my sleep and I woke up thinking, naw… it couldn't be that easy."

"But?" Rowdy asked.

"But, then, I remembered what Skeet said about the trouble with the power," Coop explained. "What if those tunnels are having issues with the power grid because this maniac is tapping into the system to power his... setup? Skeet said he always runs electricity to a platform where he chains his prisoners. The random spikes and shortages could be a result of the electrical energy needed when his victim is shocked — either during a torture session, or if she tries to escape. Then, there's the electronic door locks and he'd need some sort of light source."

"Shit," Rowdy realized his brother might be onto something. "Drive faster. If you're right, we need to save that woman before it's too late."

* * * *

Skeet nearly fell off his chair when the ringing of his phone jolted him awake. At first, he was annoyed at the interruption. He instantly grew furious at himself. Angela was counting on him and he'd fallen asleep... again. He snatched up the phone and uttered a groggy "Hello."

"I have news, but it's not good," Krueger said in greeting. "I just finished analyzing the last sample. There's nothing in there that's going to pinpoint a location. There's nothing in there that would even pinpoint what side of the city the man has been visiting. I've got sand, I've got bread crumbs, I've got clay. I've got shit, Skeet. I'm sorry, but any or all of that could have come from anywhere. The park, the mall, the beach — even the tunnels that run below the city. I tested it twice just to be sure."

Skeet sat straighter in his chair. Could it really be that easy? "Thanks," he said absently as he considered. "I appreciate all your hard work. Go home, catch a few hours. You deserve it after pulling an all-nighter."

"Why are you taking this so well?" Krueger asked, suspicious now.

"I think I have an idea," Skeet admitted. "I've gotta' go. I'll let you know if it pans out." He disconnected before his friend could press him further. As he stood, the chair tipped over and crashed to the ground.

Ryan Fulmer fell out of his chair and landed with a thud on the hard floor. "What...?" he asked as he rubbed his tired eyes.

"Go back to sleep," Skeet suggested. "Any idea where the Cooper brothers went?"

"Naw," Ryan pushed himself off the floor. "I must have dozed off, sorry about that."

"If you find them," Skeet decided. "Tell them I'm heading over to the tunnels. The place where Stanton was injured. I want to check it out, see if maybe..."

"See if someone could hide a prisoner inside?" Fulmer suggested.

"Yeah," Skeet took one more look around, then left the room, wondering where the brothers were this early in the morning.

* * * *

"You know he's in there," Rowdy accused. "We have to call Skeet. He has a right to know what we're doing."

"What if I'm wrong?" Coop asked. "Then we get his hopes up and dash them again."

"What if you're right?" Rowdy disagreed. "You know we're right. The door has one of the new locks attached. And, Skeet has a right to be here when we rescue his wife."

"You sure that's a good idea?" Coop countered. "What if she's... well, what if it's not a rescue?   What if it's a recovery?   Do you honestly think he should see that?"

"She's alive," Rowdy was sure of it.   She had to be.   Skeet would never survive if she wasn't.   "Anyway, it doesn't matter. We need to call him, anyway."   They both glanced up when a vehicle pulled down the short dirt drive.

"How did he know where we were?" Rowdy wondered.

"What are you two doing here?" Skeet demanded.

"Ask Coop," Rowdy answered instantly.   "This was his idea. I just came along for the ride."

"Coop?"

"I nodded off, I guess we all did," Coop began.   "Anyway, something hit me, and I woke with a new idea.   Maybe a new lead, but I wanted to check it out, see if it was plausible before I shared it."

"And what did you decide?" Skeet wanted to be mad, but he'd done the same thing.

"I decided someone has accessed this tunnel system recently."

"He's in there?" Skeet asked. "I was right.   It makes sense and it should have been obvious."

"What makes sense?" Rowdy asked, wanting to know what had brought the agent running.

"Krueger analyzed the samples and said they didn't have anything unique," Skeet provided.   "Said they could have come from anywhere, even in the tunnels.   That's when I realized it was the perfect hiding spot.   The secretary said nobody goes anywhere near this section of tunnel these days. They deemed it unsafe after that section collapsed. And, it would hold a great amount of significance to the guy, wouldn't it?" Skeet frowned. "Why are you here? What came to you while you napped?"

"Partially that," Coop admitted. "I realized the accident happened the same summer Eddie was visiting. It could have been the trigger."

"I agree," Skeet frowned. "Why didn't we realize that sooner?"

"Because we're all exhausted and running on empty," Rowdy provided. "But Coop also realized there could be a connection with the power issue. Skeet, you said he uses electricity on his victims. What if…"

"He's the one messing with the power grid," Skeet nodded. "He's the reason the system is acting up. He's in there and so is my wife. Let's go find them. We need to check out the area, see if we can find the right door."

"We already found it," Rowdy admitted.

"How do you know for sure?"

"The lock," Coop said soberly. "It's the same kind as he put on the warehouse. Fulmer said we were missing two. One is on the exterior door at the end of that pathway."

"I still have the code," Skeet turned and flung open his car door. He tossed papers aside for several seconds before he grabbed the document he wanted. "I have the master, let's go."

"Wait," Coop held up a hand. "We need to discuss a few things before we go inside."

"I'm not sitting out here hashing out a plan while my wife is inside fighting for her life," Skeet objected. He tried to push past Coop, but Rowdy blocked his way.

"For starters," Coop continued. "This is my case. I'm in charge, no matter what happens in there. You follow my lead. That's my one condition. You aren't even supposed to be here. You're on administrative leave. You have to agree to do what I say, without argument before we go any further."

"Or what?" Skeet asked in challenge.

"Or I'll handcuff you to my car and go in alone," Coop said flatly.

"Okay," Skeet relented. He was going inside, and he was pretty sure Andy Cooper was not bluffing. "I'll follow your lead. Now, get out of my way. I'm going to find my wife."

Coop grabbed a rifle case off the backseat of his car and the trio started up the long pathway. The trail was mostly uphill, a half-mile hike that dipped and turned before leveling out a few yards from a large wooden door that was supposed to be padlocked. The lock had been cut and discarded haphazardly on the ground below. In its place was a shiny new, electronic lock.

Skeet moved forward and quickly punched in the master code. He was holding his breath, fearful it wouldn't work until the red light turned to green. He shoved open the door and stepped inside.

"You do not draw your gun unless it is absolutely necessary," Coop called out. "We still haven't located Burns. I'm assuming he's not available if we run into trouble."

Skeet nodded absently, he was surveying the area, taking in every aspect, looking for possible danger as he waited just inside the doorway. His heart was pounding in his chest as he moved further

Subterfuge

into the damp, dark cavern. Angela was somewhere inside, he knew it, could feel it with every fiber of his being. Adrenaline pulsed through him and he wanted to run, wanted to fly down the tunnel calling her name, would have if he wasn't a cop — one that knew better. If the Scientist was inside, if he was within reach of Angie, he'd kill her the instant he heard Skeet coming. They had to be smart, had to search the area silently moving from one tunnel to the next until they located the right section. Skeet was sure being so close, but so far away... was going to kill him.

Coop cautiously stepped into the dimly lit tunnel system and glanced around. He let the outer door shut quietly behind him. In the silence, the soft click of the latch was more like a loud boom that seemed to echo forever as it traveled the empty space that surrounded them. The tunnel was narrow but appeared to be well built. Tiny lights were mounted to walls a few yards apart. They put off enough light to identify the pathway, but not enough to illuminate the tunnel. It was still dark, well... dim and filled with shadows and crevasses. Coop was on high alert and he knew his brother was feeling the same apprehension. There were too many places a killer could hide in this place, too many darkened corners that would be perfect to set up in and wait... a carefully planned ambush would be easy to orchestrate and difficult to detect before it was too late. Coop sighed, frustrated by the irregular fluttering of the tiny lights that were mounted to the walls — they were messing with his vision. He instantly realized the intermittent flickering was just another indication they were on the right track. Their killer was tapping into the electrical grid, pulling power from other areas to activate his equipment. Time was running out for their victim, they had to move. He motioned for Rowdy to proceed, then followed his brother down the tunnel. He unsnapped his holster and drew his pistol, holding it firmly as he lowered it to his side and moved slowly through the darkness. His left hand was securing the rifle case he had slung over his shoulder. He had a bad feeling about this; but, there was no turning back now. Angela Perkins needed them, and he was willing to run through fire to save her.

The group continued cautiously down the long corridor until they finally reached a door at the end of the tunnel. Coop glanced at his brother and saw Rowdy had drawn his weapon as well, they were both ready for danger. He turned back to address Skeet and saw the agent also had his gun in his hand. "Put that away," Coop ordered. "We've got this." He put a supportive hand on his friend's shoulder as he pushed to the front of the group, reached out, and opened the door.

Skeet slid his revolver into his pocket, but continued to hold on to it, ready for action if they ran into danger. He knew it would be risky to deploy his weapon, knew there would be a lot of questions, second guessing, and politics; but, he was a cop. He wasn't going to cower behind the two brothers and hope they would protect him. He held his breath as Coop swung open the door; then, let it out in a whoosh when he realized it was safe.

The three of them stepped into the large open space and carefully searched for possible traps. The place was huge, like a large dome. It was basically an underground cave with five doors — six if you counted the one they just exited — leading off in various directions. High above was a viewing platform of some kind. Two large chains had been fastened to the ceiling with large steel plates. They descended several feet before they reached a junction that split the chains into a triangle that attached to each corner of a large rectangular support made out of metal. There was a sturdy looking extension ladder welded to one side for easy access. Behind the platform was a large support beam made of concrete. Beneath it, there was some sort of drainage system surrounded by a concrete wall that stood about three feet tall. Again, there were flickering lights peppered throughout the room.

The way the lights were flickering reminded Rowdy of a haunted house or a spooky forest littered with lanterns. "Now what?" he asked nobody in particular. His focus landed on the closed doors. None of them sported a new, shiny lock.

"See if any of them are locked," Coop suggested.

Rowdy moved to the side and carefully tried the knob on the first door. "Locked."

Coop used his flashlight to illuminate each of the four remaining doors and their knobs. "One of those has to be unlocked," Coop surmised. "Let me get up there, on that platform and I'll provide cover while you check each door. Rowdy," he added.

"Yeah?"

"Be careful," Coop warned. "We don't know what's on the other side of any of them. I can provide cover from above; but, you're on your own down there. Don't start until I'm in position and give you the signal."

Rowdy focused on Skeet. "I know you want to assist, and if things get dicey, I won't stop you but give me some space and let me see what's going on behind door number two. You move over there behind that concrete wall. And, don't do anything stupid. We've got this."

Skeet frowned but moved forward as directed. Once he was in place, he took a minute to study his surroundings. One thing struck him almost immediately. Coop's position was perfect for three of the remaining four doors. But, one of them, the one positioned near the far corner of the room was obstructed by a large beam. If anyone exited that door, Rowdy would be in danger. Skeet shifted and slid his hand from his pocket, once again gripping his pistol firmly in his palm. Whatever the price, Skeet would protect Rowdy Cooper. If he was forced to use his weapon on their killer — he just hoped Burns could save him as promised. If not, he'd be looking for another job. But, wasn't he facing that anyway?

Coop settled onto the platform and set his rifle on the flat metal base as he searched for a sturdy section to snap a carabiner in place. As a member of SWAT, he'd learned almost immediately, that a marksman had to hold position no matter what happened around him. The carabiner was just a precaution, a safety mechanism attached to the metal platform... just in case there was trouble. The last thing he wanted to do was lose his footing and plummet to the ground when his brother needed him. This way, he could focus on his weapon and his target without the worry of a fall. Once he was snapped in, he shifted and took in the room. He had a clean shot in all directions but one. If anyone came through that far door, he'd be useless. "Rowdy," he called out as he picked up the rifle and settled into position.

"Ready?" Rowdy asked.

"Yeah, I'm in position," Coop confirmed. "But, I don't have a clean shot if anyone comes through that door over there. That support beam is in the worst possible location."

"Got it," Rowdy glanced around. "Let's deal with that one last. If I clear these other four, we'll know that's our pathway and you can back me from the ground as we enter." He moved slightly to the left and carefully slid to the side of the next door. "Ready?" he asked his brother. After a quick nod from above, Rowdy gripped the door knob and gave it forceful turn. Nothing happened, the thing was locked.

"You think maybe Eddie has Stanton's old keys?" Rowdy asked Skeet.

"No," Skeet said in answer as he watched Rowdy move to the next door. "If he did, there would be no reason to place that new lock on the outer door. That just makes things obvious and any

Subterfuge

employee that came across the obstacle would break down the door and investigate immediately. One of these corridors has to be unlocked."

* * * *

Eddie Hill's good mood evaporated immediately when he stepped into the partially open doorway. He was about to enter the large section of the tunnel that operated as a junction but hesitated. How was this possible? What was the man doing here? How did a local K9 officer find him and his hiding place? He knew it was the same K9 cop that he'd spotted days earlier at the park near his aunt's residence. He recognized him and his confident stance. Was it possible the man was there for him? How? And, why? His heart was pounding in his chest and fear nearly paralyzed him before he remembered the pistol. He reached into his large pocket and pulled out the heavy object, determined to escape... somehow. His hand was shaking as he raised the gun in the air and pulled the trigger. The gun jerked upward, and he nearly dropped it. In his effort to regain control, he accidentally fired again.

* * * *

Rowdy was studying the ground in front of the next metal barrier when all hell broke loose behind him. Someone fired a shot and the wall at least seven or eight feet to his right exploded. Particles flew in all directions as Rowdy pivoted, ducked and raised his gun. He was frantically searching for the threat when a second shot rang out. He watched in amazement as several things happened at once. Everything seemed to be moving in slow motion, but Rowdy knew in reality only a few seconds had passed before it was all over.

Eddie Hill stood inside the doorway brandishing a large caliber pistol. Rowdy realized immediately the man had fired both shots. He also knew Coop wasn't in a position to help. He turned to glance up at his brother and realized Coop was in trouble. The second shot went wild, flying upwards where it found an unlikely target. Dumb luck had it colliding with the chain that secured one side of the structure, where Coop was standing, to the ceiling. The chain shattered immediately, causing the right side of the base to fall – the entire thing tipped to one side and Coop was left dangling in the air by a single carabiner he'd attached to the railing. The platform swung violently left to right as Coop tried to steady himself and get into a position of defense.

Rowdy refocused on the shooter, adjusted his weapon and prepared to fire. Skeet beat him to it. Two shots rang out and the suspect, who was once again pointing the handgun at Rowdy, fell to the ground.

Rowdy didn't think, didn't consider the consequences, he didn't have time to think. He had to fix this and fast. He crossed the room, jumped over the concrete wall and snatched Skeet's gun out of his hand. Within seconds, he had fired off another shot. Then he turned to address his brother. "You okay up there?"

"I'm fine," Coop had stopped the momentum of his swinging perch and was now descending the ladder. Once he reached the ground, he moved in beside Rowdy. "This is a freakin' cluster of the first order. Now what?"

"Now, we find Angela," Rowdy said slipping Skeet's gun into his jacket pocket. He glanced at the federal agent and sighed. Skeet was still standing in the same position, shock and concern written all over his face. "Here," Rowdy took Skeet's elbow. "Sit down for a minute."

Subterfuge

Skeet let Rowdy push him onto the concrete wall. "I..."

"No, you didn't," Rowdy corrected. "I did."

Skeet's head shot up in surprise.

"That's right," Rowdy glanced at his brother then focused back on Skeet. "The man pointed a gun at me and I fired your weapon. The threat was neutralized."

"I can't let you..."

"It's not your choice," Coop decided. He didn't like it, didn't want his brother to face the stress and turmoil associated with an officer-involved shooting; but, it was the only solution to a seriously messed up situation; and, Rowdy had already complicated things when he fired another round from Skeet's weapon. "You agreed to follow my lead. Before we entered this tunnel system, you agreed I am in charge."

"But, that doesn't mean lying about the events that just took place," Skeet objected. "I can't lie."

"Nobody asked you to," Rowdy jumped in. "Did that man point a gun at me?"

"Yes," Skeet said slowly.

"Did I fire your weapon?"

"Yes, but..."

"Was the threat neutralized?"

"Yes," Skeet said with a sigh.

"Then, that's all you have to say. Stick to those facts and everything will be fine," Rowdy studied the fed closely.

"Eddie Hill was killed with my service weapon," Skeet told them. "How are you going to explain that?"

"I took your gun away from you before we entered the tunnel," Rowdy shrugged.

"Again, I won't lie."

"Look over there," Rowdy pointed to a door. "That's where Eddie came from and it leads to another tunnel. I have your gun. Therefore, I took your gun before you went into the tunnel."

"This is wrong," Skeet said again.

"I agree," Coop glanced at his brother then continued. "But, you just saved my brother's life. The shooting was justifiable, it was a clean case of self-defense. A textbook case. A justifiable shooting."

"So, let me present my case."

"That's just it," Rowdy objected. "You can't. The minute you announce it was you that killed that man, it muddies the waters. Skeet, the three of us know you were in the right. We know, without a doubt that there was no other option. But, do you think Dumas will see it that way? Eddie's family? Even the public and the media will question your motives. They'll crucify you, dig up everything you've ever done in your life. They'll talk to some kid that says you bullied him on the playground when you were six. The scrutiny is unnecessary. I fired your gun, the threat was neutralized, and we went on to rescue your wife. I suggest we do just that. Angela is back there, somewhere. She's waiting for you. She needs you. What she doesn't need is for you to be distracted, stressed out and under attack because a monster was killed during her rescue. You know as well as I do, if you admit that you were the one to shoot that man, your attention will be on your own survival instead of caring for your wife. I solved that problem, let it go. And, when anyone asks... I'm the one responsible for that," Rowdy pointed to the lifeless body crumpled on the ground before them. "I'm counting on you to back me on this. If you say anything, even hint that you were the one to shoot that man, you are going to cost me my job. I'll be fired, Coop will be fired, and it's possible - in the end - you will be fired as well. Is that what you want?"

"No," Skeet sighed. "I want to do the right thing."

"And, I'm telling you the right thing," Rowdy insisted. "Nothing good would come from the world knowing you took that shot. And besides, if you had waited about half a second, I would have been the one to take care of it, anyway. I would have taken that man out. It's settled, Skeet. Let's go find your wife."

"Coop?" Skeet asked as he stood, hoping the detective would back him on this one. He needed to get moving, had to find Angela, but this was important. It had to be settled, now. Dumas could be on his way to the tunnel at this very moment.

"I agree with Rowdy," Coop shook his head. "If I had a shot, I would have taken it. All three of us were prepared to fire. Bad luck had you in a better position to do it. It's my call, Skeet. You agreed to that before we came inside. Rowdy's the shooter. You just focus on Angela. Focus on helping her heal. Seriously, Skeet, it doesn't matter which one of us actually fired that weapon. All three of us would have. All three of us recognized the threat and tried to get into position, tried to stop a madman from killing my brother. As I see it, nobody needs to know who actually took him out. If it wasn't your wife back there, I'd let you deal with this —no question. We'd both let you tell the world you took down a killer. But, it is your wife, and that just complicates things. Add in the fact you are on admin leave and it makes it all a hundred times worse. Now, I need to make an attempt to call this in. At which time, my walkie will not function. Then, we need to get down that hallway and rescue the woman you love. You two go ahead, I'll catch up."

Rowdy moved forward, stepping over the lifeless body of Eddie Hill. He paused as he waited for Skeet to follow. The man was young, had his whole life ahead of him, but instead he chose to become a monster. His actions led to a premature and violent ending because he chose to torment and victimize others. Rowdy looked into the eyes of a dead man and realized, even in death, his eyes looked evil. He had to agree with crazy Gloria — he'd never look at blue eyes the same again.

Chapter Eight

It was easy to find the room where Eddie Hill was holding Angela. The door was secured with the final electronic lock Eddie had purchased in town. The instant they reached it, Skeet darted forward but Rowdy stopped him.

"You need to take a second to prepare," Rowdy warned. He glanced up and saw his brother walking briskly toward them. "We don't know what he's done to your wife and you need to prepare yourself for the worst. She is going to need you. For her, Skeet, you have to be strong. No matter what we find in there. Can you do that?"

Skeet swallowed hard and barely registered Coop moving in beside him. He couldn't speak, so he just nodded.

"Let's go," Coop ordered. "Rowdy, you first. Skeet and I will follow. Skeet, punch in the code."

The three men stepped into the horrible room and froze. They spotted Angela Perkins immediately. She was dressed in a flimsy t-shirt and panties, her tiny form was positioned on a large platform, the toxic liquid less than an inch away from her beautiful face. Some kind of rubber collar was wrapped around her neck; then, attached to the surface of the raised edge that held her unmoving body. There were thick leather manacles strapped to her wrists and ankles. Chains hung from each one, extended outward, and were bolted securely to the wall behind her with an electrical line running to a small box. Skeet knew the layout all too well. His stomach clenched in agony as he imagined the pain and torture his wife had endured.

Skeet called out to her; but, Angela didn't move. He rushed forward, careful not to bump or disturb the platform. If the liquid splashed, at all, it would land right in his wife's face.

"Let's get her off of there," Coop suggested. "She's unconscious, but still alive."

"No," Skeet held out a hand to stop him. "That liquid is going to be highly toxic acid. And, he always connects the chains to electricity. He uses an electrical fence kit similar to what cattle ranchers use to keep horses or livestock inside a particular area. It should be low voltage, but we have to disengage the system before we can move her. It's probably not lethal, it wasn't with the others, but it will make it very difficult to get her free. He took a step closer and carefully removed the offensive tubes sticking out of his wife's nostrils. Angela moaned, but still didn't move.

"Okay," Rowdy began to search for the power source. It took him a minute; but, he finally located it. It was easy to disengage, even though he had no idea what he was doing. Once the power was shut down, he moved back to the platform and studied Skeet's wife, and the rubber binding. He could instantly see that the collar was larger than her neck. He reached in his pocket and pulled out a Benchmade tactical knife. Within seconds,

Subterfuge

he had carefully slipped the blade under the rubber binding, with the flick of his wrist, Angela was free. Well, free from the offensive rubber thing securing her neck to the platform. Now, for the chains.

Coop spotted the bolt cutters lying on the floor a few feet from the Scientist's work area. He moved to retrieve them and let out a frustrated growl when he realized they were broken.

"Skeet?" Angela moaned. Her voice was raspy and barely recognizable. Her mouth was so dry, and she wasn't sure her husband was really there. Was this some sort of dream? A hallucination brought on by the drugs that man had shot into her? "Is that you?"

"Yeah, baby," Skeet answered. "I'm here. Don't move, we need to find a way to cut off the chains."

Angela swallowed and frowned. "I broke the bolt cutters," she croaked. "Kind of liked my fingers and wanted to keep them."

Coop laughed. "Good thinking." He started to glance around, determined to find a way to get the woman free.

Rowdy had already searched the entire area and knew they were screwed. There wasn't anything inside this room that would open those chains. Then, he had an idea. "Hill unchains his victims when he's finished."

"Right," Skeet frowned, not sure where Rowdy was going with this.

"That means, he has the key... readily available at all times. He would want to unhook the girl when she died and hook up his next victim," Rowdy knew he was right. "Wait here, I bet he has a key ring in his pocket. I bet he has the key on him."

"I'll go," Coop offered. "You stay here."

"Naw," Rowdy moved to the door. "I've got this. You're the investigator... investigate. This should only take me a minute." The instant he stepped through the doorway, he broke into a run. The sooner they got those chains off Angela, the sooner Skeet and his wife could get out of that awful room.

Skeet looked up, relieved when he saw Rowdy return. The brilliant man was holding the keys in the air with one finger. "Let's try these."

Rowdy moved forward and studied the lock, then began to sift through the keys on the ring, settling on the fourth one in; a small silver key that looked like it would fit the tiny padlock. He slid the key into the hole and held his breath as he tried to turn it clockwise. They all heard a tiny click as the locking mechanism slid open. Within seconds, Angela's left arm was free. Rowdy went to work on the other locks and soon had Angela completely free of her bindings.

Skeet lifted his wife off the platform, cradled her in his arms, and headed for the door. The instant they were out of that repulsive room, he slid down the wall and settled onto the floor. Angela was nestled in his lap as he rocked her against him. She was sobbing now; uncontrollable tears were running down her face. Skeet's eyes began to water; but, he quickly blinked the moisture away. He had to be strong, needed her to know it was okay to fall apart, and he desperately needed her to know he was sorry; and, that he would be there for her— always. "I'm so sorry, baby. I am so sorry. I am never leaving you alone again. I'm staying right here, I promise. I'm never leaving you alone, never leaving town without you. I've got you now. You're safe and I'm never going to leave your side."

Angela knew she should argue with that. She knew Skeet's job depended on his ability to travel; but, she couldn't. Right now,

Subterfuge

she needed to know she was safe. She needed to know her husband would always be there for her. So, she remained silent as she continued to weep, as she continued to hold onto him with the last bit of strength she had.

Coop silently made his way around the room. There wasn't much here, just hideous tools and that horrible platform. He wasn't going to deal with the acid or the tools. The feds could deal with all of this. The killer was dead, and his victim had been rescued. Eddie Hill couldn't hurt another soul. Coop didn't feel bad about that. As he glanced around the room one last time, the only thing he regretted was not killing this monster himself. Anger flowed through him, and for the first time since his brother fired that shot and voiced his outrageous plan... Coop knew they were doing the right thing. Angela Perkins was going to need her husband. She was going to need his undivided attention and admitting he was the one that shot Eddie Hill would be a needless distraction. One Skeeter Perkins couldn't afford and didn't deserve. He still didn't like knowing his brother would be grilled, judged and condemned for his actions; but, he supported Rowdy's decision. He was going to do everything in his power to make the next few hours a little easier.

Coop and Rowdy stepped out of the room and spotted Skeet and his wife on the floor. Rowdy moved forward and crouched in front of the couple. "We don't have much time," he began. "I'm sure word is out by now. Some citizen probably called in a shots-fired call and the whole world is on their way. Especially, after Coop's failed attempt to contact dispatch. You should take a minute, give your wife your dry shirt and get rid of that thing she's wearing. It's torn, filthy and soaked all the way through. Angela has to be freezing. We'll be right around the corner when you're finished.

Rowdy straightened and the two brothers made their way around the corner and down the hall.

Coop stopped, shifted and leaned against the wall, bending his left knee to rest his foot against the vertical surface. He studied his brother for several seconds before he let out a long sigh.

"Don't try to talk me out of this," Rowdy leaned against the opposite wall. "We both know it's the right thing to do."

"You ready for this?" Coop asked. "It's going to get pretty intense. They're going to ask you the same questions over and over. They'll try to make you slip up and say something different, fumble your story, and relay things in a different order. You have to be ready."

"I've got this," Rowdy assured him. "As long as you and Skeet stick to the story, we can pull this off. You know it's what has to be done. And, I don't think we should talk about this again." He glanced up when Skeet rounded the corner with his wife. He had removed his button-down dress shirt, the type he always wore, and was now sporting a plain white t-shirt and a jacket. Angela was wearing the button down and it swamped her; but, she was covered completely and no longer shivering. "Ready?"

"Let's go," Skeet continued down the hallway. "And, for the record, I agree. We never breathe a word of what you two were talking about again. We stick with the plan and move forward."

"Great idea," Rowdy pushed himself off the wall. "Glad you finally climbed aboard the Common Sense Express. Just remember it's a one-way ticket."

Skeet gave Rowdy a warning look and continued through the door. He stepped over Eddie Hill's lifeless body without even a sideways glance and made his way into the second tunnel.

Subterfuge

Coop stepped out of the exterior door and sighed. He couldn't say he was surprised to see SSA Dumas walking rapidly toward them; but, he could say he was annoyed. The federal agent was approaching the tunnel entrance from a second trail. Coop glanced around, relieved to see Skeet was nowhere in sight. All of their lives were about to get complicated. He just hoped they held up in interrogation because the look on the man's face screamed fury, disappointment and retaliation. He was not happy the three people he had booted from his team had brought his killer down. *Too bad.*

"Cooper," Dumas said in greeting. "Explain yourself."

Well, Coop thought. At least, he dropped the mister. "You should be able to locate the crime scene easy enough. It's all yours. My case is now closed."

"Vance, Kirkwood?" Dumas called to the men that had followed him up the trail. "Take these two into custody. I want them transported to our facility and placed in separate interrogation rooms."

"Sir?" Vance asked in question.

"Do it," Dumas ordered. "Where is Agent Perkins?"

Coop and Rowdy remained silent. They were hoping Skeet could get Angela to the hospital and avoid his boss for at least a little while.

"What's going on here?" Sergeant Hammond demanded when he came around the corner and saw two officers from his department surrounded by the feds.

"You are?" Dumas sneered down his nose.

"I'm the on-scene supervisor," Hammond said calmly. "And, those are my men."

"I'm afraid you are misinformed," Dumas motioned for Vance and Kirkwood to proceed. "These two men are currently in the custody of the FBI. They will be charged with obstruction of justice as well as possible other offenses. Your department will be notified when my interrogation is complete."

"Now, you wait just a damn minute," Hammond called after Dumas. "I'm calling the Chief."

Rowdy and Coop went willingly. It wasn't Vance or Kirkwood's fault their supervisor was making a huge mistake. They were nearly to the parking lot when Rollins, the department's Range Master, blocked their path. Coop reached into his pocket and pulled out Skeet's weapon. He passed it to Rollins and told Kirkwood to wait a minute. "That's the gun that was used inside. You have a dead suspect and I think I counted five shots... two from the killer, the rest from that gun. You might want to secure that in your vehicle immediately — before Dumas gets wind I gave it to you."

"The shooter?" Rollins frowned. "Of this weapon?"

"Rowdy shot that gun," Coop nodded towards his brother. "We'll both be at the FBI offices if you need to talk to us."

"That's not..."

"What's the holdup?" Dumas demanded as he approached the group.

Rollins slipped the weapon into an evidence bag and turned to leave. He'd take Coop's advice and secure the thing before he demanded answers. He was just closing the trunk of his vehicle when Dumas approached. He slammed it shut and turned, waiting for the trouble that was sure to come.

Subterfuge

"I understand you are in possession of my evidence," Dumas said in greeting. "I must insist you return it, immediately."

"I'm afraid you have been misinformed," Rollins said as he moved past the agent and headed for his driver's side door.

"So, we're clear," Dumas fumed. "You are not in possession of an FBI service weapon that belongs to Agent Skeeter Perkins?"

Rollins slid behind the wheel. "To be clear, I do not have your evidence. Have a good day, I have work to do." He pulled away, dialing the chief as he entered the highway. Whatever happened back there, it was now seriously messed up. The FBI had just compromised their scene and interfered with their Officer-Involved Shooting protocol. Chief Griggs was not going to be happy about that, neither would the DA.

"Don't sweat it," Rowdy whispered to Vance. "I'll come quietly, you're just following orders. I get it." They silently made their way across the parking lot until they reached the agent's car. "I'll come with you as long as you leave him alone." He motioned to Skeet who was now helping his wife into a waiting ambulance. "Let him go to the hospital with his wife. Just tell the boss they were pulling out when we got here. You tried to stop them; but, it was too late."

Vance gave Rowdy a nod and motioned to Kirkwood. The two had a brief conversation then Kirkwood approached Coop and Vance returned to Rowdy.

"Nobody will bother Skeet. Nobody saw him, guess he left before we could catch him. Maybe, his wife was injured or something and the ambulance was in a hurry," Vance shrugged as if it was out of his control. Then he sobered. "I'm really sorry about this," Vance said as he opened the passenger side door.

"Don't you want me in back like the rest of the criminals?"

"No," Vance grumbled. "I want you in your own car, driving yourself to your own house to talk to your own people. But, today I don't get what I want. Get in."

Rowdy smiled and settled into the front seat. When Vance climbed behind the wheel, he held up his hands. "You gonna' cuff me?"

"Shut up," Vance grumbled as he started the engine and pulled away from the scene.

Chapter Nine

Maggie Cooper was pacing, traveling back and forth across the entire waiting room floor. Skeet had called, notified her and Ryan Fulmer that Angela had been rescued and Dumas had intercepted Rowdy and Andy Cooper in the parking lot. He asked Maggie to meet him at the hospital with a change of clothes. They had discarded Angie's old t-shirt in the hallway of the tunnel and Skeet was feeling uncomfortable and unprofessional in just the tight white under garment he was wearing beneath his jacket. Maggie had rushed upstairs, to the guest room where Skeet had been staying and tossed a clean outfit in Rowdy's old gym bag.

Now, she was worried about her choice. Agent Perkins seriously needed a fashion consultant. Every shirt in the closet was a plain, boring button-down dress shirt. She'd snatched up a white shirt with tiny red pinstripes, threw in a clean white t-shirt and drove — maybe a little too fast — to the local hospital. Now, here she was hoping she'd grabbed the right thing. Maybe, he had casual wear in a drawer she'd missed. And, where was he? She knew he'd made it here before he even called Rowdy's house. She let out a relieved breath when Skeet stepped into the room and headed straight for her.

"Thank you for this," Skeet said taking the bag from her hand.

"Uh..." Maggie glanced at the bag. "I couldn't find a sweatshirt or anything less..."

"Official?" Skeet asked. "I know, it's all I took to Rowdy's. I was working, and I can't seem to slide into a casual t-shirt and jeans the way your husband and his brother do. For me, work is work and it's important to dress the part."

"So, it's okay then?" Maggie asked, still not sure he understood what she'd brought. "The dress shirt and a clean white cotton tee?"

"It's perfect," Skeet glanced around. "I'm going to head to the restroom and change. Do you mind waiting in here for just a few more minutes? Once I've finished, we can head to Angie's room. The doctors are with her now, so there's not really any privacy up there."

"Oh, no," Maggie moved toward a chair. "I don't mind waiting. Take your time."

Skeet headed to the nearest restroom, grateful for the change of clothes. Once he was finished, he stuffed the old clothes back into the gym bag and made his way to the waiting room. The doctors should be finished by now and he was anxious to get back to his wife.

"Let me take that," Maggie reached for the gym bag. "I'll head up with you, just so I know where to find you; but, I want to get back to my house... just in case Coop calls. It's not like him to leave me guessing this way. Do you think he'll be much longer?"

Subterfuge

Skeet frowned and wondered where the Cooper brothers were. He had expected to see them here at the hospital, thought they'd follow the ambulance over... but they hadn't. Could Dumas be responsible for the delay? "Once I get settled, back in the room, I mean... I'll see if I can find them for you."

"Oh," Maggie said in surprise. "I already called. Neither Andy or Rowdy are answering their phones." Skeet's frown deepened, now he was starting to worry.

* * * *

Rowdy was seated in a small interrogation room behind a relatively small table. He'd been directed to an uncomfortable chair and left alone for the past thirty-five minutes. He was asking himself what in the world he'd gotten himself into when SSA Dumas stepped through the door.

Dumas moved confidently across the room and casually lowered himself into a second chair... the only other furniture that occupied the room. "Mr. Cooper," he began. "You were brought in today to be interviewed regarding your participation in the attempted apprehension and subsequent death of Eddie Hill. It's important for you to understand the scope of this investigation. You are being officially interviewed, anything you say can and will be held against you. Lying during this proceeding is a felony and will be punished to the fullest extent of the law. Do you understand, Mr. Cooper?"

Rowdy didn't answer. Was that supposed to be the FBI's version of Miranda? If so, it was seriously lacking.

"Mr. Cooper?" Dumas barked. "Do you understand?"

"Do you understand," Rowdy straightened. "Mr. Dumas, that I have the right to remain silent? That I have the right to have an attorney present before you begin your official questioning? Or, did you just forget that part?"

Dumas inhaled slowly and let it out, then he did it again. "Do you wish to have an attorney present, Mr. Cooper?"

"Yeah," Rowdy decided. "I believe I do."

"That's fine," Dumas stood. "But, if your attorney has not arrived by the time I'm finished with your brother, I will be booking you on the charge of obstruction of justice."

"Do I get a phone call, or should my attorney just somehow know I'm here without being notified?"

"Please provide the name of your attorney to Agent Vance," Dumas paused at the door. "He'll make the call for you."

"Great," Rowdy grinned. Dumas... and Vance for that matter was not going to like the name he was about to give them. But, Stanley Burns was an attorney and he had said if Rowdy ever needed anything...

* * * *

"Mr. Cooper," Dumas said the instant he stepped in the room.

Coop looked up and studied the federal supervisor closely. He wasn't happy. So, Dumas had stopped in to talk to Rowdy first. He wondered what his brother had done to make the man so irritated.

Subterfuge

"I can see you have the same aversion as your brother," Dumas settled into the chair. "Is it so hard to answer a simple question?"

"No," Coop shook his head. "Nobody asked one."

"You were transported to my office today because you interfered in an official investigation and you are facing obstruction of justice charges for your actions regarding the attempted apprehension of Eddie Hill and his ultimate death. Do you understand the charges?"

"Sure," Coop shrugged. "They're BS; but, I understand them fine."

"Do you also understand that, as this is an official interrogation, lying to a federal agent is a felony? Mr. Cooper, you will be charged to the fullest extent of the law if you are not completely honest with me. You will lose your job and you will go to prison. Do you understand?"

"Sure," Coop smiled. "You do understand that as a Detective I know, without hesitation, that when a federal agent jumps immediately to lying to the FBI — straight out of the shoot... his case is shit to start with?"

"Andy Cooper," Dumas fumed. "Can I call you Andy?"

"No, Mr. Dumas you may not," Coop relaxed.

"As this is an official interrogation, you will address me as SSA Dumas, are we clear?"

"And, as you clearly stated, the nature of this interrogation is in regard to my activities and my actions that occurred in my official capacity as a detective with the Chicago Police Department, you can refer to me as Detective Cooper."

"Your actions," Dumas seethed. "Were taken while you were under my supervision. You were officially assigned to my task force and you, Detective Cooper, crossed the line."

"I disagree," Coop stretched out his legs and crossed one ankle over the other. "And, didn't you forget to inform me about my other rights? Like, oh... I don't know, I have the right to remain silent and have an attorney present during this —interrogation?"

"What is it with you Coopers?" Dumas grumbled. "Do you wish to have an attorney present, Mr. Cooper?"

Awe, Coop thought. So, Rowdy demanded an attorney. What was his little brother up to? Whatever it was, it had Dumas in a tizzy. "Naw," Coop decided. "I'm good. I'll let you know if I change my mind."

"Your call," Dumas tried to sound casual; but, he was elated. He could crush this cocky detective without even breaking a sweat. "Now, back to the obstruction case. Is it true that you obtained information that could lead to the location of a serial killer and, instead of reporting it to the task force where you were officially assigned, you decided to go out alone — unsanctioned — in an attempt to apprehend the dangerous suspect on your own?"

"No, that is incorrect."

Dumas waited, silence filled the room as he waited and glared at his target. After several seconds, he couldn't stand the silence any longer. "Could you elaborate?"

"I'm afraid not," Coop said casually. Unlike Dumas, he didn't mind the silence. He was actually very accustomed to it. He used it as a tool frequently when he interrogated his suspects.

Dumas practically growled. "You were assigned to a federal task force, were you not?"

Subterfuge

Coop studied Dumas for several seconds. How to answer that question. "Throughout my career, I have been assigned to a number of specialized teams. You will need to be more specific. Can you outline the timeline in question for me? I'm afraid I'm confused."

"You know precisely what timeline I am referring to," Dumas slammed his fist on the table. "Did your department assign you to my task force immediately following the abduction of Angela Perkins? And, were you assigned to that task force when you ventured out on your own this morning."

"Is that a trick question?" Coop asked.

"No, Mr. Cooper it is not," Dumas said through gritted teeth.

"Well," Coop considered. "Then, I'm afraid I don't understand the question."

Dumas was about to respond when there was a sharp knock on the door. He stood, practically stomped to the door and swung it open. "Yes, Agent Vance?"

"Uh," Vance shifted nervously in the hallway. He wasn't entire sure what to do about Rowdy Cooper's request. "We have a problem."

"Did you contact the attorney as requested," Dumas demanded.

"Well," Vance said hesitantly. "That's the problem."

"Why is it a problem, Agent Vance?"

"Because Rowdy Cooper has requested Stanley Burns as his attorney of record and I'm not really comfortable making that call."

"What!" Dumas yelled and turned on Coop. "Do you and your brother think this is a joke?"

Coop couldn't hide his smile. He didn't even try. So, that's what his clever brother had up his sleeve. Dumas was in a bind and they both knew it. Burns was an attorney; but, Dumas couldn't call him in on this one. He also couldn't deny Rowdy's request. If Coop read the situation correctly, Dumas was the one that had gone rogue. He needed this wrapped up before Assistant Director Burns made it back to town and shipped his sorry butt to Butte, Montana.

Dumas left the room and slammed the door behind him. He stepped across the hall and marched across the room, pressing the palms of his hands on the desk as he leaned forward to invade Rowdy Cooper's space. "Either give my agent the name of your attorney or you will be questioned without one."

"I gave him the name of the attorney I want to represent me," Rowdy didn't budge. "If you are unable to reach Stanley Burns, I'm willing to give it a go. I'll just need my phone back for a minute — well, make that two."

"Stanley Burns is not going to represent you in this interview," Dumas sneered. "Give me the name of your real attorney so I can contact him."

"Burns isn't a real attorney?" Rowdy pretended to ponder that. "He told me he was. In fact, he said he passed the bar and everything."

"Burns is a real attorney and you know it," Dumas straightened. "He's just not your attorney. Give me a name, Cooper."

"I think I'll stick with Stanley Burns," Rowdy decided. "I haven't known him long; but, he does come across as competent. Yeah, I'm gonna' risk it and take my chances with Burns."

Subterfuge

Dumas left the room and cornered Agent Vance. "Call Burns."

"Nope," Vance shook his head. "You can write me up, you can suspend me, you can lock me in one of those interrogation rooms and forget about me for days... I am not calling Burns. I am not going to be the one to tell him you arrested the Cooper brothers. You created this mess, you make the call." He turned, walked away and never looked back.

Dumas considered, Burns was out of town. Burns was inaccessible, out of reach, unable to return calls. He'd just call Burns, leave a message and inform the cocky Mr. Cooper his request was denied. He'd have to pick someone that was currently in town, that was available, that was accessible. He was smiling as he dialed the number. His smiled turned to panic almost immediately.

Stanley had just turned his phone back on and was in the process of checking messages as the private plane left Washington headed for Chicago. He glanced at the display and recognized Dumas' number. *Now what?* He wondered. "Hello, SSA Dumas. Make it quick."

"Uh," Dumas floundered. "Sir." He cleared his throat and tried to come up with a way to break the news gently. "Well, I have good news. Angela Perkins has been located."

"Why are you calling, Dumas?" Stan rejected the menu the flight attendant tried to hand him with a shake of his head. "Where is Skeet? Where are the Cooper brothers?"

"Well," Dumas said again. "I believe Agent Perkins is at the hospital with his wife. The Cooper brothers?"

"Yes," Burns barked. "Where are they? Are they with Skeet?"

"No," Dumas cleared his throat. "I have them in custody. I'm charging them with obstruction, sir. And well, that's the reason for this call. It seems Rowdy Cooper has requested an attorney before he will agree to any questioning and he has requested uh... well, he requested you, sir."

Burns grinned. "He did, did he? Very well, I'll be there in an hour."

"What?" Dumas choked. "But, sir."

"Yes, Dumas?" Stanley was furious at his subordinate; but, he rather enjoyed the clever twist Rowdy Cooper had instigated.

"Well," Dumas regained his composure. "I believe that would be a conflict of interest. The FBI is investigating the Coopers, a high-ranking attorney with our office cannot represent one of them."

"Are you giving me orders now, Dumas?" Burns said flatly. Frank Dumas had just crossed a line he couldn't turn back from. And, it was going to land him in a remote office, in a remote city, where his toughest decision was what flavor of coffee to make in the morning.

"No, sir," Dumas tried to backtrack. "I was simply pointing out..."

"Rowdy Cooper requested my services," Burns cut him off. "Am I to understand you also have his brother, Andrew Cooper in custody?"

"I do," Dumas admitted. "He hasn't requested an attorney; but, he isn't cooperating."

Burns shook his head. Dumas was out of his league with the brothers. "You will stop all contact with those two until I arrive. Are we clear, Agent Dumas?"

Subterfuge

It didn't escape either of them, Dumas had just been verbally demoted.

"We're clear," Dumas sighed.

"Take them out of interrogation and settle Rowdy in my office to wait," Burns decided. "Coop can wait in Skeet's office. And get me an update on Angela. I want details, Dumas. I want very specific, very precise information on her condition... and Agent Perkins as well. Do you understand?"

"Yes, sir."

* * * *

Stanley Burns stepped off the elevator and spotted Troy Vance loitering in his waiting area. "Troy."

"Sir," Vance said, clearly uncomfortable.

"Before I speak with Rowdy, what can you tell me?"

"Not much, sir," Vance stood. "Clear as I can gather, Skeet, Coop and Rowdy found a lead. They headed out this morning to check it out. Somehow, they ended up in the old tunnel system, the one where Stanton Proctor was injured over a decade ago."

"Clearly, I have a lot to catch up on," Stan motioned for Vance to continue.

"Sorry, do you want me to fill you in?"

"No," Stan decided. "I'll get that information later. Tell me what happened today."

"We don't know," Vance swallowed. "Sir."

"Stop with all the sirs, Vance. What do you know?"

"The three of them went in and at some point, they were confronted by the suspect, Eddie Hill," Vance added. "The suspect had a weapon and several shots were fired. Hill is deceased, and Dumas arrested the Cooper brothers for obstruction of justice. He wanted me to snag Skeet; but, I let him go to the hospital with his wife. If you have to write me up for disobeying an order, I'll understand; but, I stand by my decision. Skeet needed to be there for Angela and that woman needed her husband."

"You're not going to be reprimanded for doing the right thing, Vance."

"Rowdy's in your office," Vance motioned to the closed door. "Dumas is mighty upset about all of it; but, I'm glad you're back. Arresting those two, it wasn't right, sir."

"I agree," Burns placed a hand on Vance's shoulder. "You should go home, get some rest. It's been a long couple of weeks. You've earned a break."

Vance, once again, glanced at the closed door.

"I've got this," he turned and placed a hand on the doorknob. "You're off the clock until tomorrow. And Vance," he added.

"Yes, sir?"

"Thank you."

"No thanks needed, sir."

Stan watched as the tired, dedicated agent stepped into the elevator. He sighed, pushed open the door and stepped inside.

"I'm thinking maybe — just maybe, I overstepped a bit," Rowdy stood and greeted the man in charge.

Subterfuge

"Don't back down now," Stan moved to sit behind his desk. "I'm enjoying this little play you orchestrated."

"I hope I didn't interrupt anything important," Rowdy continued. "I was just... well, I was messing with your agent. I think he deserved it; but, I'm now wondering if dragging you into this was a bad idea."

"I was on my way home, anyway." Burns stood and moved to the window. "Vance told me our killer is dead. What I need to know is very simple. I promised Skeet I would protect him. Do I need to protect Skeeter Perkins?"

"No," Rowdy said immediately. "I'm a little confused by this whole obstruction of justice thing Dumas is pushing. He kicked Coop off the team, you need to know that. I overheard him saying something at the scene about chain of command and Coop being out of line. Coop was no longer on the team when we entered those tunnels."

"Good to know," Burns considered. Dumas was going to pay for that misstep as well. He was very specific when he spoke with Dumas before he left. Kicking Coop off the task force was stupid on the low end, a blatant disregard for a direct order on the other. "Tell me what happened."

"Are you my attorney, or are you going to use this interview as the official record?"

"Does it matter," Stan asked.

"Of course," Rowdy smiled.

"I cannot represent you as your attorney," Stan informed him. "I'm a supervisor here at the Bureau," in the near future he might be the director. "But, this is not an official interrogation either. Just tell me what happened, and I'll figure out how to handle it from there."

Rowdy went through everything from the time Coop woke with his idea to the moment Eddie was shot. He trusted Burns; but, he wouldn't put him in a position where he might have to lie. He had no doubt, Stan would protect Skeet as much as he could. But, that wasn't good enough. "Eddie Hill fired two shots," Rowdy began. "One went wide, hit the wall a few feet from where I was standing. His second shot struck the chain that secured the platform where Coop was located. He was neutralized before he could get off another round."

"Neutralized?" Stan pressed. "Who fired the shot that killed him?"

"I fired Skeet's service weapon," Rowdy said, looking Stan square in the eyes.

Stanley Burns studied the man sitting before him. It didn't escape his notice that Rowdy hadn't answered his question. Oh, Rowdy fired Skeet's gun. The question that Stan wasn't going to ask... when did he fire it? Every instinct he had told him Skeeter Perkins had killed the man that abducted his wife. And, once again, Rowdy Cooper was stepping in to save him. "Very well." Stan stood. "Let's go get this over with. We will need your statement on record. We will also need Coop's recollection of the events that occurred today. And, when I'm finished with that... I suppose I'm going to have to make another call to Chief Griggs and grovel. I don't imagine he's too happy with the Bureau at the moment. Maybe, you could put in a good word for us, when he asks."

"Are you afraid of little ol' Chief Griggs?"

"Terrified," Stan laughed. "Let's go find your brother. How is Skeet?"

Subterfuge

"He was holding it together," Rowdy said as he stepped into the elevator. "Angela is in bad shape; but, it could be worse. I'm just grateful Dumas didn't haul him in with us. Skeet needed to be with his wife."

"I agree," Burns frowned again. "This is a cluster, Rowdy. And, I'm afraid the evening is just getting started."

Rowdy just nodded as the door to the elevator slid open and the two men stepped out. They immediately spotted Dumas, who was practically running down the hallway. *Seriously?* Rowdy thought. *Didn't the man have even an ounce of self-respect?*

Dumas glanced at Rowdy then focused on Burns. "I have a forensics expert waiting," he said in greeting. "They're prepared to test Mr. Cooper for residue."

"Why haven't you completed that test already?" Burns knew Rowdy would test positive and waiting this long could only help support Rowdy's story.

"He demanded an attorney," Dumas said soberly. "It's the policy of the Bureau not to proceed with any additional questions or procedures until his attorney arrives."

"Did Andy Cooper also request an attorney?" Burns inquired.

"No," Dumas said. "And, we tested him nearly an hour ago. The tech did find faint traces of residue on the palm of his hand; but, it can be explained by the fact he handled the gun. We don't believe he fired a shot at all today."

"Where is the weapon in question?" Burns asked.

"The weapon used in the fatal shooting of Edgar Hill was removed from the scene by Detective Cooper. He then turned said weapon over to a member of the Chicago Police Department."

Burns turned to Rowdy in question. "Since I was the one to fire the weapon, Coop tried to activate our protocol team. We have specific procedures that pertain to officer-involved shootings. The weapon used to neutralize the threat was turned over to Sgt. Rollins. He's the Range Master with our department."

"The identity of the actual shooter has not been established as of yet, sir," Dumas told Burns. "I would like our forensics team to test Mr. Cooper immediately. If there are no objections."

Burns looked at Rowdy and waited.

"I'm fine with it," Rowdy shrugged. "All you had to do was ask." He was escorted by a middle-aged woman to a back room where she conducted a thorough test, looking for gun powder residue. Rowdy knew they would find what they were looking for, he fired Skeet's gun after all. The instant he stepped from the room, Dumas jumped to his feet.

"You ready to put this on the record?" Burns asked Rowdy.

Rowdy glanced up, saw his brother and the two of them exchanged a knowing look. "I'm ready."

"Very well," Burns turned to Dumas. "I'm going to let you conduct the interview as long as it doesn't get out of control. I'm watching you. One misstep and Kirkwood will be instructed to take over."

Dumas scowled but entered the room, Rowdy on his heels. Burns stepped into the observation area to watch.

"Mr. Cooper," Dumas began. "During our previous interview, you indicated you would like an attorney present before you underwent any questioning. Have you changed your mind?"

"For now," Rowdy settled into the chair and waited.

Subterfuge

"I'd like to go over the events of today," Dumas decided.   He had to tread carefully with Burns watching his every move.   One slip and he'd never get his promotion.   "Can you start at the beginning?   Tell me what happened from the moment you got out of bed."

"I wasn't in bed," Rowdy corrected.   "I was working to locate the man who had abducted a woman in our jurisdiction.   I was the initial officer on the case and Detective Andy Cooper was the primary investigator on the abduction."

Dumas gritted his teeth but didn't object.

"Coop and I had worked late.   At some point, we moved to the lounge chairs in my loft to grab a couple hours down before we started up again.   We all believed time was running out and Angela didn't have much left."

"You are referring to Angela Perkins, the wife of an FBI agent?"

"Correct," Rowdy had to work hard, but he was able to stop the grin.

"And, Mrs. Perkins, she was abducted in her home by a serial killer?" Dumas pressed.

"She was abducted from her home," Rowdy said.   "And, we believed she was taken by a man that had killed others — yes."

"An active FBI case," Dumas pressed further.

"I believe the serial killer case did fall under the jurisdiction of the FBI.   The abduction case belonged to Chicago PD."

"You know very well there was only one case," Dumas erupted.   He glanced at the window and did his best to regain his composure.

"That's not the way I understand things," Rowdy answered. "But, I'm just a dog cop. Those things are above my pay grade. Any clarification on the status of our investigation would need to go through Chief Griggs. I just know, I was officially assigned to work an abduction case for CPD."

"You were assigned to my task force, to work the serial killer case immediately after Angela Perkins was abducted," Dumas corrected.

"I was asked to join your task force," Rowdy smiled. "But, you kicked me off the team that first day. At which point, I was assigned to work an abduction case for my department."

Both men looked at the wall of glass when a brisk knock sounded from the other side. Dumas just swung and missed. Strike one.

"So," Dumas continued. "You settled into some lounge chairs for a nap."

"Coop woke me up," Rowdy tried to remember the time. "It was early, around five maybe."

"And why did he wake you?" Dumas asked.

"He said he had a lead," Rowdy shrugged. "He wanted to go check out the tunnels where Stanton Proctor had worked. Specifically, the area where he was injured."

"Why?"

"Epiphany, I guess," Rowdy shrugged. "He was thinking about the case when he dropped off and an idea came to him when he woke. Plus, we realized the problem the city was having with the electricity in the tunnels could be on account of Eddie Hill's experiments. History showed he liked to shock his victims."

Subterfuge

"Then what?" Dumas asked.   Furious with himself for not realizing the same thing.

"We headed out," Rowdy provided.   "Once we got there, we knew we were onto something.   The outer door had the same locking system Eddie had put on the old warehouse.   The secluded building where he held Angela while he looked for a place to set up his lab."

"How do you know that?" Dumas asked.

Rowdy blinked and stared at the man.   No wonder the killer was on the loose for so long.   "Angela's DNA was on the evidence collected at the scene."

Dumas decided to shift gears.   "So, you saw the lock and you did what?   You called Agent Perkins who was on administrative leave and asked him to join you.   You didn't call me, or anyone working the official case, correct?"

"We didn't call," Rowdy surprised him.   "Skeet showed up on his own.   He came to a similar conclusion that morning and drove out to investigate.   Since we now had three cops on scene, we decided to enter the tunnels and take a look around."

"Even though one of those cops was on administrative leave and was not acting in his official capacity as an agent?" Dumas pressed.

"A cop's a cop where I come from," Rowdy shrugged. "And, I'm not familiar with FBI policy, I've never worked for the Bureau."

"Clearly," Dumas mumbled.   Another knock sounded on the thin glass.

Rowdy smiled. Strike two. "Anyway, Skeet had the master code. He got it from the dealer that sold the electronic locks to Hill. Once he retrieved it from his vehicle, we approached the tunnels. It took a while to clear the place. It's a big area and we were being cautious. Anyway, the tunnel emptied out into a junction sort of thing." He proceeded to describe the room, explained how Coop took the high ground because he had his rifle and Skeet moved into a safe position while Rowdy tried to clear each door.

"You're telling me Agent Skeeter Perkins did not participate in the search?" Dumas questioned.

"That is correct," Rowdy nodded.

"Why?" Dumas demanded. "You said a cop is a cop."

"True," Rowdy agreed. "I guess for the same reason your boss is not in this room while you conduct the interrogation. His assistance wasn't required at the time. Since we were going after his wife, we thought it was better to have him stand back, not get involved in any sort of altercation but just focus on rescuing his wife once we found her."

"And did he?" Dumas asked. "Did he get involved?"

Rowdy considered the question. "Once we found Angela, he was involved in the sense that he knew the layout. He understood the platform, warned us about the acid, and knew the chains would be rigged to emit an electrical shock to anyone that messed with the thing."

"I'm talking about the room where Edgar Hill's body was located," Dumas challenged. "Did Agent Skeeter Perkins get involved in that room?"

"I don't understand the question," Rowdy said calmly.

Subterfuge

"Was it in fact Agent Skeeter Perkins that shot that man?" Dumas demanded. "Did Skeeter Perkins see the serial killer he had been chasing for over a year and gun him down in cold blood because he had the nerve to abduct his wife?"

"No," Rowdy said honestly. For a minute there, he was worried how he was going to respond but Dumas was an idiot. He had no idea how to ask a proper question.

This time the door flung open and Burns stood in the doorway. "I need a minute, Dumas. Now!"

Rowdy sat in silence for several minutes, knowing a very large piece of Dumas' hide would be missing when he returned. The door opened and a red-faced Frank Dumas stepped into the room.

"Please proceed," Dumas settled back into his chair. "Tell me what happened once you entered that room."

"Coop was up above, I started checking doors. That's when I heard the shot and a section of wall exploded a few feet away from me. I glanced up to see if Coop was okay and realized the second round had struck the chain holding his platform in place. Then Hill refocused and aimed the gun directly at me. The threat was neutralized."

"You fired Agent Skeeter Perkins service weapon?" Dumas asked.

"I fired the weapon that was turned over to our Range Master," Rowdy answered. "I fired the weapon I took from Agent Skeeter Perkins before we entered the tunnel. I have no idea if that is a service weapon or a personal weapon. You'd have to ask him."

"Why did you take his weapon?" Dumas asked. "I thought you said a cop was a cop."

"And I stand by that," Rowdy said carefully. "But, I also knew the danger. It was important for Skeet to be there when we located and rescued his wife. It was necessary. But, Coop and I also knew it would be dangerous and very emotional for Skeet. I took his weapon as a precaution, nothing more."

"Because you believed he might kill an unarmed man rather than arrest him?" Dumas asked, knowing the question would get him in hot water. But, he was right, he knew he was right. Rowdy Cooper did not shoot their killer. Agent Skeeter Perkins had turned into Rambo, tracked down the man that abducted his wife and shot him in cold blood. He didn't even believe the man had a gun on him. One of the Cooper brothers probably planted it there to save Skeet's career. He was right, he knew he was right. But, with Burns watching his every move, it was going to be hard to prove it.

"I believe Skeet is an honorable cop with a level of integrity that most will never possess. I believe it was important for him to be there when we rescued his wife. I believed at the time, it was also important to minimize the chance that his emotions would make a decision he would have to live with for the rest of his life. I simply took his weapon as a precaution, a way to balance the emotions and focus on tactics."

"I'm going to ask you again, Mr. Cooper," Dumas pressed. "Did you fire Skeeter Perkins weapon in that room? The room where Edgar Hill was killed?"

"Yes," Rowdy said honestly. "I did."

"You admit to killing Edgar Hill," Dumas questioned. "A man with no history of using or even owning a pistol or any other firearm?"

"Edgar Hill was in possession of a firearm at the time we encountered him. Edgar Hill fired on us and continued to fire on us until he was neutralized. I have no idea what you're implying with your question, but those are the facts."

Subterfuge

"I'm implying..." Dumas stopped immediately when the door opened again.

"Thank you for your cooperation, Officer Cooper," Burns stepped into the room. "This interview is now over. And, I'd like to add a personal thank you before you go. You and your brother went above and beyond in this case. Our department owes your family a great debt. One, it's likely, we will never be able to fully repay. It is my belief Angela Perkins is alive today because of your dedication and tenacity... not to mention your compassion and your professionalism. Chief Griggs will be contacted as well. Your brother is waiting down the hall, Kirkwood has finished his interview. You are both free to go."

Dumas opened his mouth to object but closed it when he saw the look on Stanley Burns' face. He'd lost this one and he was afraid it might cost him. It might just cost him that promotion he'd wanted. If it did, Skeeter Perkins was going to be the one to pay the price. And, he had no intention of dropping his request to have the insufferable agent transferred to another unit. The infallible Skeeter Perkins just might be guarding a field in Iowa before this was over. That idea was all Dumas needed to brighten his day. It lasted exactly seven minutes and forty-two seconds. Long enough for Burns to inform him... Dumas would be the one heading to a cornfield in Iowa. His career was over, and he had no idea how it had happened.

Epilogue

Angela Perkins was sitting on the back patio trying to relax but failing miserably. She had a blanket over her legs and a freshly made margarita in her right hand. And, she was more nervous than she could remember being in her life.

Skeet's friends, the Cooper brothers and Andy Cooper's wife, were coming over for a welcome home party. She wasn't in the mood to party. Wasn't in the mood for company, but Skeet had asked her to meet them, and she could see in his eyes it was important. She vaguely remembered the two brothers, two angels that had helped her husband locate and rescue her from a monster. But, to be honest, she was doing her best not to remember any of it. She wanted desperately to forget the cold, dark prison at the end of the black dirty tunnel. Wanted to forget the broken ribs, the hunger, the pain, and helplessness she had experienced there. But, her mind refused to cooperate. These days, her nights were filled with flashbacks and nightmares she couldn't escape.

Skeet kept his promise. The first words out of his mouth when Stanley and Lana Burns entered her sterile, white hospital

Subterfuge

room was an ultimatum. Either Stan figured out a way to keep Skeet in Chicago, or he was resigning — effective immediately. Stan found a way. Angie wondered just how long it would take for her husband to regret that request. They would deal with it later, she'd help him deal with it when he started to get antsy. She'd pretend it was okay when he realized he needed to travel, to be a part of the action, to track another killer. Somehow, she'd deal with it... she just had no idea how.

For about the millionth time, Angela Perkins cursed the man that had ruined her life. He didn't just take her independence away, didn't just take her sense of security... he took her desire to paint. He took her livelihood and her passion. Just the thought of picking up a brush or mapping out a new landscape made her feel nauseous. Something that had always brought her so much peace, so much pleasure, was now part of a past life she could never go back to. Knowing that, made her a little sad. But, mostly it just made her angry.

She nearly jumped out of her chair when a large male figure stepped through the French doors and paused in the shadows. It embarrassed her when she realized it was Stanley Burns, life-long friend and the newest Director of the FBI. "Sorry."

"Don't apologize dear," Stan said as he moved forward and gently took Angela's left hand. He frowned at the deep burn that still covered it completely. "These things take time. I should be apologizing to you. I didn't mean to startle you, I just wanted to say hello."

"I didn't realize you were coming tonight," Angie set the margarita on the small table next to her chair and reached out a hand in greeting to Lana Burns. "Please, have a seat and relax. Skeet's running around somewhere, trying to make everything perfect for

256

our guests. I just..." she trailed off, not knowing exactly how to explain her melancholy.

"You're going to like the Coopers," Stan promised. "I liked them right away. And, I'm the grand Poohbah."

"Those two do have a humbling effect on my husband," Lana said as she settled in next to Angela. "I like them, too. You just relax and let Skeet take care of this little gathering. It's good for him... and you too, I think."

"He's been so wonderful," Angela said, feeling a little guilty. "I'm so much trouble but Skeet, he's my rock."

The group heard voices moments before two men and a tiny woman preceded Skeet onto the back porch. "Everyone meet Maggie Cooper. You know the brothers; but, for Angela's sake, this is Coop and that guy over there is Rowdy," Skeet paused in the doorway momentarily to introduce his guests.

Angela moved to stand up, but Maggie was across the patio and by her side in mere seconds. "Stay where you are," she insisted. "Your injuries are still healing. Skeet said that maniac broke two of your ribs. This is your party and tonight... you're the queen of the castle. The queen doesn't leave her thrown to greet the peasants." Maggie lowered her voice. "In case you're wondering, Rowdy is the peasant."

"Thanks, Magpie," Rowdy grabbed a beer as he turned and smiled at his sister-in-law. "I'm going to remember that."

"I invited Ryan," Skeet said stepping from the doorway onto the porch. "But, he couldn't make it. That means the gang's all here."

The group settled in for a night of good food and good friends.

Subterfuge

Several hours later, Angela joined Maggie in the kitchen. It was odd really, but somehow, she felt like she'd known the woman all her life. She was certain the two of them were going to become fast friends. Maggie was rinsing dishes and loading them into the empty dishwasher.

"Can I ask you something?" Angela said hesitantly.

"Sure," Maggie turned at the serious tone in Angela's voice.

"Skeet's been acting... different since I got back," she began, hesitantly. "Sometimes, he seems stressed. Like, he feels guilty about something. I'm wondering, do you think... well do you think he might have killed that monster? Do you think Skeet shot that guy because he was so angry and scared about what that man did to me?"

"Angela," Maggie moved to her side. "They all said Rowdy was the one to fire that gun. That means, Rowdy fired the gun. Does it really matter anyway? A monster is dead. He can't hurt anyone else. In my world, that equates to a successful mission all around."

"Then why would he feel guilty?" Angela pressed.

"Do you really want me to answer that?" Maggie asked. "Because, I'm not sure you will like the answer."

"Meaning me?" Angela realized.

"Meaning," Maggie took her hand in comfort. "Our men are warriors. They firmly believe it is their most important mission to keep us safe. Skeet couldn't do that. Not because he wasn't capable; but, because he wasn't here. I think that makes it worse. He knows he could have protected you... but he wasn't around to do it. And since he wasn't around, the man he was after kidnapped you, hurt you, and would have killed you. It's a lot for a macho cop like Skeet to accept."

"True," Angela considered.

"You need Skeet right now," Maggie continued. "You need him here to feel safe. You need his love to heal. You need his patience to help you get through the tough times. But, he needs you just as much because he feels like a failure. The sooner you can get back on your feet, the sooner you can smile and even laugh — just a little — the sooner Skeet will start to heal as well."

"How did you get so smart?" Angela asked, knowing Maggie was right. And deep in her soul, she knew her husband would never kill anyone in cold blood. Not even for her. Questioning what happened in those tunnels, before the men got to her... that was just some irrational paranoia her mind had conjured up to deal with everything she'd been through.

"I'm a cop's wife," Maggie shrugged. "That pretty much explains it all."

THE END

Melanie P. Smith is a Multi-Genre author of Paranormal, Criminal suspense, Police Procedural, and Romance Novels.   She worked as a civilian member of law enforcement for over twenty six years and uses her education and experience to make her novels exciting, action packed and gripping.

www.ingramcontent.com/pod-product-compliance
Lightning Source LLC
Chambersburg PA
CBHW050722180626
46814CB00002B/566